Intoxication

A Steamy New Adult Romance

Erika Bradley

Edited by The Fiction Fix

Cover Design by Cormar Covers

The characters of this story are purely fictional and do not depict any actual person or event. The names of each character are not related to any person bearing the same names. The details of this book are not based on any actual event, and any reference made to anything remotely familiar is purely incidental.

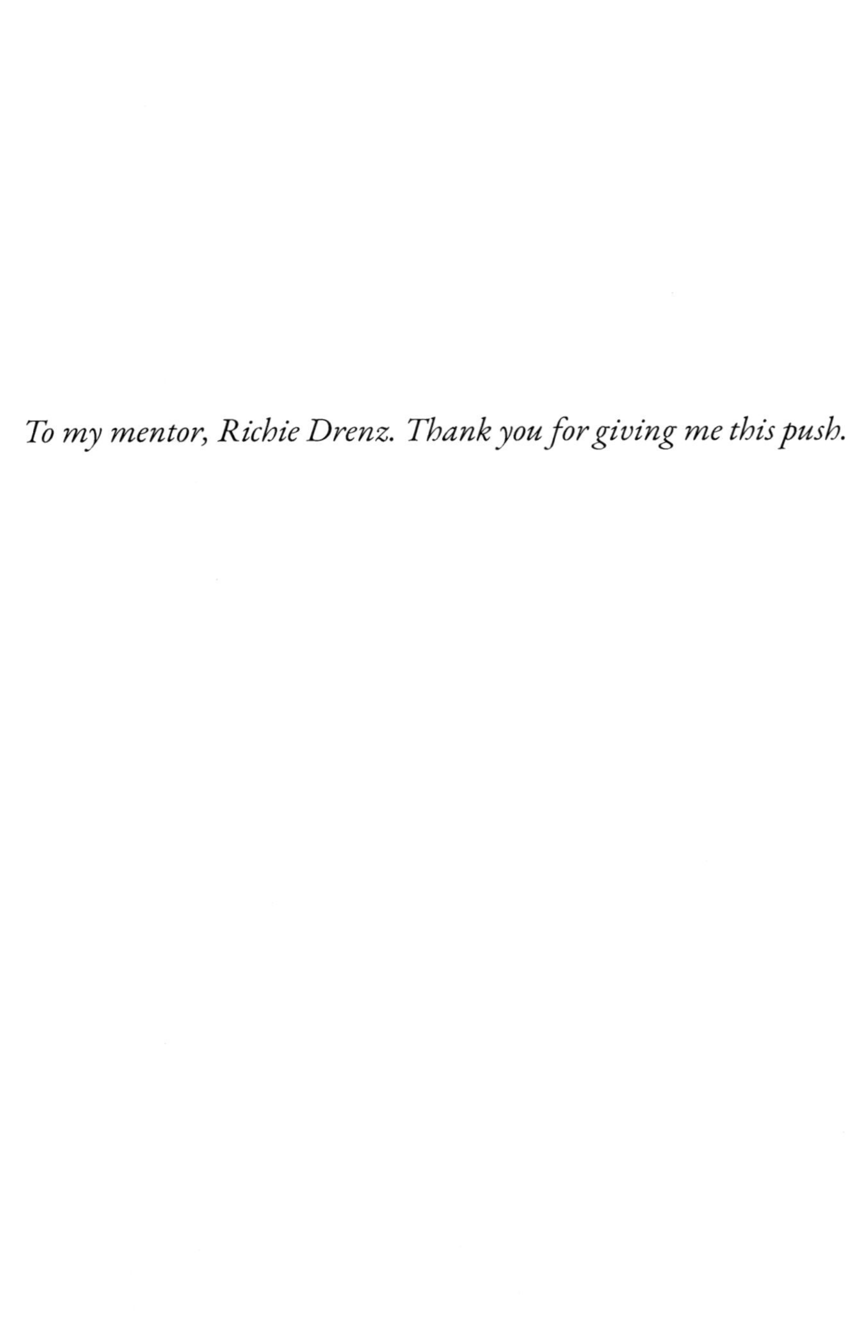

To my mentor, Richie Drenz. Thank you for giving me this push.

Contents

Playlist

Runnin'- Adam Lambert

For You- Liam Payne and Rita Ora

Forever- Labyrinth

If I Had You- Adam Lambert

Ashes- Celine Dion

Why Can't I? Liz Phair

All I Wanna Do- EN'DERA

Note to Reader

Hello reader,

Intoxication is the first book of the Damaged Hearts trilogy and is not a standalone. Books 2 and 3 will be released summer of 2022.

Trigger Warning: this story contains subject matters some may find triggering, including sexual abuse, sexual harassment (not by main characters), alcoholism, death and suicide.

Intoxication also contains explicit sex scenes and expletives.

Intoxication

I'm buried deep in my work when I hear Zyon's door open, putting me on edge instantly. I glance at the time. It's a little after two. Why is she still up?

She's moving silently, which is no surprise, considering her minute size, but without even looking up, I suspect she's coming downstairs. I glance to the stairs and she's halfway down, my T-shirt swallowing her body. It's thin enough for me to notice she's wearing nothing underneath. No panties, definitely no bra. Her nipples press against the fabric like they yearn to escape. I automatically wet my lips, and I can't help imagining them in my mouth.

Goddamnit.

1

Gabriel

My touchy-feely date removes her hand from my thigh as the car pulls up to the high-rise apartment building. *Finally.* No more lingering hands, no more surreptitious side glances, no more hints that she wants to be more than my plus one to my father's wedding. She's been pretending her touch is innocent, but I've gotten enough fuck-me looks from women to know what she wants.

It's strange. Nicole and I are like family. With both our mothers being best friends, we've been thick as thieves since we were eight years old, since the days of hide and seek, four square and Simon says. I kicked the ass of the first guy who broke her heart in high school, and she pretended to be my girlfriend in college when I wanted to get a stalker-ish one-night stand off my back. We've never had a romantic moment, which makes her flirting really weird.

"Well, this was fun, Gabe," she says when the car comes to a stop. "How about we do this again sometime soon?"

My best buddies who are also my business partners, Marcus Brady and Noah Armstrong, exchange a look from the front seat. I don't need to read their minds to know what it means. They witnessed Nicole flirting throughout the evening, too. Marcus thinks I should bang her and get it over with, but I won't take advice from a man who fucks anything in a skirt. Noah wants me to let her down gently, and while I appreciate his sensitivity, I won't listen to him, either. I can't cross the line and sleep with her, but I don't want to hurt her feelings, either. I'm going to pretend she didn't try to come on to me.

I can't help but suspect my mom's role in Nicole's behavior today. She's always been on my case to ask Nicole out on a date, but I suspect she wants more than that. I haven't forgotten how she and Nicole's mom used to talk when we were teenagers, how they wanted us to get married and have kids. At first, I thought it was just a stupid joke between two friends. By the time we got to college, I realized how serious they were. I was a little relieved when Nicole moved to Paris for her medical internship and fell in love with the city and an orthopedic surgeon named Lukas.

Now she's back in New York for good, without Lukas. There's no more engagement ring on her finger. She hasn't explained what happened, and I won't ask. But I would give anything to get them back together and take Mom's pressure off me. I've spent the last six months trying to avoid her scheming, but it was hard to deny her last night when she showed up to my apartment and insisted I take Nicole to Dad's wedding today. Never mind that the RSVPs were already sent, or that Dad and Karyn, his fiancée, would be blindsided by another guest. What Charlotte Cain wants, Charlotte Cain gets. I can never say no to her. I can't bear the look she gives me when she doesn't get her way.

I give Nicole an evasive smile, get out from my side, and walk around the car to open her door. She holds onto my hand even after she gets out. I resist the urge to pull away.

"Coming up?" she asks.

"Yeah, I'll take you to your door," I reply. Mom won't let me hear the end of it if she finds out I left Nicole on the steps of her apartment building. She draws closer to me as we walk in, and when we get inside the elevator, she sets her hands on my waist. "What are you doing, Nicole?"

She giggles, although there's no humor in what I just said. "Hugging my best friend, silly. Thanks for inviting me today. I needed to get out of the apartment."

My eyes meet the ceiling when she wraps her arms around me, her body pressing against mine. I should ease her away, but I just can't bring myself to do it. Nicole is a beautiful woman. Hands down, one of the most attractive women in my circle. Her petite frame fits perfectly against me, but it does nothing to stir my insides. Our friendship is a major stumbling block in our way.

Is it, really? Or am I just not attracted to her? If Nicole was any other woman, would I want to fuck her then?

I don't know. I'll probably never know, but sometimes, I think it's easier to give my mother what she wants. Date Nicole. Marry her, even. Give Mom those grandkids she's been riding my ass about. Anything to get her off my back. Will it ever be enough, or will she keep demanding more than her pound of flesh for what I did eight years ago?

I know the answer. Mom won't stop until there's nothing left in me, until she's gotten revenge on me for taking her most precious gift. Her favorite son. Yeah, I should probably give her what she wants. Maybe then I'll be forgiven. Maybe then she'll leave me alone.

"You are so tense," Nicole whispers, her palms pressed against my chest.

"I'm exhausted," I reply, looking down at her with a forced smile.

"You work too hard, that's why."

"This coming from a woman who's working sixteen-hour shifts on the pediatric ward." Nicole's work ethic has always been an inspiration. As the daughter of a business magnate, there's no need for her to work, but she has never been the entitled type. While the guys and I were having fun in college, she was busy doing part time shifts at a children's clinic, which continued until she left for Paris. She's only been back in New York a few months, but she's made such a huge impact, the hospital has already offered her a promotion. She's bashful about it, but it's well-deserved.

"That was a typical pot-calling-the-kettle-black moment, am I right?" she says.

"Without a doubt," I reply.

Nicole sighs as the elevator doors open, and I don't stop her from twisting her arm through mine as we walk along the carpeted hallway. We get to her door at the end, and she holds my wrist while using her free hand to slip the key in the lock. I gently pull my hand free as she pushes the door open.

"Goodnight, Nicole."

"Oh, come on," she says, pouting at me. "The night's still young, and I'm lonely."

"Take a bath. Watch TV. Call Emily. I'm sure she's still up."

"I'm one hundred percent sure my best friend's out getting laid. Don't leave me hanging. How about a nightcap? I have a bottle of sweet red..." Her voice trails and she licks her lips. My stomach churns as I ease her off me. She notices my dour expression and slaps her forehead.

"Oh, shit, Gabe, I'm sorry." She reaches for my arm and I pull away. "Being away for so long made me forget—"

"Don't worry about it."

I back away from the sadness on her face. I know where her mind's going and I don't want her to take me there, too. I've been doing a superb job avoiding the dark memories, but now they follow me out of the apartment and settle beside me in Marcus' car. I throw my head against the back of the leather seat with a loud sigh.

"Don't tell me. Nicole invited you in to scrub her back, didn't she?" Marcus asks with a chuckle. "Why don't you just put that girl out of her misery, man? Just fuck her and get it over with."

I shake my head in response. Sex has always been Marcus' answer to any woman-related problems in his life, ever since high school. Small wonder he's become such a dog. Women are never safe around him. I understand the appeal. He's a good-looking guy, tall and muscular, tattooed, and the ladies don't stand a chance when he flashes a smile and opens his charming mouth.

"Noah, come on," Marcus says, shoving Noah's shoulder. "Talk some sense into our boy."

Noah releases a weary sigh, his eyes glued to his cell phone. "Leave me out of it, man."

Marcus looks over to him and the humor fades from his face. "Why the hell are you torturing yourself like that? For the last time, get the fuck off Instagram and stop staring at engagement photos of your ex."

"That's not what I'm doing," Noah says, throwing the phone in the center console. He runs his fingers through his shoulder-length blonde hair with a harsh sigh.

"Are we going, or what?" I ask, when I notice Marcus still has the gear in park.

"Wait a minute, let me sort this out," Marcus replies, turning back to Noah. "Are you still hung up on Ana being engaged?"

"Nope. I'm happy for her." His expression says the opposite. "Ana deserves all the happiness in the world. I just hope that asshole knows how lucky he is."

"Just be honest. You feel like shit," Marcus teases.

"Fuck off. Weren't we talking about Gabriel?"

"Yup. Now we're talking about you." Marcus shakes his head, his expression pitiful as he regards Noah. "Ana is engaged, man. Still can't believe it. Honestly, I thought she would have waited for you."

"Waited for what?" I chip in. "We both know Noah didn't want to settle down."

"I wasn't completely against it," Noah grumbles. "She just wanted to get married too soon."

Well, considering they had been dating since high school, a full nine years, I disagree. It wasn't too soon. Noah just wanted the best of both worlds: a live-in girlfriend without the commitment. Ana got tired of playing the wifely role without the title. Noah, that fucking dickhead, he didn't even fight to make her stay, not until he found out she was dating someone else, but by then, it was too late. She was already in love with Colin, a guy she met while on a get-over-Noah vacation. Even then, I still had hopes she and Noah would work it out, but her engagement post on Instagram blew us all away.

"Well, she's getting her wish. You, my man, are free to sample as much pussy as you want. There's no curfew, no checking in with Ana, no worrying if a woman gets her makeup on your shirt. You're a free agent, remember that. Don't let all your hours in the gym go to waste."

"I want a woman who values more than a hot body. The single life isn't for me," Noah replies.

"You're wrong, my brother. The single life is the best thing ever, right Gabriel?" Marcus says, checking for my approval.

"No comment." I shake my head. "Just drive, goddamnit."

"Oh, right... you're on a pussy hiatus. I forgot. Boring."

"Don't you get tired of people telling you to fuck off?" I wasn't in the mood for Marcus' bullshit tonight.

"Don't you get tired of fucking your hand?"

His response gets us all laughing, and it relaxes me a little. The guys constantly tease me about my decision to abstain from sex, so I'm used to it. It's a decision I don't regret. I've gotten sick of the casual flings, the one-night stands that leave me feeling empty and alone. I'm ready for something wholesome. Well, when I find the time, that is. These days, I'm busier than a mosquito on a nude beach.

I lean back in my seat, watching the view outside my window zip by. Marcus' foot has always been heavy on the gas pedal, but tonight he seems in a hurry. I'm guessing there's a booty call waiting somewhere. Maybe two. It wouldn't surprise me if there were three. Marcus has always been the most adventurous of the three of us. Noah is a proud, certified one-woman man, while I'm caught in the middle. Well, I was. Those days are long behind me.

"Wait a minute," Marcus suddenly says, and I shift my eyes from a couple on a motor bike next to us to him. "We weren't done talking about you and Nicole, Gabriel."

"There's no me and Nicole. And we're done talking about whatever it is."

"Just take my advice. Put your celibacy on pause and give her a good, hard ride. A one-and-done," Marcus replies.

"You want me to ruin her for another man, is that it?" I ask with a grin.

Marcus scoffs. "I don't know about that. You've been out of practice for a while, so you've probably lost your touch. Hey, wait—there's a thought. Make it so bad she won't want seconds."

"You know, I wish you would grow the fuck up," Noah says to him.

"What the hell did I say that's so childish?" Marcus asks, his voice whiny.

Noah ignores him and twists in his seat, directing his attention to me. "Listen, Gabriel, just give it to her straight. I don't mean sex. Tell her you don't want to complicate your friendship. I'm sure she'll understand."

"That's the worst advice I've ever heard in my life," Marcus snorts.

"Guys, that wasn't even the highlight of our brief time upstairs. She invited me in for a drink."

Marcus slows down and our eyes meet in the rearview mirror before he returns his gaze to the road. "Shit."

"Yup."

"That's pretty fucking low," Noah says. "She knows you don't drink."

Yeah. It's quite upsetting that Nicole would offer me a drink when she knows *why* I don't drink. She was there that night in the hospital when my brother died. She witnessed how my life escalated afterwards. One drink. That's all it takes to backslide into the darkness. I don't want to ever go back there.

Oh, God, these fucking memories...

"Put some music on, Marcus. I don't want to think right now."

Marcus hums while scanning through his playlist, and soon his favorite hip hop mix tape blasts through the surround speakers. It clears my head a little, and I think about my plans for the rest of the night. There's a business plan waiting for me to complete, which will require a few cups of coffee to keep me awake. It's not the usual way a twenty-eight-year-old spends their Saturday night, but I have a dream to make our real estate developmental company the best in the city. We've been kicking ass since launching five years ago. Now, I want to take it to higher heights.

The car rolls through an industrial neighborhood decked out in imaginative street art, and we soon pass the stunning mural Noah created on a dare a year ago. He and Ana had just broken up and we wanted to lift his spirits, but it was a big mistake. I shake my head at the life-size portrait of a beautiful, half-naked Asian woman reclining on a chaise lounge, her dark hair hiding her breasts and fabric covering her lower half. He swore to God it's not Ana, but Marcus and I agreed the image fit her to a T. I glance at him now, and I can't help smirking at his attempt to ignore the mural as we drive by. He starts picking imaginary lint off his pants and doesn't raise his head until we get to the next avenue.

Yeah, random art my ass. It's a constant reminder he's still in love with her.

My mind returns to work until the music stops, pulling me back to the present. Noah clears his throat, the way he usually does when he has something to say. He turns on the overhead light and leans forward, the orange glow giving his face a healthy glow. Back in high school, we mercilessly teased Noah about his pretty face until we realized how popular he was among girls. Even then, he only had eyes for Ana.

"I know you want a little time to your thoughts, but hear me out," he begins.

I nod. "Go on."

"Marcus has been joking around about sleeping with Nicole to get her off your back, but I hope you realize how serious this is."

"I know. Mom's been working overtime since Nicole got back from Paris. I'm sure she's behind how Nicole behaved all day," I reply.

"So, what are you going to do about it?" he asks.

"What the hell should I do? She's my mom. How do I say no to her? I'd love to find out."

"It's been eight years, Gabriel." His grey eyes are filled with sad memories of that fateful night.

Sighing, I shift my gaze, staring at my palms. Noah doesn't need to say more because I've read between the lines, but I allow him to continue.

"You were young, and a little... reckless. We all were, but you are not that kid anymore. It's time to forgive yourself. Because if you don't, Mrs. C will continue to manipulate you."

Noah's talking about my mother, and he's right. Since Daniel's death, she's been using my guilt to get her way. How do I fix it? It's my fault her beloved son's not here anymore, but how can I give her what she wants this time?

"You're right, Noah. I just want her to be happy."

"By sacrificing your happiness, dude? Is that fair to you? I think you've done enough to make up for your mistake. I mean, when your dad wanted a break, you took over the family business *while* getting our company off the ground. That's a huge load, man. A great sacrifice," he says.

"Preach," Marcus chimes in from beside him.

"Do you want the perfect solution to get Mrs. C off your back? Find a woman. Settle down. The minute she notices you getting serious with someone, she'll have no choice but to leave you alone," Noah suggests.

Marcus scoffs. "I have so many reasons why that's total bullshit. For one—most important— he's not ready to settle down."

"Okay, you fucking man-whore. You can sit this one out."

I half listen to my friends arguing in the front seat while I think about what Noah said. He made a valid point, like he always does. A woman in my life would guarantee a break from my mother, but I haven't been on a date in months. Getting back in the dating pool requires time, which I don't have. Between running both companies, I hardly have time for anything, just a daily workout session with my trainer and an occasional night out with the boys.

No, there's no time for a woman in my life.

I want to change the subject, so I steer the conversation toward Marcus, my easiest target. "I saw that hot brunette checking you out tonight..."

Marcus laughs and I know it's partly because he knows what I'm trying to do. "I guess you missed the part where I checked her out, too."

"Now, that's a given, Mr. One-Night-Stand. I'm assuming you got her number, too."

"Do birds fly?" Noah asks. "This asshole can't keep his dick in his pants for a minute."

Marcus laughs while slowing down at a stoplight. "I saw the ladies checking you out, too, Gabriel. I guess they didn't approach because of Nicole. Man, she didn't give you a break." He snickers. "But I doubt that would have changed anything."

"It wouldn't have."

"How much longer do you plan on being celibate?"

"None of your business. Why don't you focus on getting us home in one piece?"

The light turns green, and he moves off. "Come on, man. Let me hook you up. I got a fine-ass girl in my apartment building that's definitely your type. I promise, I didn't hit it. I'm saving her for you."

"I don't need your help—"

My body jerks forward when Marcus suddenly hits the brakes and my face slams against the back of his seat. A blood-curling scream pierces the night, sending an ice-like sensation through my veins. Someone's in trouble. Big, big trouble.

"What the?" Noah murmurs, leaning forward to peer out the windshield.

Pushing myself between the front seats, I lean closer to take a look. There's a woman in the middle of the street getting dragged by a man twice her size. Narrowing my gaze, I realize he's trying to take her purse.

I immediately reach for the door handle and Noah stretches over to stop me. "What the hell are you doing?"

"Are you blind? There's a woman who needs our help!" I try to shake off his grip, but it's too secure. "Let go of my arm, Noah."

"Don't fucking get involved. You don't know what's going on out there. What if he has a gun? Marcus, just drive by on the other side."

But Marcus is already opening his door, too. "Looks like she's being robbed, guys."

"You sure?" Noah asks warily, releasing his grip on me as the woman gives the mugger a solid kick in the groin. Still, it's not enough to stop him. He's got a solid grip on her purse strap, pulling so hard I'm sure she's about to get yanked to the other side in a minute.

I jump from the car into a run, dashing past Marcus as she loses her hold on the purse strap and falls to the asphalt. The thug moves toward her, his curled fists revealing his intent to hurt her. It triggers an emotion I haven't felt in years. A vicious fury takes over me in a heartbeat, pulling me to the darkness I've been fighting to keep at bay. I surrender to it, running smack into him, the tackle reminding me of my high school linebacker days. He hardly puts up a fight, not that he stands a chance. My height and weight advantage allows me to overpower him with little effort. My knuckles connect with his cheekbone, and each blow creates a cracking sound, echoing into the quiet night. I feel the wetness and metallic scent of blood telling me his face is a bruised mess.

"Alright, alright. Enough already," Noah says, pulling me off the half-conscious man. I shrug him off to finish what I started, but Noah gives me a hefty push that stops me in my tracks. "Chill the fuck out, Gabriel. I don't intend to bail you out of jail tonight. Neither does Marcus. You've done enough."

I glare at him, my fists curled at my side. I know he's right, but I don't care. There's still some fire left inside me. I'm still itching to pound the prick into the pavement.

Noah must have read the anger on my face, because he raises both palms at me. "I'm not in the mood for a tussle tonight, so just chill."

Noah and I have a similar build; broad shoulders, thick arms and legs, but I'm a few inches taller. A fist fight would be brutal, and definitely not worth it. He's not the enemy. He's just trying to calm me down. "Fine. I'm chill," I reply, backing off.

Marcus yanks up the asshole and he staggers, blood running down his jaw from a cut on his cheek. Noah reaches for his phone to call the cops and I turn my attention to the woman on the ground. I extend my hand and she immediately slips hers into my palm. She looks even smaller standing up, but she's got more curves than a winding road, especially in the skin-tight black dress she's wearing. I'm trying not to stare too hard, but I can't help it. My curious eyes get busy taking in every detail of her figure. There's a slight swelling already starting on the side of her face, but it doesn't take away from how stunning she is. Her brown skin looks soft, and I am battling the urge to stroke her arm, just to confirm its smoothness. My eyes scan the many piercings on her small face. From a quick count, there's ten. Her nose looks cute with a tiny loop ring attached to her nostril. Her ears are decorated with tiny diamond studs. Her thick, curly hair reminds me of a bird's nest, but I still want to bury my hands in it.

It takes me a moment to notice she's assessing me too, with a soft smile on her full lips. I reluctantly release her hand. She surprises me by wrapping her arms around my waist, pressing her soft curves against me and resting her head on my chest. Her pleasant, jasmine scent washes over me. My body feels like it's emerging from a deep slumber, reminding me of my teenage years when it took nothing to arouse me. Hell, I can already feel my cock stirring in my pants.

"Thank you," she whispers, staring up at me.

She wets her lips and the action steals my attention, leaving me wondering about their taste. I catch myself. It's the last thing that should be on my mind, considering what just happened.

"No problem," I reply.

My commonsense prods me to ease off and check the bruise on her face, but she feels so good against me. I just want to hold her. Then Noah, that fucking dickhead, clears his throat behind me, ruining the moment, and she pulls away a little.

Just a little.

I'm in for another surprise when she pops up on her tiptoes and captures my mouth for a blood-heating kiss.

2

Zyon

Danger.

There's something about it that gives me a high. It's like a drug. I think I'm addicted to it. There's no other explanation for what I decided to do tonight. Walking alone in the middle of the night in a barely-thigh-length, body-hugging dress, that's asking for trouble, isn't it? So, why am I not scared when it finds me?

I think there's something wrong with me. My mother would agree. She's been saying how crazy I've become.

If she's right, it explains why I'm so aroused watching the stranger go to work, beating the shit out of the asshole who tried to steal my purse. Every blow sends heat rushing between my thighs, leaving my panties soaked. From my seated position on the pavement, I squeeze my thighs together to ease the throbbing. It doesn't help. There's only one thing that can soothe this tension. The one thing my therapist thinks I shouldn't have, which makes me want it even more.

Sex. Not just any sex. Random sex. The best kind. One-night stands with strangers, no names exchanged, no attachments, no romance, just a good, hard fucking that gives you a head rush for a moment. Then you're done. It's over. You move on without another thought to that nameless stranger who just rocked your world. For a while, that was my life. The alcohol, the sex, the fun.

Until it wasn't.

Therapy forced me to face my demons, not overcome them. I'm still a work in progress, still searching for that high. And right now, I'm getting a double dose. My attacker never stood a chance. The gorgeous stranger is almost double his size, with fists that resemble sledgehammers. He was down for the count after two blows. Now, it's just brutality.

I fucking love it.

"Alright, alright, that's enough."

I'm just starting to notice we've got company. Two men, clearly his friends, both dressed in a black tie ensemble just like him. The long-haired blonde guy pulls him away while a brown-skinned man hauls the assailant to his feet.

My savior shrugs off his friend and looks at me for the first time. Dark pools lay where his eyes should be, and for some reason, I can't look away. I don't want to, either. He's the high that I've been searching for all night. I can feel the energy radiating from his body. He runs his fingers through his dark hair, offering me his free hand. I take it, and my body comes alive at the first touch. It seems to have a mind of its own, pressing against him without warning. There's a soft, sensual moan, and I can't tell if it came from me, or him.

Goddamn. It should be a sin for a body to feel this good. Hard as a rock, telling me he's quite active. I wonder how active he is in bed.

One way to find out, Zyon.

I can hear my therapist's warning in my head. This is definitely not what I should be thinking of right now. I don't need this high. What I need is my life whole again.

But when has it ever been whole, anyway? When have I ever fucking listened to anyone?

Behind him, the blonde guy clears his throat, trying to ruin the moment. I give him a defiant glare before looping my arms around my savior's neck and tasting his lips. Well, it's more than just a taste. I'm hungry. A tiny sample isn't enough.

He doesn't respond for a moment, and I know he's surprised, so I give him a reason to kiss me back. I moan against his mouth, using my tongue to press against the seam of his lips; he lets me in immediately. I prepare to do all the work, but a low growl escapes his lips before he cups my cheeks with his enormous hands to deepen the kiss.

Holy fuck.

This isn't a kiss. It's a soul-stealing ritual. Every single, skillful stroke of his tongue takes a little piece of me, and I fear there'll be nothing left when he's done. I don't care. He can take whatever he wants as long as I get my fill; I'm getting that and so much more. I'm overwhelmed by the spicy warmth of his cologne, aroused by his body pressed against me. His cock, hard and ready, grazes my stomach, and I would give anything to have it inside me.

Anything.

"Okay, okay. Break it up."

The blonde guy again. Is he a cock blocker, or what? My savior releases me with a harsh sigh, staring down at me like he's seeing me for the first time.

"Noah, Noah. Always ruining the moment," the brown-skinned man says from the sidewalk. He has my attacker in a comfortable head lock, unaffected by his struggles.

"Look, man, she's in shock. You're taking advantage of a vulnerable woman," Noah says.

My savior takes a step backward with a soft "fuck," and runs his fingers through his hair again, messing up the neat hairstyle. A few stray locks fall over his forehead, adding an extra tousled sexiness that makes me ache to kiss him again. I won't. I will behave. There are other things pulling my attention right now, like the pain on the side of my face reminding me of my faceplant onto the pavement earlier. *Shit.* There's a burning on my elbow, too, and it prompts me to tilt it upwards to examine it. *Great, blood.*

"Damn it. You're hurt."

He takes my hand before I can reply and leads me off the street. Under the streetlights, he tilts my face to the side. A soft curse escapes his lips as he studies my face then he takes my elbow, shaking his head. "Marcus, do you still have the first aid kit in your car?" he says to his friend.

"Nope," Marcus says. "Forgot to put it back in."

"It's okay, honestly," I speak up. "I barely feel a thing. Plus I live around the corner. I'll have it taken care of in no time."

He slowly nods, but he doesn't seem too pleased by my response.

"I'm Zyon, by the way." I extend my uninjured hand.

"Gabriel." He wraps his hand around mine. Our eyes meet for a split second before he glances down, squeezing my hand before letting go.

"Thanks again for saving my ass, Gabriel. I owe you one."

"Don't mention it."

An emotion flashes across his face so fast, I barely catch it before it disappears. It looks like regret. I wonder what it means. Sirens interrupt our moment, and a squad car pulls up beside us. The cops immediately take the thug into custody, no questions asked. Apparently, he's been wanted for a very long time. Good fucking riddance.

"What's your address?" Gabriel says to me after the cops take our statement and drive off. "I'm taking you home."

I give him my address, and after a quick official introduction to Marcus and Noah, we leave the godforsaken spot. Within minutes, we arrive at the apartment I share with my best friend Roshell, and I feel a little disappointed we got here so fast. It's crazy, but I'm not ready for this night to end. But Gabriel is already looking impatient, like he can't wait for me to get out of the car. Which is odd, considering the way he just kissed me. Hungry. Desperate. Like he'd been trapped underwater and I'm the air he needed to breathe. I'm getting wet just thinking about his tongue stroking my mouth.

I need to go before I do something crazy, like free his cock from his pants and impale myself with it, right here on the backseat of Marcus' car. I swear I'm done with the impulsive lifestyle that got me dragged into therapy. I don't want to be the out-of-control girl anymore, but I can't help my impulses when there's such a gorgeous man sitting beside me.

I can hear my mom, Dineo, in my head once more. Annoying. I can't seem to shut her out this time.

It's time to go.

"Thanks for the ride, boys. I wish we'd met under different circumstances, but it was nice meeting you, anyway."

"Wait a minute," Gabriel mumbles. The back door opens, and he gets out from his side. He goes around the car, heading to my door.

"Take care of yourself, Zyon," Noah says. "No more walking by your lonesome so late at night."

"Thanks for the tip."

"Nice meeting you, too," Marcus chips in. "Although I have an inkling I'll be seeing you again."

I consider asking him what he means by that, but Gabriel is opening my door. He lets go of my hand the second I'm on my feet. Shit, he's not even looking at me. I'm not used to this hot and cold behavior from a man.

I walk past him without a word, taking the steps to my apartment two at a time and digging for my keys as I go. My hand hits the bottom of the purse, and I don't hear the telltale jingle of my keys. I stop, wiggling my hand around, still not hearing anything. Where the fuck are my keys?

"You okay?" Gabriel asks from the bottom of the steps, surprising me. I thought he would be on the other side of Brooklyn by now.

"Just... great." I pull my hand out of my purse with a frustrated groan. Did I lose my keys when that prick tried to get my purse?

This is what you get for rebelling, Zyon. Disobedient girls get punished.

Shit.

"Are you sure everything's okay?"

Gabriel's coming up the steps, and his body fills the tiny patio within seconds. My stomach flutters violently as he stops right in front of me.

"Yeah, I just—" I tear my eyes from him to rummage through my bag once more. "I just need to have my roommate let me in."

I retrieve my cell phone and turn it on. It immediately shrills with notifications, most of which are missed calls from Dineo. No surprise there, seeing as I missed her ten o'clock check-in. I know she's probably losing her mind right now. Good. She should. I dial Roshell's number, hoping she's already back from her date with her new boyfriend, Terrence. She answers on the second ring and I hear music in the background.

Romantic music.

Damn it. This is not good.

"Girl, I was just about to turn off my phone," she says, her voice barely above a whisper. "What's up?"

Definitely not good.

"I'm locked out of the apartment, Rosh. I can't find my keys," I reply, and wait for my words to sink in.

There's a beat, then the music fades in the background. "Why are you locked out, Zyon? Where did you go?"

To a bar... the last place I should have been. "Out," I reply simply.

"Are you drunk?"

"No."

"Hold on, let me rephrase the question. Did you drink?"

Silence.

"Zyon!"

My eyes flicker to Gabriel, who's patiently leaning against the brick column watching me. I'm not enthused about a total stranger overhearing my personal struggles, but it's almost one in the morning. I don't want to be here alone.

"I just had one drink, okay?" Lie. I lost count after the seventh shot, but I can hold my liquor like it's nobody's business. My mental clarity is still on point.

Still, Roshell and I have been best friends since middle school, so she knows me better than anyone else. Better than Dineo, even. "You did not have just one drink."

"Fine. I had a few, but I swear to you, I'm okay. I just need to get inside."

Roshell sighs, and immediately I feel guilty. I'm fucking up her night. She hasn't been with a man in a year. She was probably looking forward to breaking that dry spell before I called. I can't ruin her night, not for my careless ass.

"Look, girl. I'll figure it out, okay? Enjoy your night."

"But how—"

"Don't worry about it. I'll call Dineo or something." Another lie. I'd rather sleep on the steps than ask my mother for help. Plus, she can never know I drank tonight. I'm not ready for another family intervention, or worse, rehab.

I hang up the call with Roshell and send Dineo a quick message. *Fell asleep. I'll call you in the morning*. I hope that's enough to placate her. Tucking the phone inside my purse, I give Gabriel the customer service smile I perfected on my previous job. "I guess I need a place to sleep for tonight. How about you give me an invitation?"

In hindsight, it's probably not the *best* decision to go home with a stranger, especially after what I went through last year. But for some reason, I trust Gabriel, and it's not just because he saved me. There's something about him that makes me feel safe.

A tiny smile tugs the corner of his lips. "How about you ask like a normal person?"

"I'm not a normal person, Gabriel," I reply, lightly touching his chest. He gently takes my hand and moves it to my side, but he doesn't let go.

"You know what? I'm inclined to agree." He shakes his head, still with that ghost of a smile. "You are definitely not a normal person."

"For some reason that doesn't sound like a compliment."

"It's not." He moves off, taking me with him. "Lucky for you, I have a spare bedroom. Plus I won't be able to sleep if I leave you here alone, anyway."

I don't know why his last line touches me so much, but it does. I can't help smiling as he guides me back into the car.

"Change of plans, guys," he says in response to his friends' puzzled stares. "Zyon is coming with us."

"My place or yours?" Marcus says, giving me a wink.

"Christ, don't you already have your hands full tonight?" Noah asks.

"Whoever says three's a crowd has never had a threesome," Marcus replies, pulling away from the curb. "I doubt tiny Miss Zyon can handle me, anyway."

His reply earns a loud snort from me. People, especially men, often underestimate me because of my size. Usually, they get a huge awakening, but Marcus won't be one of them. He's not my type. He's a little too cocky for my taste. I glance at the man beside me, who's staring out the window, clearly lost in thought.

Now we're talking.

I wouldn't mind sampling this hunk of a man. No, not just a sample. I need an entire meal. Something to satisfy me until the next craving sets in.

"What's that for?" Marcus asks in response to my snort.

"Nothing."

"Are you saying you can take me on?"

"All I'm saying is, don't judge a book by its cover."

He meets my stare in the rearview mirror. "Is that a challenge? I can cancel my date within a minute."

"The fuck you will," Gabriel snarls beside me. He's sitting straight, his dark frown directed at Marcus.

Marcus chuckles. "He's awake. I was wondering how long before I got your attention."

Gabriel leans back in the seat, looking even more pissed than before.

"Don't sleep on this, man. I swear to God, if you slack off, I'm going in." Marcus quickly twists to look at him, then back at the road. "I mean it."

"Of course you do," Gabriel mutters.

"You are the worst influence alive. You know that, right?" Noah adds.

Marcus flips his middle finger at him. "I've never claimed to be a saint. Now, I'm giving my best friend major life advice. It's time to end that hiatus before this opportunity slips away."

"Why don't you concentrate on the road and get the hell out of my personal life?" Gabriel says.

"Don't be mad when I cut those legs from under you. That's all I'm saying."

"I hear you. Now leave me the fuck alone."

It doesn't take a genius to realize they are talking in code. Which means they don't want me to understand, but I'm not slow. I know what they mean. Gabriel doesn't seem enthused about screwing me like his best friend wants him to, which is fine: it's his loss. Whatever. All I need is a bed for the night. In the morning, I'll be long gone. We enter a posh, residential area with elegant brownstones that probably cost more than my lifetime salary. Well, *if* I had a job. I haven't been employed since my anxiety attack six months ago. It's not something I want to think about right now, so I push it to the back of my mind.

Marcus pulls up to a stunning townhouse and looks back at me. "Goodnight, Tiny Zyon. Don't do what I wouldn't do," he jokes as Gabriel opens his door. He shoots Marcus a dirty look as he gets out.

"I have a feeling that list is a short one. Probably non-existent," I say.

"Only one way to find out." He winks at me.

I'm about to reply when Gabriel pulls me from the car. I can hear Marcus laughing as Gabriel guides me up the stairs. He opens the front door and I'm immediately transported into opulence. The high-ceilinged foyer leads along a gallery to a light-filled living room twice the size of my bedroom, with floor-to-ceiling windows giving me a view of the manicured garden outside. I turn from Gabriel and check out the entire space. Beautiful watercolor paintings on the walls, expensive-looking accent furniture, a geometric crystal chandelier in the center of the ceiling... it doesn't quite feel like him, but I don't know him well enough to make that judgement. The dining and kitchen areas are on each side of the open concept room, just as beautifully furnished, with a stairway leading upstairs.

I turn around and Gabriel has already removed his jacket and tie, his collar turned up, brushing his chin. His arms are even bigger than I thought, and I can't help noticing them flexing as he bounces the tie on his palm.

"You have a really nice place," I say.

"Thanks. It's all my mom's doing. Interior decorating isn't really my thing."

"Well, she has good taste."

He gives me that hint of a smile again, and it eases the tension in his face a bit. "Come on. Let's get that wound cleaned up."

"I can handle it myself. You've done enough for me already." In truth, I can't handle him touching me because I don't trust my body. My impulsiveness is reigning supreme tonight.

He seems about to argue but changes his mind. Instead, he gives me a stiff nod. "Let me show you to the guest room."

He gestures ahead and I follow him up the stairs. There are several open doors, but he leads me to the closest one. I enter behind him, stepping into a space that rivals a five-star hotel. There's a king-sized bed that's just calling my name, reminding me how exhausted I am. I drop my purse on the armchair while Gabriel opens the walk-in closet.

"There are extra blankets in here, in case you need any. The bathroom's through that door. First aid kit's in the medicine cabinet behind the mirror."

"Do you have a bathrobe, or something I can change into? Although I don't mind sleeping in the nude," I reply. I smirk; I just couldn't help myself.

His eyes do a slow-motion scan of my body and I wonder if he's imagining me naked. "Sure. I'll bring you a T-shirt," he says.

He walks from the room and I kick my shoes off, plopping down on the bed. I wince a little when I irritate my elbow and the tender spot on my face. I try again, lying on my good side instead. The bed is firm, yet comfortable, and the sheets smells amazing. I don't know what the scent is, but it's definitely something exotic and expensive.

"Here you go."

His voice makes me jump. I didn't hear him return. For a big guy, he sure moves quietly. I pull up from the bed and take the T-shirt from him. "Thanks."

He nods. "I'll be downstairs if you need anything."

"Cool."

The T-shirt lands on the pillow as I toss it aside for later. I move to the bathroom and find the medicine cabinet, then dress the wound on my arm before remembering I should have taken a shower first.

Idiot.

The water makes the pain sting even more, but I bear it, quickly washing my underarms and lady parts before rinsing off. If anyone had told me I'd be showering in a million-dollar apartment tonight, I'd tell them they were crazy. I've never been in a space so luxurious.

Tonight has been quite interesting. Dangerous, too. I'm quick to admit I've been reckless. Walking an entire block from the bar at midnight was the stupidest thing I'd ever done. No, scratch that. My silliest blunder was going to a bar in the first place, especially when I promised I wouldn't take another drink. I called for trouble, and it found me. Thank God Gabriel came along just in time. I don't even want to imagine an alternative outcome.

My thoughts wander to him as I wrap a towel around my body. I've never met a man who had conflicting feelings about wanting me, and Gabriel seems to be battling with a double dose. What's his problem? Does he have a girlfriend? Is he engaged? I don't think he's married. There's no ring on his finger. Gabriel is a challenge I'd love to take on. But I'm damaged. I need fixing. Sleeping around won't do me any good. Oh, how I wish I could climb his body like a tree and give him a good, hard screwing. Something to fuck with his head like he did mine with that kiss.

All I need is one taste. Just one.

It won't do any harm.

Right?

3

GABRIEL

Agony.

It's like a cloak wrapped around me, heating my body to a feverish degree. There's no way to escape the tension, not while the source is still under my roof, probably naked in the shower right now, the warm water caressing her body the same way I'm tempted to. I'm itching to spread her gorgeous body on my bed and fuck her until my night feels normal again.

Hell.

It feels like hell in this house. It's the first week of April and I haven't used the heater for days now, but it's like a sauna wherever I go. Maybe I need to take a shower. A cold one. Something to cool my blood and clear my head. I should have called Marcus' bluff and let him take Zyon home. Anything to keep from losing my mind. Although, I doubt I could handle Marcus being so close to her. Call me insane, but just the thought of my best friend touching her makes me want to run his head into a wall. I experienced a similar urge when he flirted with her in the car. I know he didn't mean it. He was just trying to irritate me, but even knowing that, I still wanted to fight.

This instant surge of violence disturbs me greatly. Twice in one night. No, three times. My knuckles still hurt from when I pounded the shit out of that prick mugger. Granted, he deserved that beat down and so much more, but I hate losing control. I've spent years putting the darkness behind me, trying to be a good guy. No drinking and definitely no getting into fights like I used to.

Until tonight.

The cold shower doesn't work like it usually does. My body is still on fire, still burning with need.

For her.

Sighing, I pull my boxers on, covering my erection. A pair of pajama pants follow, then a T-shirt, and I move to the living room while drying my hair. I need to work. Not only for the distraction but to make up for the three days I lost attending my father's bachelor party and his wedding.

Besides managing the development company with the guys, I'm also temporarily running my father's manufacturing business while he takes a short-term break. A well-deserved break, I might add. For as long as I can remember, Dad worked himself to the bone. There's no doubt I got my work ethic from him, along with the drive to leave my mark. His rags-to-riches story motivates me every day. Dad was just a struggling kid from Queens with a business plan and a dream; now he's a multimillionaire with a company among the best in the entire industry. He's been my idol since I was a kid and that hasn't changed, although our relationship has been strained over the years. Most of it's my fault, so I don't blame him for pulling away.

Despite the tension between us, I know he's proud of what I've accomplished. The guys and I were fresh out of college when we launched the company with our combined trust funds and our skills. It's been five years since we vowed to dominate the New York City real estate game.

So far, so good.

Business has been extraordinarily great. Within five years, we've launched several developments around the city. We've built a few apartment buildings and a shopping mall, and we're currently completing our first business center. I don't want to stop there. I'm always thinking big, and I have this plan to expand our business into uncharted territory.

Hotels. Resorts, specifically. The guys think it's a crazy idea. Too risky, they say, especially Noah, which doesn't surprise me. He's always hated taking risks, but I'm the finance major; I know what I'm doing. He's the architectural genius, and Marcus heads the IT arm of our company. We all have our strengths, and this is mine. The research will prove it's worth taking a chance. Real estate market conditions are trending upwards and they probably will be for a long time. There's also the possibility for high income from long-term ownership. So yeah, it would be one hell of an investment. The best we'll ever make. I just need to get my facts together.

After pouring myself a cup of coffee, I settle on the couch. The exhaustion settles like a weight on my shoulders. Even with the coffee,

I probably won't last until three a.m. like I had planned. I'm counting down the months until Dad reclaims his position, because running two companies is no joke. I don't have a life anymore.

The sixteen-hour workday never used to bother me, but it's been ages since I've been on a date, taken some time off, or even watched a game with the guys. There's a part of me that wants to tell Dad to end his break early, but it would defeat the purpose of why I agreed to take over. I want to strengthen our relationship, not make it worse.

Eight more months, and I'll be free. I just need to stick it out.

I'm buried deep in my work when I hear Zyon's door open, putting me on edge instantly. I glance at the time. It's a little after two. Why is she still up?

She's moving silently, which is no surprise, considering her minute size, but without even looking up, I suspect she's coming downstairs. I glance to the stairs and she's halfway down, my T-shirt swallowing her body. It's thin enough for me to notice she's wearing nothing underneath. No panties, definitely no bra. Her nipples press against the fabric like they yearn to escape. I automatically wet my lips, and I can't help imagining them in my mouth.

Goddamnit.

I put my iPad down as she approaches, her eyes already latched onto me. It feels like I'm under a microscope as she looks me over. She moves to the couch, and I pull my feet up just in time for her ass to hit the spot where they were a few seconds ago. She smiles at me, a wide, sneaky grin that makes me realize she intended to sit on me. Shaking my head, I swing my legs to the floor.

"Can't sleep?" I say to her.

"Nah. Too many voices in my head. How about you?"

I point to the iPad on my lap. "Working."

"At two in the morning?" She's looking at me like I'm insane. "Is your boss an asshole, or what?"

"Oh, he definitely is," I reply with a chuckle.

From her incredulous stare, it's clear she doesn't get the joke.

"You need a new job, because that's crazy."

"Maybe I do." I set the iPad on the center table and prop my foot up on the couch again, resting my chin on my knee. "Tell me about those voices in your head."

She immediately wags her finger. "Uh-uh. You don't want to hear about them, believe me. Your life will never be the same."

"Isn't that a little dramatic?" I ask, snickering, but her face remains serious.

"It's not." She curls up on the couch, giving me a glimpse of her upper thighs. I immediately start thinking about the bare flesh between them. I force my attention to her face and she's smiling now. "I'd rather hear about you, my knight in shining armor."

"There's nothing interesting about me."

"I don't think that's true. But..." She makes a sudden move to push up on her knees, facing me. "If you don't want to talk and I don't want to talk, we could do something else instead..." She cocks her head, fiddling with the hem of her shirt, and my gaze locks onto it, watching, waiting, hoping she'll tug it upwards. Disappointment rushes through me when she plops back down on the couch.

"Wow, you're so fun," she says in a dry voice, reaching for the remote on the center table. "How do you work this thing?"

Taking the remote, I show her how to work it and she soon gets the hang of it. I'm surprised when she settles on a fantasy film and not a chick flick like I expected. She catches me staring and frowns. "What?"

"Harry Potter and the Deathly Hallows? Really?"

"Are you judging me?"

"No, I just didn't peg you for a Potterhead."

She draws back as her face lightens. "I'm not a Potterhead. I'm only mildly obsessed with the books and the movies. I get the feeling you're a fan as well."

I shrug. "I've only read the series three times since I was a kid."

"Get out of here!"

The next half an hour involves a healthy, sometimes heated debate of the series, both agreeing the books are better. Soon, Zyon shushes me while she settles to watch the movie—her fifth time—and I reach for my iPad once more. I feel content, comfortable, like this is a normal nightly occurrence. There's a crazy desire for more of this. Something permanent.

Yeah, this is weird, and I must be more fatigued than I thought. It's the only explanation for wanting a life with a woman I don't even know.

I continue working until my peripheral vision catches movement. I glance to my right as Zyon's upper body slumps to the arm of the couch, her mouth slightly open, her eyelashes fanning her cheeks. There's none of that sassy, tough girl look. Instead, her features are soft and vulnerable. I resist the urge to stroke her cheeks, but I can't let her sleep on the couch. I'll have to touch her anyhow.

She stirs a little when I grasp her underarms and lift her to my chest, and before I can slip my arm under her knees, she makes a surprising move and wraps her legs around my waist. A soft groan leaves my mouth when I feel her pressing against my stomach, knowing she's wearing nothing underneath. Zyon sighs, but she's not quite awake. Her head drops to my shoulder as I move. It's torture walking up the stairs, but I can't bring myself to switch.

When was the last time I had sex?

It feels like forever. Maybe that's why I'm so triggered by her body against mine. Every step creates a friction that makes me want to move her further down. I need to feel her against my crotch. I'm aching to sink my cock inside her, but common sense screams at me to behave, get Zyon to her room and leave her the fuck alone. One-night stands have never ended well for me, which is why I don't do them. Although something tells me it wouldn't be the same with Zyon.

No, it would be worse.

Zyon lifts her head when I enter the bedroom, her beautiful, sleepy eyes taking me in. I pause at the foot of the bed, knowing I should let her go, but can't bring myself to do it. She feels so good against me. Too good, like she belongs right here. Her eyes drop to my lips as her tongue darts out to moisten her own, the action making my pulse trip. My arms tighten around her. The battle between right and wrong grows more intense in my head.

Don't do it, Gabriel. Let her go. Now!

Oh, to hell with it. I can't help myself. I need to taste her for a minute. Just a simple kiss.

Our lips collide in a violent rush, both of us hungry, neither of us holding back. Zyon's arms lock around my neck as she matches my hard strokes, her nipples brushing my chest, her center rubbing against me. *Fuck*. There's nothing simple about this kiss. I'm not prepared for the raw emotion coursing through me, or the flutters in my stomach making it so hard to breathe. This is too much. I can't handle this.

I break the kiss with a grunt, moving to deposit Zyon to the bed, but she tightens her legs around me. Reaching behind, I try to pry them apart, but she locks them even tighter.

"Unlock your legs."

"Why?" she asks, her expression sexy and naughty, triggering the filthiest thoughts in my head. I shake them off. There will be no bending Zyon over my knee tonight.

"You need to get some rest, Zyon, and so do I."

"I don't need sleep." She grinds herself against me and I curse out loud. "What I need is you inside me."

Her soft, seductive tone sends blood rushing to my cock. I don't need to touch it to know how hard I am right now. "Zyon..."

"Talk to me." She leans in and whispers against my ear. Goosebumps fill my skin. "Tell me what *you* need, Gabriel."

It takes everything in me to grit out, "I need you to let me go."

"Why don't you say it like you mean it?" She takes my earlobe between her teeth, gently tugging.

Fuck. I close my eyes, sucking in a breath.

Zyon pulls back, and I open my eyes to meet her gaze. "What are you afraid of?"

"Afraid?" I scoff. "Who says I'm afraid of anything?"

"It's right there in your eyes."

"You're seeing nothing but exhaustion. Plus, I have an early morning meeting." Not true, but she doesn't need to know that. I'm not going to give in to the urge to sleep with her tonight.

Zyon sighs. "It's just a fuck, Gabriel. I'm not asking you to marry me."

"I don't do random hookups, Zyon. Not anymore."

She gives me a long, hard stare, then unwraps her legs. "Oh, screw you." She lands on the floor and turns away from me, angrily peeling the duvet back. "You can't handle a woman like me, anyway."

She's trying to bait me, and I won't fall for it. I turn on my heels, muttering as I stalk toward the door. "Sleep tight, Zyon."

How she gets to the door before me, I don't know. But she's standing there blocking the way with a hurtful expression that makes me feel bad. "Admit it," she says. "You don't want to sleep with me."

Is she for real? Blind? Is the hard-on in my pants invisible? I'm quite positive it's not, so she's definitely trying to push me over the edge. The question is, do I allow it, or do I ease her aside and go on my way? A sleepless, horny night, or a one-night stand I'm sure will be as spicy as the woman offering it? Do I really want to go back on my word?

No. A single retraction could open the door for every buried impulse to escape. I can't allow that to happen again. I can't afford to lose control.

"Get out of my way, Zyon."

"Make me."

I reach to move her aside as she hauls the T-shirt over her head. My hand freezes in midair before it falls to my side. I'm trying to tear my eyes away, but it's probably easier to pull a horse through a needle. God, she's stunning. Full, round breasts. Perky nipples. A flat, toned stomach with a tiny, glittery navel ring and a cute butterfly tattoo below it. My eyes fall lower, settling right between her thighs, my cock hardening even more. She's bald down there. There's nothing else that turns me on more than a woman who's completely shaved.

Zyon runs her fingers down her tiny waist and over her hips before she palms them with a smirk. "Like what you see?"

I swallow, not intending to answer. Her knowing smile confirms she already knows the truth.

"Good." She dips and picks up my shirt from the floor. "Because you missed your window, Gabriel. All you get to do is look."

She tries to get past me, and I grip her upper arms. "You're a fucking tease, you know that?"

For some reason, my response irritates her. She violently tugs her arm from my grip and shoves against my chest. The gesture is a forceful one, but it doesn't faze me. "Don't you *ever* fucking say that to me again, got it?" When I don't answer, she pushes me again. "Got it?"

I grip her wrist when she makes another attempt to shove me, and I drop them before cupping her cheeks. The fire in her eyes is the last thing I see before I close mine and capture her lips, getting another taste of heaven for the third time tonight. When she closes the gap between us, encircling me with her nakedness, it seals my fate. There's no going back now. I'm already too far gone.

4

ZYON

Please Gabriel, don't stop kissing me. I'm begging you, don't pull away.

The words flow through my head like a prayer, but I'm hoping he hears them somehow, because this kiss... it's even better than the ones before. It's deeper, more intense. His large hands are everywhere; kneading my breasts, cupping my ass, gripping a cluster of hair while he explores my mouth. I surrender to his erotic takeover. I couldn't resist him if I wanted to, anyway.

He releases me with a gasp, like he's coming up for air, and he backs away with the agony stamped on his face. "Fuck."

He's obviously conflicted, and my conscience— the fragmented parts that still exist— wants me to let him go. But I'm so aroused, my body wound tighter than the strings of a guitar. I can't sleep like this. Masturbating won't do it for me, either. I reach for his arm, relieved when he doesn't pull away. It encourages me to move closer to him.

"Don't think, Gabriel." I run my hand down his chest, grazing over his hard cock in his pants. "Just feel. That's all I ask."

A soft curse leaves his lips before he hauls off his T-shirt, blessing me with a full-on view of his gorgeous torso. His pecs are firm and muscular when I run my hands over them, and the lust intensifies in his eyes when I pinch each puckered nipple. He doesn't stop me, encouraging me to swirl my tongue around the bud before taking it in my mouth.

Gabriel groans, and it's so sexy, making my pussy clench so tight it hurts. My lips move lower, peppering his tight body with kisses, licking his abs, fingering the waist of his pajama pants as I drop to my knees. I want his cock in my mouth. *Fuck*, I can already taste him on my tongue.

He grips my wrists before I pull his pants down, lifting me off my feet and throwing me on the bed, where I land with a healthy bounce. My protest flies back down my throat when he tugs his pants down and his cock springs free. I push up on my arms, already salivating from the sight. It's lengthy, thick, and erect. *For me*. Yes, he's aroused *for me*. I can feel the moisture gathering between my thighs as I impatiently rock my hips. I'm ready for him, burning for every inch of him inside me.

Gabriel moves toward the bed and I open like a flower for him. He falters, his gaze dipping and lingering, then a soft curse leaves his lips. The brief resistance on his face makes me worry; is he changing his mind?

I push to a sitting position again. "Gabriel—"

"Condoms. I'm completely out," he says, and I'm pleased that he sounds disappointed.

"I have that covered," I reply, jerking my head over to the armchair. "Hand me my purse."

An expression resembling a scowl flashes across his face before he turns and walks to the chair. Maybe I imagined it. He seems fine while handing me my purse. I fish out the condom, tearing the package with my teeth, and he allows me to slip it on. He releases a shuddering breath as I slide it down the base.

A sudden, overwhelming nervousness takes over me. My shaking hands release Gabriel's cock and I wipe my damp palms on my hips. It's not unusual to feel like this before sex. Sometimes, I have to psych myself up before spreading my legs. Sleeping with Gabriel doesn't require a couple shots of liquid courage or a pep talk with myself in the bathroom mirror, but I'm still a little jittery. I can't walk away, though. I need this. I need him.

This is new, this desperate ache for him. I've never experienced it before. Sex has always been physical, never emotional. It was just a symbol of taking control. For the first time, I want to completely lose myself in a man and it makes me anxious. Scared. Gabriel must see it on my face because he tilts my chin upwards and asks, "Are you sure you want to do this?"

"Yes," I reply with a forced smile, pulling him in for a kiss. He responds briefly, pushing at my shoulder to force me backward on the bed. Within a few seconds he's over me, settling between my thighs. He gently kisses my collarbone, my throat, moving upwards to my chin, along my jaw, then nibbling on my ear, the action releasing bursts of pleasure inside me. It feels like I'm being pulled into a deep, sensual trance, and I don't ever want to emerge. With my eyes half-closed, I run my fingers through his silky hair as he moves down my body.

Balancing his weight on one arm, Gabriel gently trails his fingers between my cleavage and over my stomach, leaving goosebumps on my skin. I bite my lips to stifle a moan when he grazes the seam of my sex before sinking two fingers inside me.

"Fuck," he mumbles, his eyes darkening as he strokes me. "You're dripping, Zyon."

I'm too overwhelmed to reply. The onslaught of emotions makes it hard to think straight. My hips slowly churn, matching the rhythm of his skillful fingers. If this is Gabriel's foreplay, I can't imagine the main event, but I don't think I'll last long enough to get there. His fingers are fucking me so well; I swear I'm about to pass out from the fire-hot passion that's consuming me. I pinch my nipples as he adds another finger, digging deeper, thrusting harder, his thumb brushing my clit.

The first pre-climatic wave rushes over me just as Gabriel withdraws his fingers. He surprises me by licking them off then leaning down to kiss me, and the taste of me on his lips makes me moan. I doubt I could get any more aroused than this.

But then his lips start wandering, kissing my neck, licking my throat, raising my body's temperature. By the time he gets to my nipples I'm on the verge of bursting into flames. He grips an erect bud with his teeth, roughly tugging. His fingers sink inside me again, the movements deliberately slow. Teasing. The contrast is messing with my mind. Holy fuck, he's about to drive me insane.

"You're killing me, Gabriel," I whisper, my eyes half-closed, overdosed on pleasure. He rubs my clit with his thumb, and I moan as another orgasmic surge runs through me. I increase the tempo of my hips, fucking his fingers, pushing myself toward climax. God, I just want to come. My eyes fly open as Gabriel withdraws his fingers. From the wicked grin on his face, he knew I was about to pop off. Breathing hard, I push up to a sitting position while giving him a dirty glare.

"That was cruel."

"This is what you get for fucking with my head." His smile disappears and he pushes me back to the bed, straddling me once more. Pushing up on my elbows again, I squirm, wildly aroused as he teases my clit, his head glistening with my juices. I'm trying to be patient, but it seems he's hellbent on driving me insane.

"Gabriel, please..." He inches in a little then quickly withdraws, the wicked gleam in his eyes getting more intense. Our eyes lock in a stare-down as he rims my entrance with his cock, grazing along the seam, repeatedly brushing my sensitive clit. "Damn it—"

Gabriel places my leg over his thigh and sinks inside me, taking my breath away. Literally. The emotional connection is so swift and intense, I forget to exhale for a moment. A soft curse leaves Gabriel's lips before his eyes fly shut. His fingers dig so deep into my thigh, I'm sure they'll leave a mark, even with his short fingernails. For once, I don't mind. I'm so caught up in the sensation of being *full*, it takes a few seconds to realize he's not moving at all. I brush the hair from his forehead as he opens his eyes to meet mine. The emotion I see leaves an unfamiliar ache in my belly and again, I'm struggling to breathe.

What the hell is happening to me?

Gabriel pulls out to the tip, hovering, his gaze still locked with mine. Growling, he fills me again, the rough stroke taking me by surprise.

From some reason, he's furious, but I don't mind. I'm here for the wild, angry sex. I don't need him to make love to me. I just want to be fucked. Tomorrow, I'll forget he ever existed, just like the others. Another notch on my bedpost, that's all he'll be.

Gabriel soon picks up the pace, his slim hips rolling, his powerful arms flexing as he makes deep, deliberate thrusts. I bite my lips, stifling the moan when he hits a sensitive spot only my vibrator has ever reached. There's an instant explosion of pleasure that spreads to every inch of my body, and it barely subsides when I experience another burst, then another. My fingers curl around the sheet when he digs a little deeper.

"Jesus, Gabriel."

He's moving even faster now, getting rougher, breathing hard. Sweat decorates his gorgeous torso, giving it a sheen that makes his skin glow. Each skillful thrust leaves me battling with an indescribable emotion swiftly rising to an unbearable point. I'm aware of my racing heart, the tightening in my chest, the tears trickling down the corners of my eyes.

What the fuck is wrong with me?

Uh-uh. Whatever this is, I'm not having it. I push against his shoulder, intending to get on top where I can take control. "Stop."

Gabriel pauses at once, his mouth slightly parted as he takes uneven breaths, his face softening with concern. "Did I hurt you? Do you want to stop?"

"No, I'm fine. I—"

"Good."

His cock starts knifing through me again, the ferocity of his thrusts matching his expression. Sweet agony envelopes me. *Fuck*. He's good.

No, amazing—goddamnit, he's picking up the pace. Goosebumps form on my arms, which makes no sense because my body feels like it's burning up. I feel like pulling my hair, or sinking my teeth into something, or screaming—ugh, I have no clue what to do with myself. I'm definitely going crazy. Every single, delicious stroke from his cock pushes me closer to insanity.

"Yes, Gabriel," I whisper. "Don't stop."

Gabriel grunts in response, sweat dripping from his body, the droplets decorating my torso. His hot stare lashes me as he heeds my request. I moan as he hits my sensitive spot, the action sending electric tingles through me. My pelvic floor tightens as he flicks my clit with his thumb, pushing me over the edge. The orgasm hits me like a lightning bolt, surging from my center to my nipples. My fingers grip the sheets as my mouth spews the filthiest words. I'm too far gone to care. The unfamiliar high is so thrilling, I never want to come back down.

Gabriel's sexy groan tells me he's not far behind. He grips my ass, thrusting into me so hard it blurs my vision. It's over too soon. Gradually, I descend, returning to reality. Gabriel rolls off me with a loud sigh, flopping on his back.

"Oh, my God," I mumble between breaths. "That was amazing."

Gabriel doesn't reply. I turn on my side while still catching my breath, watching as he removes the condom and drops it in the waste bin by the bed. When he glances at me, I glimpse the anger that was there before. It flits across his face so fast I barely catch it.

"You regret doing this, don't you?"

"Nope." He swings his legs off the bed and reach for his clothes on the floor.

I quickly push to a seated position. “Stay. Please. I hate being in a strange room all alone. I won’t be able to sleep.”

Gabriel stares at me for a beat, then surprises me by dropping his clothes on the armchair and coming back to bed. “Only until you fall asleep, okay?”

“Okay.”

There’s a smile on my face when he pulls me against him, his hand splayed across my stomach. This is comfortable. It feels good. It's just the post-sex, euphoric residue, but I don’t care. I want to bask in it for as long as I can.

I soon relax in his arms, feeling safe for the first time in a long time.

My eyes fly open as rough hands grip my throat, clutching tighter, tighter, making it hard to breathe. I try loosening his grip but it's no use. It's iron-clad. I refuse to panic. I can’t show my fear. He can never realize how terrified I really am.

Still, evil recognizes fear, doesn’t it? He's clearly getting off on what he's doing to me. His erection presses against my thigh, making me sick to my stomach. I wiggle my body to dislodge him, but it only makes him laugh.

His hot breath fans my face, his voice cruel as he whispers, “You’re such a fucking tease, Zyon, you know that?”

My scream comes out in a gurgle. I claw at his face, but it's no longer there. Just darkness. Nothing but darkness. Where the hell am I?

I can hear my loud panting as my eyes adjust, and I glimpse dim light coming from the right. Getting out of bed, I rush toward it and yank the curtains aside to stare at the approaching dawn brightening the street. The memories quickly return, bringing a familiar guilt.

Damn it, another one-night stand. I broke my promise. Again.

The guilt slowly dissipates as I make my way back to bed. Last night wasn't like the others. I didn't plan for this like I usually did. Gabriel wasn't handpicked from a bar or seduced in a club before I took him home.

My world has never been rocked like this.

Sitting on the edge of the bed, I think about the nightmare, the one that haunted me for months, leaving me with sleepless nights because I was too afraid to fall asleep again. I haven't had one in weeks, and now I'm worried. Did sleeping with Gabriel resurrect my greatest fear?

No. What Gabriel and I shared was unexpectedly amazing. I won't associate such a wonderful moment with the worst night of my life.

Ugh.

I don't want to think about it, or him. The piece of shit who destroyed my life. He doesn't deserve a rent-free space in my head. I reach for my phone and text Roshell to pick me up. It's a little past six and she's an early riser. I just hope she wasn't fucked into a coma last night. I dress and head downstairs. There's no sign of Gabriel, which means he's probably still asleep. A well-deserved sleep, if I may say so myself. I can never repay him for what he did for me.

Entering the kitchen, my eyes scan the well-stocked pantry, and a fabulous thought occurs. For the next twenty minutes, I get to work preparing a batch of breakfast egg muffins. It's my favorite morning meal and I hope he likes it too. If not... well, I won't ever find out, because I will never see him again.

The sudden tightening in my chest is no surprise. I've been a little depressed since waking up, and it has little to do with the terrifying dream I had. It's the thought of saying goodbye. It leaves an ache in my stomach that makes no sense, but it's there and it's strong. It makes me want to do crazy things, like go to Gabriel's room and spend the entire day in his arms. It makes me want to see him after this. To date him. It's surreal. Definitely not like me.

I put the muffins in his warmer while banishing the thought. No. There will be no talk of dating or anything remotely close to it. I made rules for a reason, and I'm going to stick by them.

One: no making love, just fucking.

Two: no spending the night.

Three: absolutely no contact after sex. None.

Yes, I've already broken a rule with Gabriel, but this wasn't a typical one-night stand. I needed a place to stay and he offered one. What happened next wasn't a part of my plan.

Well... not really.

My cell phone rings as I close the warmer. It's Roshell, and she sounds puzzled. "Why do you need me to pick you up?" she asks. "Can't Dineo take you home?"

"I'm not at Dineo's. I'm in Brooklyn Heights," I reply, leaning against the kitchen counter and bracing for the inevitable outburst. I hear the sharp intake of her breath, then a door slam. The sound of a car horn tells me she stepped outside.

"What the hell, Zyon? Didn't we talk about those one-night stands and how you won't do them anymore? Are you trying to get yourself killed? What's wrong with—"

"Are you picking me up?" I'm not interested in a lecture. I just need to get out of here, to escape these crazy feelings for Gabriel.

Roshell sighs. "Lucky for you, I'm just a few blocks away. Otherwise, your ass would walk home for all I care."

I know she doesn't mean that. She's just angry, and I understand why. It took a lot of work to put me back together after I fell apart. She's the only friend that stuck around. I can't lose her.

"Listen, Rosh, it's not what you think, okay? I'll explain when I see you."

"Fine. It better be good or I'm kicking your butt."

I hang up the phone with a grin. There's still no sound from upstairs, which means Gabriel is probably still asleep. It's for the best, although a part of me wants a final glimpse before I walk away. Ignoring the urge, I search downstairs for something to write on and spot a notebook and a pen on a table near the hallway. Flipping over to a clean page, I scribble a quick note.

Hey Gabriel,

Thanks for everything. Check out my appreciation breakfast in the warmer. Hope you like it!

Zyon.

Simple. To the point. No emotion involved. Just how I want it. I just wish I could control the emotions inside me, too.

5

ZYON

"What the hell?" Roshell exclaims as I ease onto the seat of her car. "What happened to your face?"

"Nothing worth talking about, believe me."

Closing the car door, I give her a once-over, taking in her hair that looks more disheveled than mine. Her lucky bamboo hoop earrings are missing, a clear sign my best friend got screwed real good last night. Those earrings were a gift from her granddad before he passed. She never goes out without them.

"From the look of things, it seems *you* have plenty to talk about. You look like a woman who had a hell of a night."

She blushes, then gets serious again. "Do not change the subject. Who hurt you?"

"Can we talk about this when we get home?" The longer we linger in front of Gabriel's apartment, the more I regret leaving without saying goodbye and the more I want to go back inside. It's time to put some distance between me and the man who's triggering the strangest, most insane feelings I want no part of. A warm shower and decent sleep will put me in my right mind.

Roshell doesn't seem pleased with my response, but she doesn't argue. She shoots off from the curb and the sudden movement makes me wince. Damn it. I'm really sore. I can't believe I underestimated Gabriel. I mean, he looked like a guy who could handle his business, but he didn't just take charge. He fucking *dominated*. My body starts warming from the memory of his cock inside me and I squirm a little in my seat.

Oh, God. Make it stop. Please.

"Seriously. What's up with you, Zyon? You're clearly uncomfortable," Roshell asks, concern stamped across her face.

"Nothing." I fiddle with my seatbelt. "I'm fine. Can you put some weight on that gas pedal, please?"

"And get another ticket? No ma'am. I'm not about to join your suspended license ass."

"*Temporary* suspended license," I correct her. I lost my driving privileges when I ran off the road and into a convenience store last year. My alcohol level was two times the legal limit and I had just finished smoking a blunt. It was the last straw after a DUI charge a few months before. The judge wanted to sentence me to jail time, but Dineo hired a decent lawyer—the least she could do, considering she caused the mess I'm going through. I ended up with a three-year suspended sentence, including a two-year suspension on my license and mandatory AA meetings, which, by extension, means no drinking at all.

Oops.

Okay, so last night was a major setback. I'm human, aren't I? I'm still a work in progress, but I'm really trying to get the old Zyon back, I swear. Slowly but surely, I'm checking off all the things on my to-do list. I've done rehab. I'm almost finished with therapy. My AA meetings... well, there's room for improvement in that area. I haven't been to one in weeks. My sponsor's number is on my blocked callers list for the moment. Probably permanently. I don't think I have a problem with alcohol anymore.

"Whatever. Bottom line, I don't want to be stuck in passenger mode like you. I'm keeping this baby below the speed limit," Roshell says.

"Oh, come on, Rosh. I need to be home like yesterday. Knowing Dineo, she's on her way to check if I jumped over the balcony last night."

"Damn it. No. I'm not going another kilometer until you tell me what the fuck is going on." She pulls off the road and parks near a gas station, then lashes me with a stern look. "What happened last night, Zyon? I left you curled up under the covers, half asleep. Which, I might add, was the best idea ever. How the hell did you end up in a bar? Or on this side of town? With a *bruise* on your face?"

Sighing, I relax in the seat and turn my attention to the line of cars waiting for an available pump at the gas station. "I couldn't sleep."

Roshell sighs too. "Oh, girl. It's hard. I know. But violating your probation isn't the answer to outrunning those demons. Drinking only makes them stronger than before." She pats my thigh with her free hand. "Promise me you'll just settle for Netflix and a bag of banana chips next time."

"I'll try."

"Zyon—I mean it, okay? I heard the slur in your voice last night. You were drunk, which means anything could have happened to you. Well, other than whatever gave you that bruise."

I bite my lower lip, knowing all hell is about to break loose when I tell her the truth. "I was almost robbed while walking home from the bar."

"Oh my God! Zyon!"

"Don't look at me like that."

"How? Like I want to bitch slap your stupid ass? Because I do. Luckily, I'm not your mother because girl..." Her fingers curl around the steering wheel as she shakes her head.

"Speaking of my mother... can you do me a solid and not tell Dineo? If she ever finds out, it's back to rehab I go."

"Frankly, I think it might be what you need. That asshole could have done so much worse."

Just like that, my common sense gives me the bitch slap Roshell threatened earlier. Damn it. She's right. I could have been hurt way worse. That mugger could have damaged my soul even more than it is right now. I don't want to think about the what-ifs when they make me so sick to my stomach, so I brush her comment aside with a flick of my wrist.

"On the bright side, I'm still in one piece. No real harm done, okay?"

"Except you left your keys inside the apartment and had to sleep at a stranger's house." She gives me a quick, withering glance then turns her eyes back to the road, merging into traffic. "Something tells me that's not all you did."

"I plead the fifth."

"Zyon!"

Bewildered, I look over at her. "What?"

"I thought you were done with this. Didn't your therapist ban you from having casual sex?"

"Correction; she *suggested* I heal first, then try having a meaningful relationship instead of jumping into bed with a hot guy." I roll my eyes. I'm twenty-four years old, just coming into my prime. I'm not ready for a meaningful relationship. I don't want one, either. Men are assholes. Useful for a good time, but that's it.

"You say it like there's something wrong with settling down."

"For me, there is."

"Listen, Zyon—"

"I *really* don't need a lecture right now, Roshell. I think you've ripped into me enough for one day."

Roshell is a middle school guidance counselor who's always in work mode. I often appreciate her opinion, but today isn't one of them, especially when it's making me feel so guilty.

"Oh, shut it. I'm just giving you a bit of advice. You've been through shit, Zyon. I get that, but men are not the enemy. Don't paint every guy with the same brush because of what A—"

"No. Stop. Don't even say his name."

"When will you stop giving that asshole power? Huh? Say his name, Zyon. Talk about what he did to you. That's the only way you'll truly heal."

"I'm healing quite well without doing that, so I'm good. Let's just drop it. Okay?"

"Fine." Her mouth tightens, the way it usually does when she's not pleased. "So... how was your little one-night stand?"

"Oh, girl..." I relax with a grin, resting my palms behind my head. "It wasn't little at all."

"Oh, shit."

"That's all I'm going to say."

"Come on!"

"How about you tell me about your night? Although it's quite clear how your night was from the look on your face."

Roshell's eyes sparkle, and I can't remember the last time I've seen her so happy. "Babe, I can't begin to describe how amazing it was. I think Terrence could be the one."

"Oh, wow. I'm happy for you." I am. Ever since we were kids, Roshell has always wanted the happily ever after, the kids and the husband and the penthouse suite. I've met Terrence and he seems great. He's really into her, too. Plus, he's loaded, so it seems she's on her way to her dream.

"Now, back to you," she says.

"Uh-uh. I'm not talking about it."

"Then I'll form my own conclusions. I saw how you waddled to the car. Is the headboard still intact?"

"Oh, fuck off, Rosh." Still, I can't help smiling, and my face heats when I remember the banging headboard last night.

"Your face, sis..."

I cover my face with both hands, chuckling. "It was so fucking good."

"Oh wow."

"I made him breakfast. Left it in the warmer."

"Holy cow," she says in an exaggerated whisper, looking over at me in shock. "Zyon, you've never cooked for a man."

"I know."

Roshell grins. "You're thinking of sleeping with him again, aren't you?"

"I'm done talking." I twist my body and turn my back to her. She laughs out loud.

The truth is, I can't think of anything *but* sleeping with Gabriel again. I can't get him off my mind. Not that I'm trying much, anyway. His touch, those lips, that *cock*. I'm still coming down from that high. There's no cocktail that has ever intoxicated me like this. There's still lingering regret over how I left, but it's for the best. I don't trust the way I feel right now.

Roshell turns onto our street and pulls up to the curb, giving me another stern glare. "I'm glad you're okay, Zyon, but don't ever do this again, you got that? I can't handle if something happens to you again."

"Aww." I reach over and wrap my arms around her torso. "I'll be careful from now on, I promise. Thanks for looking out, sis. I love you."

Her body relaxes and she hugs me back. "Love you more."

I'm almost done with my shower when Roshell comes barging into the bathroom. "Dineo's here, and she seems pissed. Did you guys have a falling out again?"

I shake my head while quickly reaching for the towel on the rack. "Dineo is always pissed at me. It should be the other way around."

My mother and I weren't always like this. I'm her only child. She's been playing the dual-parent role for as long as I can remember, after Dad ran off with another woman. Financially, we had little, but I lived a contented life because she constantly showered me with love. Everything changed when her restaurant kept hemorrhaging the little savings she had. Despite her most ambitious efforts, she kept losing, until the bank threatened to take it all. I was a few months away from graduating college, buried up to my neck in student loans. I had no job, no way to help her escape financial ruin. She reminded me of my uselessness every single day. The more depressed she got, the worse the insults, which were usually followed by apologies and tears. I was constantly involved in a tug-of-war between helplessness and fury, between wanting to give her a hug and telling her to fuck off.

I didn't deserve her anger. I was a good girl, always had been. There was no sneaking out of the house to go partying when I was a teenager. No making out with boys in my room. I was a straight-A student who never succumbed to peer pressure, never got pregnant in my teens like my cousins did. It angered me that even after all I did—or didn't do—she never saw my worth. She tried to make it up to me when things started looking up, but it was too late. I was already scarred. Our relationship would never be the same, and she made it worse when she invited that monster into our lives.

I take my time slipping on a comfortable pair of leggings and a T-shirt, and I linger in front of the mirror trying to untangle my hair. I spot a cute little love bite on my neck, resurrecting the memory of Gabriel's mouth on me, nibbling and licking—

"Girl, can you hurry up already?" Roshell whispers through my open door. "I'm running out of small talk. Plus, she's asking what we did last night. Are you sure you don't want her to come up? It would make things so much easier."

"I'm sure." Dineo's not allowed in my personal space anymore. Not after what she did to me. It was her actions that caused—

"I wish you would just talk to me," Roshell interrupts my thoughts, closing the door. "I've been waiting an entire year for you to open up. What's going on with you and Dineo? Why do you hate her so much?"

"I don't hate her. Just her decisions."

"That's still not saying much."

I sigh out loud. "We'll talk about it when the time is right, okay?"

"You keep saying that, but cool. I'll wait."

I cover the bruise and my love bite with makeup, then wrap an oversized scrunchie around my giant mop of hair. I linger in the bedroom a few minutes longer before getting this meeting over with. Dineo gets up from the couch as I approach, and like always, I can't help admiring her. She's stunning, and with that smooth, dark-brown skin, high cheekbones, and long legs, she could have been a supermodel. She looks like an African queen in a dashiki dress, her hair done in neat Bantu knots. How she gets her waist-length dreadlocks into that hairstyle is beyond me.

Her sharp eyes look me over. She lingers for a beat on my upper body, and I cross my fingers, hoping the makeup did its work to hide the marks. I'm not ready for a lecture on abstinence. I don't need to hear that I should heal before letting another man between my thighs. I wouldn't need to heal if she hadn't been so generous with her spare room. I know what her visits mean. She's not really interested in my welfare. She's trying to assuage her guilt. I'm a mess because of her mistakes.

"Zyon," she says, leaning her head to the side, "don't just stand there. Come give your mother a hug."

I move at once, unable to withhold my sigh as she wraps her arms around me. I settle against her warm body, and for a moment, my bitterness evaporates.

Just for a moment.

"Why do you feel so thin? Have you been eating?"

I pull back while stifling the urge to roll my eyes. "I eat fine, Mommy."

She's looking like she doesn't believe me. "I keep telling you to come home for dinner. Especially when I'm cooking jollof rice with goat stew. Always been your favorite, hmm?"

As if I would ever set foot in that God-forsaken apartment ever again. I respond with an evasive smile.

"I was worried about you last night," she continues, worrying a loose lock of my hair through the scrunchie. I bear her invasion of my space, knowing it won't last.

"I started assuming the worst when you didn't answer your phone. You always pick up."

My stomach churns when I realize what she's implying. "Mommy, I wouldn't..." I trail off with a harsh breath, battling the memories of the night I tried to take my life. From the disturbance on Dineo's face, I know she remembers it too. That was six months ago. I've made major improvements since then.

"I'm just glad you're okay, that's all."

"I'm fine, I promise." I move to the kitchen to escape the guilt from being out while she was worried about me. Granted, it doesn't happen often, but I don't like feeling like I'm the one who's wrong. That's Dineo's forte. Not mine.

"So..." she begins while I set the kettle under the open tap. "How's the job hunt going?"

"Not great. I sent out several applications this week. I'm waiting to see what bites."

"Are you okay with the bills for this month?" she asks, and I reply with a stiff nod, feeling a drop in my stomach. Every month brings the harsh reminder that I'm surviving on *his* blood money. Hush money. Payment for my pain.

"Good." She comes over and affectionately rubs my shoulder. "I know you don't agree, but I still think we did the right thing. His family would have made the case disappear; you know that. We would have gotten nothing in the end."

Again, I nod, but inside I'm angry. I sold my soul because Dineo got scared. He should be rotting in jail for what he did to me. My life spiraled out of control because he couldn't take no for an answer. My screams had no effect. I was his for the taking. Now I'm left trying to escape the demons, trying to piece my life together again. I haven't been doing a great job of starting over. It's been a year since the incident, and I don't recognize who I am anymore.

Dineo moves to a stool under the kitchen island, and I suspect she sensed the anger boiling inside of me. She says nothing for a few minutes while I busy myself with making a sandwich for breakfast.

"So, how was your session with Anita?" she asks after a while.

"Okay, I guess. She thinks I'm not expressing myself enough. You know how she is."

"She's just trying to do her job."

"I know. It's just difficult talking about shit."

She cocks her eyebrows at me, and I release a conceding breath. "*Stuff*. I don't want to be there. I sure as hell don't want to relive the memories."

"She's there to help you heal, Zyon. Your stubbornness isn't helping one bit," Dineo replies, sounding impatient.

I drop the knife down on the counter and turn to her. "I wouldn't need to heal if you hadn't let that piece of shit into our lives."

"Zyon!"

"No! I don't need to hear your self-righteousness, Mommy. I had a decent job, a car—a license. My sanity. I had my entire life ahead of me. Now, I have nothing. My bills are being paid by the man who raped me, and it's all your fucking fault!"

Dineo stands abruptly, her face barely containing her anger. "My fault? Was I the one walking around the house with my ass hanging out? Those half-done blouses with that disgusting belly button ring... was that me, or you?"

My mouth falls open. *What did she just say*? Is she blaming me for what happened?

Dineo's face sobers and her arms falls to her side. "Zyon, I—I—"

"No, don't say a word. It's quite clear how you feel. Now I know why you were so quick to take his money. You think I asked for it."

She takes a step toward me. "No, I don't, baby."

"Whatever." I push past her and out of the kitchen. She calls my name as I run up the stairs, but I don't look back. I feel awful inside. I just want to curl up in bed until the tension goes away.

There's a knock on the door and I pull my head from under the duvet as Roshell sticks her head inside. "I won't ask if you're okay. I'm here for you, cool?"

"Cool. Is she gone?"

"Yup. She says the invitation to dinner is still open if you want it. Which, from the look on your face, is definitely not happening."

"You know me quite well." Dineo and I lived in that apartment since I was five years old. It was my safe space until she let him in. Now I can never go back there. Not unless I want to lose my mind.

I don't want Dineo's olive branch. What I need is a job so I can get my life back. I can't bear living off the blood money anymore.

6

Gabriel

A knock on the office door grabs my attention and I shift my eyes from my computer as Marcus steps inside.

"You ready?" he asks. "Lauren has already called twice. She's asking what time we'll be there."

Marcus's referring to the party my mother's throwing in my sister Lauren's honor for graduating first in her class with honors, from Stanford. "She's just trying to not get caught in the crossfire. I'm still trying to figure out why Mom invited Dad and Karyn."

There's no love lost between Mom and Dad's new wife. She thinks Karyn tricked Dad into getting her pregnant and marrying her six months after they met because she wanted his money, but I suspect Mom's just jealous he moved on so quickly after the divorce. A divorce *Mom* insisted on. She didn't care that he wanted to fix what was broken. She just wanted to be free. From what, I have no clue. I'm not privy to my mom's private thoughts. Not anymore.

"Mrs. C is just a classy woman, that's all," Marcus says.

"I hope you're right," I reply, rubbing my temple. "The last thing this family needs is more drama."

Marcus glances at his watch, giving me an impatient look. "What's the hold-up, man?"

"I'm just booking a meeting with Dad's board of directors, then I'm out of here."

"Wait a minute. Did you lose another assistant?"

I shrug. "Something like that."

"What did she do this time, bring you a cold cup of coffee?"

I slide him a dirty glare. "You make it sound like I'm high-maintenance."

"That's because you are. You're too goddamn picky. No one's ever going to replace Matt. Just get that through your thick skull."

Matt was my assistant since day one, back when I was a nervous mess, convinced we were crazy to launch our own company. If it wasn't for him, I probably would have burned the building down the first week. He was my backbone, always ensuring I remained on top of things. We gelled so well, he anticipated what I needed before I even knew I needed it. He was always on time, and always pleasant. I never imagined him leaving. It crushed me when he resigned a few months ago and moved to LA with his new husband. So, yes, I've been a little hard on his replacements because I'm still looking for the synergy Matt and I had. Sue me. If they can't handle the heat, well... not my problem.

I get up from the desk and reach for my laptop bag. "The perfect assistant exists, Marcus. All I need is to find him. Or her. I won't settle for less."

"Speaking of finding someone... still haven't heard from Zyon?"

"Nope. I don't want to talk about it." It's been a week since I woke up to a well-made bed in the guest room and a handwritten note from Zyon. I'm still pissed she didn't have the decency to say goodbye.. Those egg muffins were delicious, but they weren't enough to soothe my irritation.

I'll admit it, my pride is a little bruised. Before Zyon, I had experienced nothing like that. Women didn't leave my apartment without saying goodbye. It was always the other way around. I've lost count how many times I snuck from a woman's bed in the middle of the night, leaving them with nothing but the memory of me. No cell phone number, nothing. Is this karma?

Karma has been giving me a beating for years. It's time for a break. I earned it. Five years sober, my man-whore days over. I haven't lost my temper or gotten in a fight in ages. Well... except the night I rescued Zyon. I'm *trying* to be a good guy, goddamnit.

Marcus's cell phone rings as I slip my laptop into the bag. "It's Noah." He puts it on speaker and moves closer to me. "What's up, my man?"

"Just had a conversation with the consultant we hired to run the SWOT analysis, and Gabriel, you were right. It's very profitable to launch a resort chain in the Caribbean. Way to go, dude."

"Hell yeah!" Marcus says, fisting the air. I can't contain my joy. The smile on my face spreads from ear to ear.

"Okay, okay, let's hear the I-told-you-so, you prick," Noah grumbles.

"I'll leave the gloating for the end when we're in full operation. There's plenty of work to be done. When are we getting the actual report?" I ask.

"Next week," he replies. "We can finalize the business plan then. Enough about work. I'm going downstairs to celebrate. Finally, something to do in this goddamn place." Noah is away at his father's ranch in Texas for a weekend family reunion. From the grumpiness in his tone, I'm guessing he's not too enthused about being there.

"You're overreacting. I'm sure there's plenty to do in Plano," Marcus says with a sarcastic chuckle.

"Oh, screw you. I'm pissed enough as it is."

"Hurry back to Brooklyn so we can officially celebrate," I say. "Talk to you later. We have a party to catch." It won't be a party at Mom's apartment, but I'll say anything to get under Noah's skin.

"Yeah, way to rub it in asshole," he grumbles before hanging up. Marcus and I head out to his car. He starts fiddling with his shirt when we pull up at my mom's apartment. He's tense; Marcus doesn't fiddle. We take the lift upstairs and he's still fussing with his sleeves.

"Relax, man. It's just family," I say, shaking his arm lightly to get him to stop.

He pauses, and the look on his face reminds me of when his dad caught us smoking weed when we were sixteen. "I know."

I wait for him to say more, but he doesn't. That's a first. Marcus has always been talkative, which means he's definitely nervous. It instantly puts me on edge. I didn't find it unusual when Mom invited him to the party. Marcus' dad and my family are quite close, as are Noah's parents.

But Marcus is behaving like a guy on his first date with a girl who's out of his league.

Someone like my mom.

No.

Fuck no. I'm just exhausted. I'm overthinking this shit. Marcus is a dog, but even he wouldn't dare cross the line and date my mother. I glance at him again and he's doing a breath test with his hand. Uh-uh. I can't hold it in any longer.

"Marcus. Be straight with me. Are you sleeping with my mom?"

He stares at me like I've just sprouted two heads. "What? Hell no! Mrs. C could be *my* mom, you weirdo. What makes you think I'd do such a thing?"

"Because you've checked your reflection in the mirror five times since we got in here and you keep fidgeting with your goddamn clothes."

The elevator opens on the top floor, and we get out.

"I just want to look the part, that's all."

"What part? Do you see what I'm wearing?" I sweep my hands over my body. Before leaving the house this morning, I slipped on a pair of distressed jeans and a sweater. On my feet are a pair of simple, dark sneakers. "You're overdressed, dude."

That thought quickly goes out the window when I enter my mom's living room; *I'm underdressed*. Mom's wearing a dark blue dress with sparkly straps and her blonde hair is in an updo. She usually wears her hair up when she means business. Oh, boy. Please don't cue the drama.

Mom gives me a disapproving glance before greeting Marcus. "So nice of you to come, my dear. Thank you for making an effort with your outfit." She shoots a cool look at me again. "I can't say the same for all of us."

"I was at work, Mom, busting my ass, thanks to Dad offloading on me."

She raises her brows at me. "Don't get smart with me, young man. And don't be ungrateful, either. Your father and I worked hard to create a foundation for you to enjoy, to give you the luxury to start your own company. We're asking for the bare minimum in return. God knows you owe us so much more."

Here we go again. She never fails to take a dig at me, reminding me of what I've done. It's subtle, but I get the hint.

"Would it kill you to put a dress shirt on, huh?" she says as I walk past her.

"You know what, Mom? It probably would. I don't see what's the big deal. I'm here, aren't I?"

Mom opens her mouth to reply but her face brightens, and I realize she's looking behind me. Turning, I see Lauren coming down the stairs. Her hair is a little darker than mine, but we have the same golden-brown eyes. She's definitely overdressed. The sparkly dress brushes her knees and it's a little too tight, but at least she's not leaving the house.

"Don't tell me you two are at it again," Lauren says when she reaches the foot of the stairs.

"She thinks I'm underdressed."

Lauren surveys me a little. "You kind of are, bro. Now, Marcus, he's definitely dressed for a party. You look sharp, dude."

"Thanks." His response is a little dry, but his light-brown skin is now red. Marcus hates getting compliments. For a cocky chick magnet, I find that completely odd.

"At least someone agrees with me," Mom says.

The doorbell rings and her smile disappears. "Gabriel, be a dear and get the door. I'm sure it's your father and his... companion."

She immediately moves to the dining table, reaching for a wine bottle as I walk to the door, wondering for the millionth time why she bothered to invite Dad and Karyn. She's clearly not okay with seeing them together.

Shaking my head, I open the door with an arranged smile. Dad and I had been close before Daniel's death. Best of friends, actually. I understand how losing a son pulled us apart, especially when it was my fault. I remember what a nightmare I was afterwards, so I don't blame him. I'm working my ass to the bone to get back into his good graces. Lately, it feels like I'm bending over backward to please him. I hate it, especially when it's becoming clear my sacrifices will never be enough. The more I give, the more he requires. Like Mom, I suspect he's trying to punish me.

I give him a quick hug then turn to Karyn. There's a genuine smile when I greet Dad's new wife. Karyn and I got off to a rocky start, but she won me over with her cooking and her motherly warmth. Which is weird, considering she's only four years older than me, but I like her. She seems great for Dad. Karyn pulls me into a big hug—or tries to. Her baby bump keeps getting in the way, so I hug her sideways instead and get a whiff of her flowery scent. She eases me off, taking in my outfit.

"I told Sam we were overdressed," she murmurs.

"It's the other way around, actually," I say, letting them into the apartment. "You look amazing, by the way."

"What, this old thing?" she replies, doing a little twirl, missing the glare Mom gives her. "Just a little something I threw on."

I chuckle, because I suspect just like Mom, Karyn went all out for dinner tonight. The shimmery gold dress stops just above her knees and compliments her dark-brown skin tone. Mom stands stiffly as we approach, and she makes no effort to hide the fakeness in her smile. Watching Karyn, I realize she's giving one as well. Dad gives me an uncomfortable glance as the women exchange air kisses and I realize he doesn't want to be here. Yes, this is my family. No one says what they really feel. We are all guilty of sweeping things under the rug.

"Can we eat already? I'm starving," Lauren says, after greeting Dad and Karyn. She moves to her place at the table and Marcus hurries to pull out her chair. I follow suit and pull Mom's chair out.

"Thank you, honey. I'm glad to see you have some manners left."

"Mom, come on," Lauren says.

"What?" Mom gives her an innocent look, then sighs. "Fine, it's a celebration. Let's just relax and enjoy the wonderful meal Helena has prepared."

"And me," Lauren adds. "I did the roast chicken, remember?"

"Yes, yes, you did," Mom replies. "Marcus, say grace, please."

Marcus looks a little dumbfounded at being put on the spot. He instantly clasps his hands and fumbles through a prayer. By the time he finishes, his face has gone red again.

"That was wonderful, Marcus," Mom says. "Now, how about we all take turns saying what we're thankful for. Starting with you, Gabriel."

"This isn't Thanksgiving," Dad says.

"My house, my rules." Mom gives him a glare that makes it clear there's no room for arguing. "I say we're giving thanks, and that's exactly what we're doing. Gabriel, you're up."

God. Why the hell can't we just eat? "I'm thankful for families and friends," I say in a dry tone.

Mom gives me a deadpan look but says nothing.

"I'm thankful for my bonus family and this wonderful spread before me," Marcus adds.

"Typical Marcus, always thinking of food," Lauren says with a giggle.

"Food's not the only thing I think about," he murmurs.

"Ok, man-whore, we get it." Lauren rolls her eyes and continues, "I'm thankful for my new apartment and my freedom."

"Wait, you're getting an apartment?" I look from her to Mom. "Why am I just hearing about this?"

"I said I'll *think* about letting you lease an apartment, Lauren." She glances at Dad before adding, "Your father and I need to talk about it. When he's done with..." Her eyes flicker to Karyn, "...whatever else he has going on. God forbid he tries to focus on two things at a time."

"Don't talk about me like I'm not here, Charlotte," Dad mumbles, his forehead creasing.

Lauren groans. "Guys, please don't start."

"What did I say that was so wrong? He hasn't had time for his kids lately—at least, not the ones already in this world— and we all know why."

I glance at Karyn, the discomfort obvious on her face. Again, I wonder why Mom bothered inviting them.

"Maybe it's because they are both adults," Dad says to Mom. "One's busy running two companies and the other's just finished college. They have no time for me, either."

"So it's their fault you haven't been around?"

I throw my napkin down. "For Christ's sake Mom, just stop. We've barely started dinner and it's already a shit-show."

"Language!" Mom and Dad shout together. It's a habit they developed in my mid-teens when I would curse like a sailor. Thankfully, it eases the tension when they both smile.

It didn't surprise me when my parents announced they were getting a divorce. I had seen the signs for years; the separate bedrooms, the tense conversations. It all pointed to trouble in their marriage. Things got even worse after Daniel died. Mom was inconsolable and Dad struggled to handle her grief while dealing with his. There was no coming back for them after that. A part of me will always blame myself for their breakup. What if Daniel hadn't died? Would they have continued trying to make their marriage work?

Sadly, I'll never know.

"So, Samuel. It's your turn. What are you thankful for?" Mom says.

"My lovely wife, for one," Dad immediately replies, taking Karyn's hand. They exchange a loving glance and Mom takes a large sip from her wine glass. "I'm also thankful for my kids and for you, Charlotte."

Mom pauses, taking another sip and raising her brow at him. "No, seriously," he says. "It means a lot that you invited us to dinner."

The dry smile appears again, and she mumbles, "You're welcome." Her eyes sweep over the table, and she continues, "Well, I'm thankful that my kids—my *living* kids—are healthy. I'm still alive to see them thrive. I'm also thankful for the future, to see them get married, have kids, and all the happiness in the world. I'm also thankful for my own happiness." She smiles mysteriously and takes another sip from her glass.

"Speaking of babies, Gabriel, I thought you would have invited Nicole to dinner," she continues.

"Why would I do that?" I ask.

She frowns at me. "What do you mean? I thought you were getting closer again now that she's back."

"We're just friends, Mom, nothing else."

Mom slowly places her napkin on the table. "Oh."

When I hear that tone, I know what's coming. I brace for it.

"Nicole is such a lovely girl, Gabriel. I don't understand why you're not interested in her. She's stunning, successful, she has a good heart working with those babies... and she was there when you needed her the most."

Yes, she was there for me when Daniel died. I haven't forgotten. Maybe that's why I can't hurt her feelings, but there's no spark between us and I'm not going to force it.

"Kelly and I talk about it quite often, how we would love to see you two married."

"Charlotte, you and Kelly have been talking about hooking them up since they were kids. Let it go. It's nothing but a best-friend fantasy that's never going to happen," Dad chips in.

I give Dad a grateful look, while Mom shoots him one that's sharp enough to slash tires.

"You'll never find a woman like her, trust me," she says.

An instant image of Zyon flashes across my mind, instantly stirring me. I remember my fingers running through her wild curls as I capture her lips with my own. I can still feel the toe-curling sensation of her pussy gripping my cock. I don't know if it's just the sex or something else that makes me feel so alive, so... high. She makes me high, but it's not like the intoxication from smoking weed or drinking alcohol. This is different. It's liberating.

It's also crazy. I'm pining after a woman I'll never see again.

Lauren reaches over and palms my hand. "I think we should be free to date who we want, Mom, not forced into an arrangement that's not for us."

"Thanks, Lauren, but Mom can't force me into anything I don't want. She knows that," I reply.

"Just think about it. That's all I'm saying," Mom says. "Will you?"

"For God's sake, Charlotte, give it a rest!" Dad thunders, and Mom's face darkens at once.

Sensing an argument, I quickly reply, "Fine, Mom. I'll think about it."

She smiles at me. "That's all I ask."

"Now can we eat?" Lauren says, looking just as annoyed as I feel. "The food is getting cold."

Mom nods and declares the table open. Marcus gives me a solemn look as he passes the salad bowl to me and I can tell that like me, he's expecting a long, tense dinner.

7

Zyon

"Oh, screw my life."

"What's wrong?" Roshell asks, peering over my shoulder. We're in my bedroom, and I'm curled up in bed, browsing on my laptop while she's digging in my closet for an outfit for her date tonight. She leans in closer while I open the email I'd gotten thirty minutes ago.

"What the hell? Girl, you got a job interview!" she says when she's done reading.

"I know."

She frowns at me. "Try not to jump for joy, please."

"I am happy, believe me." It's my first interview since I started applying for jobs three weeks ago. It's for a sales position, right up my alley, and the salary is enough to get me back on my feet. "I just wish it was somewhere else."

Roshell dips and reads again. “Cain Industries? What’s wrong with them?”

“Remember the one-night stand I had last weekend?”

“Yeah?”

“Well, he’s the interim CEO.”

I click on the web browser to bring up the website I had been scouring for the last twenty minutes. The company's executive page pops up, showing a full-sized image of Gabriel leaning against a large desk and staring into the camera, his thick arms crossed on his chest. There's a half smile on his lips that makes him look incredibly sexy, and I instantly remember his taste and the heat his lips left on my skin.

“Oh, wow. He’s gorgeous, Zyon. How the hell did you walk away from all that?”

“Easy. I put one foot in front of the other, then I repeat the motion,” I reply with a grin.

“Smart ass.” She gently shoves at my head. “But I don’t see the issue. Enlighten me.”

“The purpose of a one-night stand is to do the deed and move on. To forget. I’m not supposed to see him again.”

“So what if you do? You’re both adults. I’m sure you both can coexist in a professional space. Besides, this is a job we're talking about. A job you need. Are you willing to let it go because you're scared to see him again?”

“Bitch, I’m not scared,” I say, impatiently clicking my tongue. Still, I silently acknowledge the flutter in my stomach.

I will never admit how often I’ve thought of Gabriel since leaving his apartment last Sunday morning. Not out loud, anyway. This is a first.

My one-night stands are usually a distant memory by the next morning. For some reason, he got under my skin and stayed there, and it's not just from the exhilarating sex. This lingering feeling isn't carnal. It's more emotional, unfamiliar, and very, very disturbing. Try as I might, I can't stop it from taking over.

"If you're not scared, then do it. Go kick ass in that interview and get that job. It's time for you to stop taking that blood money."

Her response immediately sobers me. I set my laptop on the bed and turn to face her tight expression. She's angry, just like she was that night when I came pounding on her apartment door, hysterically sobbing and bruised in places that had never been touched by a man. She wanted to kill him for what he did to me, and she had three brothers who would have gotten rid of him in a heartbeat. We decided to let the cops handle him. She's still mad at me for letting Dineo change my mind.

"You still think I made the wrong decision, don't you?"

"Aaro—*he* should be rotting in a jail cell, Zyon, not jetting off to the Maldives or taking cruises around the Caribbean or whatever the hell he's doing, wherever he is." She sighs. "I don't agree with your decision, but I understand. The Murphy family has law enforcement tucked in their back pocket. You probably didn't stand a chance. Besides, you really needed the money... I don't know, I'm torn."

She's right. I needed the money for rehab, therapy, to clear the mountain of debt from when I lost my job; the monthly bills that included rent, utilities, groceries, student loans—

"Listen, sweetie," Roshell says, taking my hand. "I don't judge you, not even for a second, but the longer you take this money, the harder it gets to be free from him."

I nod. "You're right." Which means I can't worry about running into Gabriel again, or these weird feelings for him. I need to focus on getting my life back on track. This job could be the first step in the right direction, so it's worth taking a chance.

My phone dings with a reminder and it makes me groan out loud. It's time to meet Anita for another therapy session and I'm not looking forward to her poking around in my head, pushing me to bare my soul. Some things are better left buried. I know that better than anyone.

"So, tell me about your week," Anita says when the initial pleasantries are over and I'm comfortable on her couch.

She toys with her ponytail, her dark eyes locked on me as I casually shrug, fidgeting with my fingers. "It was alright. Uneventful. I mostly stayed in bed and binge-watched a fantasy series. Took a little walk around the block for fresh air. Prepared for an interview I have on Tuesday. That's basically it."

"Mhm." Anita's hint of a smile puts me on edge. She types something on her tablet then looks back at me, her lips spreading across her face. "How long have you been seeing me, Zyon?" she asks after a beat.

"Six months..."

"Right. This is the most you've said in one sentence. Why is that?"

"I thought you wanted me to be more open."

"Or maybe you're stretching the truth a little."

"You're calling me a liar?"

"Are you?"

I huff, glancing at the clock on the wall. Fifty-five minutes to go. "Why would you think I'm lying?"

"That doesn't answer the question."

I back down. What is she going to do when I tell her the truth, anyway? Lock me up? "Okay. I slipped a little on the weekend."

"What did you do?"

"I had a couple drinks and I... I slept with someone."

Anita purses her lips, then releases a soft sigh.

"Look, it's not like I didn't try. I've been abstinent for like, two months. Give me some credit here."

"I'll give you credit when you admit you have a problem *and* start working to fix it. You've been living in denial since the first day you sat on my couch."

"I'm not living in denial. I'm not an alcoholic or a sex addict. You want me to admit I am, but I'm not."

"No, I want you to realize you're using both methods to mask your pain, that you're trying to put a band-aid over a deep gash. It won't work. What you're doing will make things worse."

"I'm not masking the pain! I love having sex. Consensual sex. It makes me feel like I'm in control. It's the only thing that feels better than a cocktail going down my throat. Ask any twenty-four-year-old and they'll tell you the same thing."

She's staring at me patiently, like I'm a child having a tantrum and she's waiting for me to calm down. I run my fingers through my hair, wanting to rip it out in frustration.

"You're not a regular twenty-four-year-old, Zyon. You experienced some serious trauma, and your promiscuity is a distraction from dealing with it, but sleeping around won't make it go away."

"I don't want to talk about this anymore. Please."

"Okay. Tell me why."

"Isn't it enough that I don't want to talk about it?"

Anita crosses her legs and relaxes in her seat. "Zyon, your mother hired me because you've been spiraling out of control. Three DUIs in six months and you totaled your car. You could have killed someone. You could have killed *yourself.* It's my job to help you fix whatever problems you've been having so that you can have a normal life."

"I *am* living a normal life. My best life. Life is good and I can't complain." I almost bite my tongue with the lie and Anita is clearly not buying it.

"Zyon, you were raped. You had your virginity stolen by a man you thought was a family friend. It's okay not to pretend. Being vulnerable—"

I'm already on my feet, reaching for my bag before she can finish. "I told you, I don't want to talk about it."

Anita gets on her feet, too. "Where are you going? We have another half hour left."

"Why don't you use the time for something more constructive? Better yet, why don't you shove it up your ass?"

I slam the door on my way out, ignoring Anita's calls for me to return. I storm through reception, my eyes blurry with angry tears, internally cursing myself for losing my temper and walking out. I know Anita's right, I just don't want her to be. The darkness feels terrifying, but finding the light requires facing the demons and I can't handle them right now.

8

Gabriel

It's a little past six when I finally break from work. I'm not quite satisfied with the untouched items on my to-do list, but they'll have to wait. Rome wasn't built in a day, and neither will the new development we have in the works. Time for my work out, the only time I can turn my mind off, even if only for an hour. Based on the time, I'm almost thirty minutes late. It's too much to hope my trainer won't kick my ass for running behind—again. I feel bad for messing with his schedule, but what can I do? Work is work. I'm lucky to get off early as it is.

It would be easy to hire a private trainer, someone flexible to my crazy life, but I hate wasting money when there's a cheaper alternative. My friends call me frugal, but I don't care. I'd rather give to people in need than waste money on something totally unnecessary. Like a new car. I can never understand why Marcus changes his ride every two years, or why Noah is attempting to assemble a fleet. My 2017 Lexus Hybrid has been serving me quite well, and I have no plans to buy another until this has run its course. It purrs to life when I press start, and the ride to the gym is as smooth as butter. Nope, I don't need another car.

A dark-haired, middle-aged woman flashes me a smile when I open the gym door for her. It's Mrs. Elliott, a regular, and she's been trying to set me up with her daughter since my first day. If only she knew I'm not Sara's type. Or any other man, for that matter. I won't be the one to enlighten her darkness. She'll find out soon enough.

She squeezes my arm in passing. "Such a thoughtful young man."

"Have a great evening, Mrs. Elliott."

"I will, but you know what would make it even better?" she asks, coming to a stop.

"I already told you, Mrs. Elliott, Sara's not interested," I reply, putting half my body through the door to make it clear I'm in a hurry.

She looks me over, her lower lip caught between her teeth, her licentious stare giving me a chill, and not in a good way. "I find that hard to believe," she finally says. "But uh... why don't you drop by the house sometime? Maybe we can convince her together."

"Sorry, Mrs. Elliott, I'm a busy man. I'm already late for my session. Catch you later, okay?" I hurry through the door before she pulls me in with her tentacles. I'm starting to suspect she already knows her daughter is gay.

As I guessed, my trainer makes me pay for being late. Richard is usually aggressive during our sessions, but today he's rougher than ever. I don't complain. I need the extra push, anyway. It's the perfect distraction from the wild thoughts of Zyon rolling around in my head. I don't know why the hell I can't stop thinking about her. It's not like she's not the first woman I've been with and I'm sure she won't be the last.

Who am I kidding? Sex with Zyon was the best I've ever had, hands down. All I keep thinking of is her face contorted in ecstasy, the soft, sexy moans she made, her legs wrapped around my waist—

Fuck. I'm doing it again. *Come on, Gabriel, focus.*

The hour feels like a lifetime as Richard pushes me through the most grueling leg workout I've ever experienced. The pain is intense, but I endure the squats, the tension leg presses and the deadlifts until my entire lower body screams. Finally, the torture is over, and I cool down. I'm almost done with my

stretching when I feel a presence beside me.

"I'm sorry, is this spot taken?"

The familiar female voice makes me straighten. I face Nicole's smile with a deep frown. She's tried reaching out since the night she offered me a drink, but I keep ignoring her calls. I'm still a little ticked she made an advance, knowing what she knows. A stranger would have gotten a pass, but not her. She knew better. She witnessed how alcohol fucked up my life.

"From that scowl, it's clear I'm still in the doghouse," she says, giving me a puppy dog stare with her big, blue eyes.

"What are you doing here?"

Nicole's dressed for the gym in high-waist yoga pants and a sports bra, her blonde hair in a ponytail, but she hates working out. This is nothing but a front. It just shows how desperate she was to get to me.

"I know your workout schedule, remember? You weren't taking my calls so..." She shrugs. "I had no other choice."

I turn away from her and reach for the towel on the bench.

"Come on, Gabe. How many times do I need to apologize? I'm sorry for offering you a drink. I don't know what I was thinking."

"You weren't."

"Yes, you're right. I was a little messed up, missing Lukas, having too much to drink at the wedding. I messed up. I promise, it will never happen again."

I take a deep breath while wiping my face with the towel. I have no intention of staying mad at Nicole for long, just long enough for her to understand the severity of what she did. Our friendship has too much history for me to walk away. Her, Noah, and Marcus are my tribe. They had my back when the rest of my family turned theirs. There's nothing I won't do for them.

Nicole's staring at me, her lower lip extended in a pout, her body gently swinging to each side. Shaking my head at her cute attempt to wear me down, I draw her in for a hug. "Never again, Nicole. You can't pull that stunt ever again. I don't care how messed up you are."

"I promise I won't." She tightens her arms around my waist and presses her face against my chest. "I really missed my friend."

"I missed you too." We break apart and I lead her to a bench while I remove my damp shirt. The gym has a changing room and a shower, but I've never used them. I prefer showering at home. I grab a spare shirt from my nearby locker and tuck the damp one in my gym bag. Glancing at Nicole, I notice she still looks a little sad.

" Are you alright? I meant it when I said you're forgiven, okay?"

She gives me a quick smile. "I know."

"It still doesn't explain why you look like they just canceled Christmas."

"It's about Lukas. I'm sure you don't want to hear about my love life."

"Try me." I put my bag on the bench then sit beside her. "What happened between you two? I was getting ready for my man-of-honor role, practiced catching the bouquet and everything."

Nicole snorts. "Now, that would be a sight. You, battling with my bridesmaids... I would definitely pay to see that."

"I'm sure you would."

I take her hand in mine, waiting for her to talk. "He's not ready for a commitment, Gabe. He thinks it's too early."

"Wait a minute. He proposed. You set a wedding date, bought a dress— I don't get it."

"I don't either. He loves me, but he's too young to settle down. Those are his words. Not mine."

"Wow... and that never occurred to him before he asked you to marry him?" It's pissing me off, especially when I see the tears forming in Nicole's eyes. He deserves a beatdown for making her cry.

"Hey, hey... fuck him." I pull her into a huge hug and she starts sobbing into my shirt, her voice carrying around the gym. Everyone seems to mind their own business as she dampens the front of my shirt with her tears. I patiently hold her until the crying subsides. She eases from me and wipes her face.

"I'm sorry. I know you don't like undue attention."

"It's okay. All that matters is how you feel."

"I'll be fine," she says, getting to her feet, her expression a little lighter than before. "Ask me a few months from now and I'll be saying, 'Lukas who?'"

"You've got that right." I stand, slinging my bag strap over my shoulder. "Someday, you'll find a man who truly deserves you. I'm sure of it."

"Who knows? It might be sooner than we think," she replies, locking her arm with mine as we walk out.

9

Gabriel

"Ashley, I'm heading to Rosemead for a meeting," I say to the floor receptionist as I walk past her desk. "Please take my messages, and reschedule my one o'clock with the finance team. I have an open slot tomorrow at noon."

Ashley forces a smile, but I can see the frustration in her eyes. She's overworked from juggling her normal duties and the additional ones I pile onto her each day, which means I need a new assistant. *Pronto*. The HR department has been sending me resumes of potential candidates but I'm even pickier than before. It's hard to choose from a screen filled with generic information. I want more than qualifications or experience. I need someone who gets me.

"Sure thing, Mr. Cain," Ashley says.

For once, I don't remind her to call me by my first name. She has enough on her plate. It's weird being addressed like my father. The culture in this company is a little too formal, even for me. It's such a pity I won't be around long enough to change it. My phone beeps with a text from Noah. He's reminding me that our meeting with the shareholders will start in half an hour. I'm cutting it close, but I'll make it. The company driver is already parked on the curb waiting for me.

I text Noah a quick reply. *On my way. But in case there's heavy traffic, just start without me.* He could have handled the shareholders on his own, but I want to be there. This venture is my baby; I'm a little possessive over it.

My eyes are glued to my phone as I scroll through unread messages. The ding of the elevator alerts me, but I'm still reading a text from Nicole as I step into the lobby. I hear someone shout, "Look out!" and I lift my eyes from my phone just in time to crash into a woman with a thud.

My reflexes kick in and I grab her, pulling her against me to stop her fall. I immediately catch a whiff of her perfume, and the familiar jasmine flavor resurrects the steamy memories I kept trying to bury. Wanting to escape, I release her. She stumbles back, staring up at me with wide, familiar eyes.

Zyon.

In the flesh.

Bad choice of words. Now all I remember is my lips on her silky thighs, and how wet she was around my fingers.

Damn it. Wrong place for an erection. Definitely wrong time.

There are so many things happening in my head—and my body—all at once. I'm trying to connect the conservative-looking woman before me with the sensual temptress who seduced me several nights ago. She's wearing a pencil skirt that falls to her knees and a sheer buttoned top. Her piercings are all gone, except for a cute pair of gold studs in her ears. The curls I loved plunging my hands into are all gone, too. Her hair is silky straight, falling over her shoulders. Her entire visage seems forced, even the smile on her face. Somehow, I feel like the woman I met that night is the real deal. The one before me isn't less beautiful though, and she's stirring the same reaction inside me.

"Gabriel Cain, this is a surprise," Zyon says, but her tone tells me it's not. She knows I work here.

"The feeling is mutual," I reply. "I thought I'd never see you again."

She shrugs with a grimace. "That was kind of my plan..."

Ouch.

She catches my expression. "No, no, no. It has nothing to do with you. You were great. It's me. I'm just—never mind. But you're good."

"Thanks for restoring my ego." I chuckle.

She smiles; it instantly lightens the mood but creates a tension inside me. I acknowledge the sudden flutters in my stomach, then I disregard them. They have nothing to do with the woman standing in front of me.

"And thanks for breakfast," I add.

She shrugs again. "It's the least I could do for your help."

I take her in more closely. She's wearing a visitors' badge and carrying a folder tucked to her side.

"Are you here for an interview?"

She nods. "It just ended. Don't ask me how it went, please."

Which means it didn't go well. I can see the disappointment in her eyes. "What position?" I ask.

"Does it matter?"

"It does to me."

Her expression softens. "Customer service representative. Sales department."

"Okay. Well, why don't you have a little faith? Who knows, it just might work out."

Zyon scoffs. "Faith? Nope, not for me. I did really terrible in there. I'd be mind-blown if I actually got the job."

While Zyon's here wallowing in negativity, an idea forms in my head. If she's looking for a job, and I need an assistant...

Hiring Zyon means I can't touch her. That intimate night between us would definitely be a one-and-done. Could I handle working in such proximity to a woman I desperately want to fuck?

I have to. I need to, because Zyon is the assistant I'm looking for. The connection is already there, plus she's tough. I'm sure she can handle the demanding work-Gabriel. She did a superb job handling my cock. Yes, I'll hire her. I'll look, but I won't touch. I'm a professional, through and through. Although the thought of bending her over my desk sounds so appealing, it will remain a fantasy.

"It was nice running into you, Gabriel, but I have to drown my sorrows in a glass of milk or something. See you around." Her shoulders slump in defeat as she turns to go. "Or maybe not."

"I'll certainly see you around, Zyon." I'm not saying goodbye, because I have the perfect solution, a win-win for us both. It's a little risky having her so close with these conflicting feelings, but it's one I'm willing to take.

I'm flirting with being late for my meeting, but I can't resist turning around. I head back upstairs to the human resources department on the third floor. The HR officer jumps to her feet when I push the glass door open. I hear the crackle of a snack bag and she quickly wipes her mouth.

"Mr. Cain. Uh... is everything okay?"

She looks worried, but I'm not puzzled by her response. My presence in HR is never a good sign, but today I come in peace. "Everything is fine, Olivia. I'm going to see Emily."

Emily Cain is the HR director and my insufferable cousin. We've never really gotten along, so I know she'll give me hell before giving me what I want. I move before Olivia's done nodding her head, pressing my access card to the scanner and walking through the open door. A few people scramble when I appear, some staring from their cubicle as I go by. I don't find it strange. I was a hurricane the last time I stormed this path, which I still regret. I hate losing my temper, particularly in public. Especially in a professional space. Granted, my behavior was warranted, but I still get a dip in my stomach when I think about it. It felt like I took several backward steps toward the guy I used to be. Angry, violent, out of control. I never want to go back there.

I enter Emily's office after a brief knock, and she looks up with a frown that deepens when she realizes it's me.

"Come to try your luck again, cousin?" she asks with mocking amusement. "If that's the case, then let me save you the trouble. I won't fire Deacon. Not without reason."

"If the word of several witnesses isn't enough to get him out of here, I don't know what is," I reply, bracing my hands on the back of the seat before her. "You made a mistake, Emily. He will try again."

My reply seems to irritate her more than I expected. She's upset enough to run her fingers through her immaculate dark hair, ruffling it a little. Her eyes are like glaciers staring me down.

"You're just jealous because Uncle Samuel thinks of him as a son, way more than you."

I sigh. Emily always tries to get a rise out of me, ever since we were kids. It used to work back when I couldn't control my temper. Now, I refuse to let her under my skin. Of course, I find it odd how Dad and Deacon Miller got so close overnight. We'd never heard of him until Dad introduced us a few years ago. Within a few months, Dad set him up with a cushy job in the company and he climbed the corporate ladder at breakneck speed. He's now a HR manager without a college degree. Something's off. I just know it. I don't buy Dad's explanation that he's just an old buddy's kid.

"I'm not here to discuss your failure to do your job, Emily. About the search for my assistant—"

"A search for another victim, you mean." She snickers, clearly pleased with her witty reply.

"Ha, ha. Well, your search is over. I've found someone."

Her expression settles. "Okay...well, he would still need to experience the interview process for official purposes, but if you're satisfied with your choice, then I guess it's a go."

"It's not a man. It's a woman."

Her eyebrows slightly lift. "Oh."

"Why would you assume it's a guy, anyway?"

"Because you worked so well with Matt. I thought you wanted a replica of him."

"I want someone capable enough to handle the pressure, that's all."

"Mhm." Emily purses her lips and rolls her eyes.

"What?"

She huffs. "Nothing. I'll need her phone number so Olivia can contact her for the interview."

"No need. She already came today, so her number's on file. Zyon Stewart."

Emily forehead creases as her eyes narrow at me. "Zyon Stewart... as in the girl I interviewed earlier?"

"Yup."

"Are you joking?"

"Do I look like I'm joking, Emily?"

"She's not qualified for an executive assistant post, Gabriel."

"Says who?"

"Says her resume. She's barely out of college and she's only been employed once. A job that lasted for three months before she quit. Her reason for leaving wasn't even substantial. She's not capable of handling the workload you have upstairs."

"It's not brain surgery. Ashley will show her the ropes and I'm sure she'll catch on fast. She's a smart girl."

Emily reclines in her seat, her fingers tapping the arm of the chair. "When did you realize how smart she is? Before or after you slept with her?"

I didn't expect *that*, and I'm aware of the sudden heat on my face. Emily clicks her tongue and shakes her head.

"Oh, boy."

"I don't need your opinion, Emily. The decision was mine and I made it. Now, do as I ask."

Emily scoffs, glaring like she caught me drinking straight from the family-sized milk bottle. "Men..."

"What's that supposed to mean?"

"You think with your dicks, not your head."

"I still don't get it."

"You still haven't denied sleeping with her."

"It's none of your business, and it has no bearing on my decision to hire her."

"Mhm. Did you ever think about how Nicole will feel? She's my best friend. My only friend. I don't want to see her get hurt."

Now it's my turn to roll my eyes. Emily and Nicole have been attached at the hip since they were both in diapers. Like Mom, Emily has this weird desire for Nicole and I to be together. She can't stand me, but she still thinks I'm good enough for her friend. I'm struggling to see how that makes sense.

"For the last time, Emily, Nicole and I will never be a thing."

"Does Aunt Charlotte know that? Because the last time I checked, she's practically planning your wedding."

Oh, screw my life. There are meddlers left, right, and center. I back my way out of her office because I don't need to hear any more. "Just do your job, Emily. That's all I ask."

I start having second thoughts while rushing out the front door to get to a meeting I'm already late for. Is this a good idea? I know what Emily's capable of. We're family, but she's a spiteful bitch. She could make life hell for Zyon if she wants to. Enough to make her quit. I'll be too busy to watch Zyon's back, although I doubt she'll need it. I think about the silkiness of her skin when I held her in my arms that night. Outside, she's soft, but inside, she's like steel. I can tell she's been through some crazy shit. It's there in her eyes, eyes that seem too old for her age. Yes, Zyon can hold her own.

There's a part of me that's intrigued. I'm tempted to peel away her layers and discover what's beneath the surface. But I can't ignore my instincts telling me to stay away from her. I can handle trouble. I've battled it for years. Zyon seems like more than trouble; she's a nuclear weapon, capable of doing serious damage. She's dangerous.

Especially in that goddamn skirt.

10

Zyon

I give the security guard a smile when he hands me the temporary pass and I head to the glass-enclosed elevators. It's been a week since I got the call from human resources, a call I didn't expect after I completely flopped in the interview. It's clear I performed much better than I thought, which means I've been in my head, doubting myself. My confidence has fluctuated ever since the night—

No. I'm not thinking about it, not on the day I've decided is a fresh start. I can't take the negativity with me because I can't afford to lose another job. I press the button to summon the lift and wait. Cain Industries is a manufacturing conglomerate, which means there are constant opportunities for growth. If I work hard enough—and I will—I can certainly move from the sales position to one that pays a better salary in no time.

Baby steps. Today is my first, but it definitely won't be my last.

"OMG, I love your skirt," comes a chipper voice behind me.

I turn around. There's a dark-haired, curvy girl in horn-rimmed glasses smiling back at me.

"Thanks," I reply, looking down at the skirt Roshell picked out for me this morning. It's a little fitted, with a daring split, but it gives me the boost of confidence I need.

"I'm Olivia," she says as the elevator doors open.

"Zyon." I reach for the button for the HR department on the third floor. Olivia beats me to it while giving me a smile.

"I knew you looked familiar. You're my nine o'clock. I'm supposed to get you logged into the system, get your permanent access pass and ID before I take you upstairs."

"Upstairs?" I ask, as the doors open again. I follow her out. "What's upstairs?"

She gives me a weird look before pressing her key card against the door. "Your workstation is upstairs, or have you already forgotten?"

There's a slight beep then the door slides open, revealing a posh lobby with an elaborate white desk and a high-back chair against the wall. In the far corner lies a white couch with a small coffee table in front of it.

"I thought the sales team worked on the first floor."

"They do, but—" she looks at me, then up to the ceiling, before dumping her handbag on her desk with a heavy sigh. "Damn it. Camille."

I don't like this. I don't like this at all.

"It seems my intern gave you the wrong information when she called you last week. You didn't get the job you applied for. You're being hired to assist our interim CEO."

I blink at Olivia. Once, twice, three times, waiting for her to tell me this is a joke. I'm being hired to work with Gabriel, the man I've been trying to get out of my head? Nope. I can't be near him. My head and body both agree it's not safe.

"Between me and you, this post is way cushier than the one you applied for. You're a lucky girl."

I don't feel lucky. I want to make a U-turn and get the hell out of here. I've just gotten a handle on the tumultuous emotions fucking with my head since our one-night stand. I don't want to backslide into that torment again.

Olivia gestures for me to sit on the couch and says, "Want to hear something even better? It's triple the salary."

Again, I blink at her. "Say what now?"

"Yup," she replies with a smile. "Now you really know how lucky you are."

Oh, wow. Triple? Does my inner struggle matter at this point? Who cares if I have stupid, confusing feelings for my new boss? I'm getting paid, damnit. Paid *real well*. Olivia is staring at me like she wants to say more, but she doesn't. She moves to her desk to create my credentials, after which she hands me an access pass.

"This is an inclusive pass. It will get you anywhere in the building. There's only a few of us with high-level access so please keep it safe."

"Got it." I grab it with a flourish and tuck it inside my bag.

"Sit tight. I'll have someone take you upstairs in a moment. Mr. Cain has been waiting for you."

I nod at her, trying to appear calm but feeling like there are a million butterflies in my stomach. I don't know if it's from the anticipation of what's ahead or the thought of seeing Gabriel again. Whatever it is, I won't let it get the best of me.

I pick up the tablet and start reading through the company handbook. I'm halfway through when a door opens to my right and a tall, brown-skinned man enters. I straighten in my seat as I do a quick scan of his figure. He's extremely good-looking, with a smile that probably makes women drop their panties in a heartbeat. He gently bites his lower lip as his eyes roam over me with undeniable interest. I'm flattered, but he's already earned a big fat X. I can't stand cocky men. The stench of his arrogance is so strong it makes me uneasy.

He taps Olivia's desk in passing and I catch the dirty look she gives him. He's totally oblivious because he's still staring at me. He's still wearing that arrogant smile when he stops at my feet.

"First day?" he asks, and I nod. He sticks out his hand. "I'm Deacon Miller. Nice to meet you."

"Zyon Stewart." I slip my hand in his; he gives it a gentle squeeze but doesn't let go.

"Nice to meet you, Zyon. What department are you in?"

My eyes flick to Olivia for the answer, and the same look appears on her face. "It's the CEO's office, Deacon."

"Mhm. Cain is such a lucky bastard." His eyes sweep over me again. "So lucky."

"She's trying to read, Deacon. Can you give her some space, please? I'm sure you have a million things to do."

"None as important as ensuring our newest team member is all settled," he says, flashing her a sweet smile. "I'm the learning and development manager after all."

“She's in good hands. Camille is on her way.”

“Camille's hands are quite full scheduling upcoming interviews. Why put more on her plate when you have a volunteer right here?”

Watching them, I catch the tension, and there’s a contrast between their expressions that makes me sense something’s really wrong. Not my business, though. I have enough to worry about. Like co-existing with a man who triggers feelings I don’t want.

“I’m taking her up, Olivia, and that’s final,” he says in an authoritative tone that makes it clear he's above her. She purses her lips but doesn’t say another word. Deacon gestures to me with a smile and I gather my things and push to my feet. I give Olivia a quick wave on my way out; she responds with a slight head shake and a worried look. Maybe I imagined it. She's already gone back to work.

Deacon's palm gently touches the center on my back as we walk through the front door to the elevator. “So, Zyon, where are you from?”

“Brooklyn.”

He chuckles. “How about you be specific? Brooklyn's quite a large borough.”

The elevator doors open, and I enter ahead of him. “Just Brooklyn.”

“You know I have access to your employee file, right? I could just go take a look.”

I turn to peer up at him. He’s still smiling, but there's something that puts me on edge. Something disturbingly familiar, and it resurrects my PTSD. I move as far away as the lift will allow and the smile disappears from his face.

“I’m sorry. Did I offend you?”

I shake my head. “Don’t worry about it.” It's my first day here. I’m not looking for drama. The last thing I want to do is step on the toes of a senior team member.

“I’m just trying to get acquainted, that’s all,” he says. “I apologize if it's too forward.”

“It’s fine. I promise.”

The doors fly open, and I step into a lobby that’s smaller than the third floor, but no less exquisite. There's no one at the front desk, but it's clearly occupied, with a large computer, a few scattered files, and a steaming cup of coffee.

Deacon gestures to a frosted glass door, but it flies open before I reach it. Gabriel prowls out, looking like he's ready to hurt someone. There’s an instant dip in my stomach when he takes my arm. His gentle hold surprises me, considering how vicious he looks, but his eyes aren’t on me. He's glaring directly at Deacon. What's even more surprising is Deacon's responding glare. I’ve never seen an employee show such open hostility toward their boss. What the hell is going on here? Do I even want to know?

“I'll take it from here, Miller,” Gabriel grits through his teeth. “I’m sure you’re a busy man.”

“Not too busy to take a beautiful woman where she needs to go, Cain.” Deacon is smiling again, but his eyes are empty. There’s something about him that gives me chills, and not in a good way. He slowly backs away while deliberately running his eyes over me.

“Nice meeting you, Zyon,” he smirks. “I’ll see you around. Maybe we can grab lunch or something. I’ll tell you all about how things work around here.”

Gabriel's hand tightens around my arm, and he directs me toward the door. He keeps his hold until we walk through a small office and into an adjoining space twice the size of my bedroom. Suddenly, he lets me go so fast that I almost gasp, like my arm is a hot skillet he accidentally touched. I wouldn't be surprised if he checks his hand for a burn.

Ugh.

I don't like the feeling that rushes over me. I should be relieved. He's making it easier for me to resist my attraction to him. So why do I feel so disappointed?

It takes a moment to realize Gabriel's speaking to me. "I'm sorry. What?"

He gives me a deadpan stare before gesturing to a large desk by the window. "Have a seat, Zyon."

I move toward a chair but make an abrupt stop before I get to it. "Wait a minute. I have a question."

"Okay. Shoot."

"Why me?"

His expression settles, and it's clear he understands the curt question. I'm positive we wouldn't be standing here without his influence. Why did he choose me?

"It's simple," he says with a slight shrug. "You needed a job, and I needed an assistant. Now both our problems are solved."

"I'm sure you've had your pick from a long list of candidates. Many, if not all, more experienced than me."

He nods. "That I did."

"So, again, why me?"

Again, he frowns. "Do you have a problem with my decision?"

"No, I don't. In fact, I'm glad for the opportunity. It's just that—I don't want you to get the wrong impression," I say.

"Which is?"

"I'm not interested in any quid pro quo. I just want to work and earn my pay like everyone else."

Gabriel stares at me blankly for a moment then he chuckles. Now he's laughing and moving past me. I turn and watch him reach into his desk drawer for a MacBook and a cell phone. His laughter fades as he hands both to me.

"I'm going to introduce you to Ashley Henriques in a minute. She's our receptionist out front, but she's been working as my interim assistant as well. You'll shadow her for a week until you can manage on your own. That cellphone means you'll be available whenever I need you. Keep it charged. Do not turn it off."

"What about—"

"You will be required to work overtime, occasional weekends. You're also expected to accompany me on business trips. Some are impromptu, the rest you'll be informed about in advance."

He must have seen the bewilderment on my face because he adds, "Don't worry, you will be compensated for all the above." He rests against the desk and crosses his arms on his chest, ruffling the front of his neat suit. The slight imperfection makes him appear less... stiff, more approachable, but his expression says the opposite. He looks a little mad. Mad at *me*.

Was it something I said?

"Any questions?" he asks, and I shake my head. The quicker he's done with me, the sooner I can get my emotions in check. There's so much to process. Being on call, working overtime, weekends—when will I get a break?

"Good. Let me call Ashley so she can show you the ropes." He reaches for the office phone and places the cradle to his ear, then he pauses and looks at me. "Contrary to what you may believe, Zyon, I'm not in the habit of giving favors for sex. I'm quite capable of getting a woman without them."

My eyes flicker over his delicious body in the suit and I nod. "I'm sure you do."

Again, he raises the phone to his ear, then pauses again before dialing. "Although, a recent fling makes me wonder if I can keep them."

Our gazes lock with heat I didn't expect. I'm usually good at holding my stance but I'm the first to look away. Damn those mesmerizing eyes.

"Look, I'm not good with goodbyes, okay? I thought it would be less awkward if I left before you woke up."

He shakes his head and raises a palm to stop me. "You don't need to explain, Zyon. I got the message loud and clear."

Now I feel terrible, which is new for me. I never think about one-night stands. I never see them again, either. This is new, confusing. I hate being confused. Gabriel finally makes the call to Ashley, telling me she's waiting at the front desk. When he's done talking, I gather my things and head to the door.

"Did I thank you for breakfast?" he asks before I reach for the handle. I turn around to see a tenderness on his face that surprises me.

"Yeah, you already did. It's the least I could do for what you've done," I reply. I want to tell him I had no complaints about that night. Quite the opposite, actually. I wish the sex was mediocre, that he didn't rock my world. It would be easier to dismiss the desire flaring inside me if it was terrible. Plus, the way he's looking at me is not helping one bit.

I turn to go, but his voice stops me again.

"Zyon. I need you to stay away from Deacon Miller, okay?"

Again, I face him. "Why?"

Gone is the tenderness. He's back to looking like he's ready to give someone a beatdown. "I'm not at liberty to say. Just... keep the door closed if he comes calling."

I wait for him to say more, but he doesn't. I reply with a slight nod before I exit, but that was for his benefit, not mine. His warning makes me curious. Is there a valid reason for his advice, or is he just jealous because another man seems interested? Why am I hoping it's the latter? Do I want Gabriel to feel something for me?

The answer is no.

He was my one-night stand, now he's my boss. I don't need to further complicate my life by blurring those lines. My only goal is to use this opportunity to start my life over again. Hopefully it's enough to leave the demons behind.

11

Gabriel

"Hey." Noah claps in front of my face. "Focus, Gabriel. Where the hell have you been?"

"I'm here, okay?" Blinking, I straighten in my seat and look at the architectural model displayed on the table. It's the mockup of the Jamaican resort we want to build next year. Hopefully. Convincing our shareholders was the easy part. Meeting the legal requirements for the island, leasing the land, getting construction permits... the list is a mile long. There's crazy work ahead but I'm looking forward to accomplishing each milestone.

Right now, though, it's extremely hard to focus on work. Not because I'm exhausted, or because I haven't eaten since breakfast. It's having Zyon in my space that's been fucking with my head all day. I've been a mess since she stepped into my office this morning. I'm aware of my attraction. I'm attracted to many women, but they don't affect me like this. I can control myself around them, but with Zyon, it's a struggle keeping my hands to myself. All I wanted to do was peel that skirt down her gorgeous legs and relieve my tension with an afternoon between her thighs. I can't explain this insatiable need for her. It's like needing air after running a long distance sprint. I'm desperate for it, *for her*, and I have absolutely no idea why.

So what if she's extremely easy on the eyes? I've been with women who were even more good-looking. What is it about her that makes me lose my mind?

Even now, I'm still seeing her legs in my head. I couldn't take my eyes off her ass as she walked away from me. I didn't want to remember how firm it felt in my palms when I gripped her. I didn't want to remember her taste, how her lips felt like coming home.

Fuck. Maybe I should look into transferring her to another office. Would it offend her? Do I even care? My sanity is more important, isn't it?

"Gabriel."

I refocus, staring up at Noah. "What were you saying?"

He gives me a weary look but doesn't pry. "Marcus suggests we build the pool overlooking the ocean, so it creates that infinity effect. What do you think?"

"Sounds solid to me." I glance over at Marcus, who's reclining on the futon that usually serves as my bed when I work late. His eyes are locked on his phone, his fingers busy typing a mile a minute. "I didn't think you had a creative bone in you, Marcus. Well done."

Marcus doesn't reply. He's still busy typing with a sneaky smile that brightens his face. I'd bet my last dollar the conversation on his phone is rated X.

"Glad to know I'm not the only one distracted," I say, and Noah moves to shake Marcus's shoulder. Marcus quickly turns the phone down, and I catch a glimpse of guilt on his face. It makes me curious. I tuck it in the back of my mind to ask him later. Noah's already pissed at us for not paying attention; no need to make it worse.

My eyes shift to the window as Noah returns to his display. It's almost eight at night, but the darkness has just begun to settle in. I wonder where Zyon is now. Is she home, getting ready for her second day on the job, or is she out with someone else, another willing victim?

I wipe my face with a deep sigh. I don't know why Zyon's actions bother me so much. We had a one-night stand and it's over. Now she's my employee. Completely off limits. Sleeping with the staff has been a no-go from day one and I'll never change that personal rule. Who am I kidding, anyway? Zyon has no interest in sleeping with me again. It was clear as day this morning. Her indifference irked me a little; I'm not used to anything other than eager acquiescence from women. I'm sure my ego can handle it. She has already moved on, and so will I.

"Gabriel. For the love of God," Noah says, clearly frustrated with my short attention span. "Go home, man. Handle whatever's distracting you so badly."

"Zyon," Marcus mutters. He swings his legs off the couch dramatically. "She's the distraction."

"Still?" Noah asks, frowning at me. "I thought you were over her disappearing that morning."

I roll my eyes as Marcus snickers. "Didn't he tell you he hired his one-night stand?"

Noah's eyes widen. "You did *what*?"

"Can we finish discussing the mock-up, please?"

"Oh, no, no, no. You weren't focused on our discussion, so we are tabling it for tonight. Tell me it's not true. You didn't hire Zyon."

"And if I did?" I ask as he takes a seat across the desk while staring at me like I'm crazy.

"Then you made a mistake. You need to undo it."

"Like hell I will."

"What's gotten into you, Gabriel? You're the least impulsive person I know, but since you met that girl, you've been making the craziest decisions. Did you even give it a second thought before hiring her?"

"Oh come on. Stop being dramatic," Marcus chimes in. "So what if she's on his payroll? She seems like a nice person. Plus, she probably needed the job."

Noah shakes his head even before Marcus finishes talking. "There are plenty of jobs around New York. Use your influence to get her one, I don't care. No good will come from having her around you all the time."

"What's your problem, man?" Marcus says before I open my mouth. "Why are you so hell bent on painting her as a villain?"

"Because she's trouble. I can sense it. Gabriel hasn't been himself since he saved her that night. He's been distracted, making errors left and right. He lost his temper and almost beat the shit out of that guy. It's been years since he's gotten—"

"Angry like that, I know; but you can't deny the asshole deserved it." Marcus seems irritated, but it doesn't compare to how I feel right now. I'm getting sick of Noah's self-righteous attitude.

"That's not the point."

"Then what's your fucking point?" I fly up from my seat; the guys exchange a *here-we-go-again* look, pissing me off even more. "Fuck you both. Don't treat me like I'm a lit fuse. I'm fine. I've been fine."

Am I?

When was the last time I got a good night's sleep? I'm exhausted. Edgy. My body's wound tighter than a goddamn string, and it isn't just because of Zyon. It's the demand of straddling two jobs, the constant pressure from Mom to date Nicole, the overwhelming fear I'll never get back in my parents' good graces, no matter how hard I try.

"For what it's worth, I support you hiring Zyon," Marcus says. "Hell, you can keep banging her for all I care. As long as you're okay."

"You're not okay," Noah adds. "At the risk of sounding like a grumpy grandpa, I don't think you should fuck around with her."

"There's no fucking involved, believe me. She's here to work, that's it."

"Right... until you screw her on your office floor," Marcus says, and the disgusting pervert has the nerve to laugh out loud at his poor joke.

My head drops back against the chair, and I sigh loudly. I didn't need that visual, damn it. Now all I'm thinking of is Zyon bent over on the office couch, her perfect ass high in the air, her glistening pussy waiting—

"See? Just like that, he's gone again."

"I'm just exhausted, Noah. Don't blame Zyon for me being overworked."

"I'm not blaming her. I just think it's inevitable. Zyon seems like the kind who trouble follows. Hell, she probably thrives on it too. Call it male intuition or whatever, but I sense a darkness around her."

"Wow, negative much?" Marcus contributes.

"Call it whatever you want, Marcus. I'm just protecting our boy. We both know what happened the last time he lost control."

The smile disappears from Marcus' face. I close my eyes once more, letting them argue without my input.

"Dude, the way you hit that guy, the anger... I haven't seen that in years. It took just *one* encounter with Zyon to resurrect it. I can't imagine what long term exposure would do."

"She's not some toxic chemical, Noah," Marcus scoffs.

"She *is* toxic. I just know it," Noah replies.

Marcus shakes his head. "You've always been a judgmental asshole, but this... this is brand new."

"It's obvious you're suffering from memory loss. Have you forgotten what happened after—"

"Stop. Don't talk about me like I'm not here. I'm perfectly capable of handling myself." The chair rolls back as I stand. "I've done the work. The anger management classes, the AA meetings. I'm better. I'm not weak. I don't appreciate you thinking a woman can push me over the edge."

Again, Marcus and Noah exchange *that* look.

"What?" I ask them.

"You seem a little agitated, that's all," Noah says.

"And?"

"Nothing," Marcus replies, giving Noah a don't-push-it glance. But I can read the silent message between them, and it makes my stomach sink. They don't believe I'm okay. They think I'm slipping.

"Guys, I haven't touched a drink in years. I can't believe you think I would backslide like that."

"Can you blame us? You been off for a while now," Noah says, and he gives me a direct stare. "Ever since that night."

Sighing, I scrub my face with my hands. Noah is right. I haven't been myself since Zyon left my apartment. I don't know why. It can't just be about the sex, but whatever it is, Noah's probably right. It's possible there's a negative correlation between Zyon and I, like gas and fire.

"You're right, Noah. I haven't been myself since that night, but I won't blame Zyon for the shit I'm going through. I won't fire her, either."

Noah sighs. "Okay. So maybe I was a little dramatic. You don't need to fire her. Just leave her alone."

"Okay, Father, I hear you. I'm already one step ahead of you. My relationship with Zyon is strictly professional."

I don't feel as confident as I sound. Working with Zyon is going to be an interesting ride. She doesn't even know it, but she has the power to bring to me to my knees.

12

Zyon

The ringing of my cell phone wakes me. With half-closed lids, I grope along the bed for the device, frowning when I notice it's not lighting up. It takes me a few more seconds to realize the sound is coming from my bag. It's my work phone. *Gabriel*. He's the only one who calls me on that phone. What does he want at two in the morning?

I force myself out of bed with a groan. It's not the first time he's called after work hours with instructions, but he has never contacted me this late. I'm tempted to turn it off and go back to sleep, but I'll have to deal with him in the morning. There's only so much biting my tongue I can do.

Working with Gabriel has been an unexpected hell. It's not because of my growing attraction to him, although that's enough to drive me up the wall. I thought Ashley was exaggerating when she told me how demanding he could be, that several other assistants had quit because they couldn't handle the pressure. It took a week to realize she wasn't lying.

The phone stops ringing as I reach into the bag. When I pull it out, it starts ringing again. *Let's get this over with.* "I'm going to assume you don't have a working clock. Or a watch. In case you weren't aware, it's two in the morning," I greet him.

"I know." Gabriel's voice sounds a little husky, like he's sleepy or just woke up. After getting to know a little more of him this last month, I think it's the former. Sometimes I wonder if he even sleeps.

"I need the itinerary for our weekend conference in Vegas," he says.

"I emailed it when you asked yesterday."

"No, you didn't. I need it now."

I huff, putting him on speaker before opening the email app, and I find the message right away.

"Three twenty-three. That's the timestamp on the message. Check your spam, just in case."

There's a pause, then an embarrassed, "Oh."

"Oh, what? You woke me at two am for nothing. I deserve an apology.'"

"Sorry," he says, not sounding sorry at all. "It must have slipped past me."

"I bet. Is that all? I need my beauty sleep. I have a boss who gets grumpy when I'm late."

Gabriel softly chuckles. "I think he might give you a pass this one time."

I would love to see his expression right now. His eyes are probably soft with laughter, a huge contrast to the iciness that's usually within them. He hasn't smiled at me since my first day. He's been distant, very boss-like, driving me crazy with his constant demands. A week of training with Ashley wasn't enough to prepare me for *this*. Managing his calendar, preparing expense reports and itineraries are just the tip of the iceberg. There's a chair at my desk that's hardly used because I'm always on the go.

"Is that all?" I ask again.

"No," Gabriel replies, and there's a sound like a door is being shut. "Talk to me for a bit. I can't sleep."

"That's not my problem. Not unless I'm being paid to miss *my* beauty sleep."

"I don't think missing sleep will make a difference. You're beautiful anyway. Especially when you wear your hair loose; it softens your face."

There's an instant silence on his end and I swear I hear a soft curse. I return to bed, slipping my nakedness under the covers. "Thanks for the compliment, but cash is the only payment I'll accept."

He chuckles again. "You would really charge for lending a listening ear?"

"It's not like you can't afford it."

"Is money a requirement for a relationship with you?"

I pull the phone away from my ear, stare at it, then place it back against my ear. "That's kind of personal, don't you think?"

"Oh, come on, Zyon. Let's be real. That question is a little lukewarm, considering—"

"Okay. Fine." I know where he's going, but we don't need to mention our one-night stand. Ever. "I've never had a relationship, so the answer is no."

"Why?"

I sigh. "We still haven't discussed compensation for my time."

"Name your price. But," he says as I open my mouth, "if I'm paying, then I get to ask anything I want, and you can't refuse an answer."

Meaning he can ask me anything at all. Maybe things I don't want to discuss. I cross my legs and lean against the headboard. The sleep has completely left my body. "I should charge you double."

"You probably should." I sense the undercurrent of something in his tone and it puts me on edge.

"Keep your money. I'm not interested in an interrogation."

"Me either. I'm just trying to get to know the woman I hired."

"You couldn't care less about getting to know me at the office, so why now?"

"Why not now? There are no phones ringing off the hook, no meetings to run off to, no demands on my time. It's perfect if you ask me."

"No, it's not. You're just full of it. You're looking for company because you can't sleep."

"Has anyone ever told you how feisty you are?"

I roll my eyes. "I just say what I mean and mean what I say. If you don't like it, don't let the door hit you on the way out."

He sniggers. "Well, I just learned something about you without having to dig for it. Or pay you."

"That's all you're going to get. I'd recommend some warm milk to help you sleep. If that doesn't work, take a shot. Scotch or whiskey, either should do the trick."

There's a deep silence on his end. If it wasn't for his soft sigh into the phone I'd assume he had already hung up.

"I'll try the milk, thanks. Goodnight, Zyon. See you at work," he says, his voice strangely tight.

Just like that, he hangs up without waiting for my reply. It leaves me confused as ever and wondering, was it something I said?

Five hours later and I'm in zombie mode, my eyes feeling like they are carrying dead weights. I switch the hot coffee in my other hand, willing the elevator to arrive so I can catch a couple minutes rest at my desk before Gabriel gets in with his list for the day. I probably should have brought another cup of coffee. One isn't enough to get me through the day, not after the night I had. I'm mad at Gabriel for waking me up from my peaceful sleep. When he hung up, he took my peace of mind with him, leaving me with a restlessness that made sleep impossible. My mind got busy trying to find possible reasons for the abrupt end to our conversation. He was pleasant one minute, back to his old broody self the next.

Ugh.

I shouldn't care about what he thinks of me. My only goal should be getting my life back on track. I just got my first paycheck, and for the first time in six months, I don't need the blood money in Dineo's bank account. I paid my own bills, bought my own groceries. I don't feel *guilty* anymore. Now, if only the remaining negative emotions would leave, I'd be good as new. Speaking of which, I need to postpone my appointment with Anita. I'm looking forward to the company's annual conference in Las Vegas this weekend. The human resource department labels it as a motivational seminar, but it's a mini vacation for me. I hope there's no real work involved, but knowing Gabriel, there will be.

I shift the coffee to my other hand as someone touches the back of my arm, startling me. I almost drop the cup as I whip around with a frown. Deacon's standing with his palms raised, wearing a shit-eating grin. I arrange the most serious expression I can manage on my face.

"Don't hit me, please," he says jokingly, and I relax.

"I don't like people touching me without my permission, okay?"

"Fair enough." He moves closer, looking me up and down. "Permission to touch you."

"Permission denied."

The elevator comes and I quickly move inside, aware that he's following me. I don't know if it's Gabriel's warning that makes me nervous, but Deacon puts me on edge. If I wasn't in such a hurry, I would have waited for another lift.

"Don't tell me you're one of those women who plays hard to get," he says, facing me in the confined space.

"Sexual harassment is a serious offense in this company, is it not?" I ask, my fingers curling around the coffee cup.

His smile disappears. "Am I harassing you?"

"You're making me very uncomfortable."

"Oh, wow. I swear to God, Zyon, that wasn't my intention. I suspect we have our wires crossed. I thought we had a moment that first day. Guess I was wrong, and I'm sorry."

I look up at him and he's wearing a repentant expression that seems genuine. "Apology accepted."

He sticks out his hand. "Friends?"

I glance at his hand then back up at him. "I don't know about that, but I'll say hi if I see you around."

"I can work with that." The door opens to his floor. "See you around, Zyon."

I watch him go, acknowledging how great his butt looks in his tailored pants, but that's it. There's no spark. No urge to break my promise to keep my legs closed. Deacon is hot, just not my speed. Anita's words come back to me as I step from the lift. This is not the time to think about getting my next fix. I should focus on healing. Using one-night stands to erase what he-who-cannot-be-named did to me is not the way to heal.

I've barely downed my coffee when Gabriel walks in, as if nothing has changed. In fact, it's worse. He's more distant than ever, barely saying good morning loud enough for me to hear. Maybe I'm imagining things, but he seems pissed at me. I watch him enter his office while still trying to figure out what I said last night to tick him off so much. It makes no sense. Hot one minute, cold the next, shutting me out.

I should thank the stars for his icy response. He's making it easier for me to stay away, but instead of relief, I feel a little down. For the first time in my life, I'm genuinely attracted to a guy, but he's off limits. Am I that unlucky? Is life playing a sick joke on me?

13

ZYON

"This session is like watching paint dry. Boring. I'm going for a smoke," Olivia whispers while digging through her purse. She finds a pack of cigarettes then looks at me. "You in?"

"Not unless you have some weed stashed in there." That's another item on my list of things not to do, but I'm in Vegas, miles away from anyone who knows about my boundaries. I don't want to waste this trip locked in my hotel room. I want to go clubbing, have a drink and dance like I've never done before. God knows I deserve some fun.

"Sorry, just cigarettes," Olivia says.

"No thanks." If I'm going to fuck up my lungs, it needs to be worth it.

"If anyone asks, I've gone to the ladies' room, cool?"

"Cool."

Olivia's whispered 'excuse me' gets fainter as she eases down our row of seats. I turn my attention back to the podium as she quietly scuttles to the exit. Maybe I should have gone with her, just to get a break from the monotony.

Empowerment conference, my ass. The only thing I feel empowered to do is take a nap.

This wasn't what I expected when I read the email. I saw nightclub images, sparkly lights, and roulette tables and thought one thing: fun. Not one boring session after another. It's almost noon on a Saturday and I'm stuck in a conference room with my team members and a star-studded list of motivational speakers. I had already gotten an inspirational push from the first presenter; now it's just overkill. I tune the current one out, reaching for my phone and scrolling through my Instagram timeline. I'm reading through the comments on a popular gossip site when a text comes in.

Pay attention.

It's Gabriel. My head shoots up as I scan the room searching for him. He's not supposed to be in here. His itinerary puts him several floors up at a virtual leadership session. Based on the time, there's still thirty minutes left. So why is he in here?

I spot him standing in the back with one hand in his pocket, the other holding his cell phone. He smirks when our eyes meet. Another example of his hot and cold behavior. We've all been in the same hotel for twenty-four hours and I haven't seen him once. I don't know if he was just busy or deliberately avoiding me, but it's irritating.

He dips his head as he types again. My phone vibrates with another message.

Stop idling on company time and pay attention.

This is a perfect example of the pot calling the kettle black, I reply. *Don't you have a session right now?*

I'm the boss. I can do whatever I like.

Shaking my head, I tuck the phone back in my bag and turn my attention to the stage. I hear the creaking sound of a door opening behind me, and without looking back, I know it's Gabriel making his exit.

I'm reclined in my seat on the staff bus heading back to our hotel room when my cell phone rings. Dineo. I consider not answering at all. We haven't really spoken since that morning in my kitchen, and she's yet to apologize for her victim blaming. I'm not holding my breath. I don't recall her ever being genuinely sorry for anything.

Even knowing I'll regret it, I swipe the green 'accept' button and press the phone to my ear. "Hey, Mommy. What's up?"

"Where are you?" she sounds a little panicked, triggering a rush of fear. I straighten my seat from the reclining position in a rush; I'm glad there's no one sitting beside me.

"What's wrong?"

"Zyon, just answer the goddamn question. Where are you?"

"Uh... I'm in Vegas for a work thing."

"Oh, thank God."

"Are you going to tell me what's going on?"

She's silent for a beat then she says, "Aaron is back in town."

I close my eyes, the sudden tightening on my chest making it hard to breathe. Taking a deep inhale, I switch the phone to my other ear. "You told me that was a part of the deal, that he would leave New York for good. That's why I didn't press charges. What the hell do you mean *he's back*?"

"I know, baby. I know. But there are things beyond my control—"

"No." *Fuck.* I want to get off this bus so I can express myself in private. "Don't give me that, Mommy. He made a promise. It's the only way I can exist in that city without losing my mind, without watching my back wherever I go." I catch movement on my right and notice a guy from IT watching me. *Shit.* I'm getting loud. I drop my voice and whisper, "What the hell am I supposed to do now?"

"Nothing's changed, baby. You can go on living as normal. He promised to stay away, and he means it."

"Wait, what? You saw him?"

"Just briefly. He won't give you any trouble."

"Then why did you call me in a panic just now? Like you were scared for my safety?"

"Everything's fine, Zyon, I swear. Enjoy your trip, okay?"

Her quivering voice makes my stomach churn. "Don't lie to me, please. What did he say to you? Did he hurt you?"

"No, he didn't. I have to go."

"Mommy—"

She hangs up. I dial her number, resisting the urge to throw my phone when her voicemail chips in. I hang up and return it to my bag. My body's trembling and I can't seem to stop it. Rage, fear, sadness, emotions flood my system, heaving it into turmoil. I hate being mad at

Dineo. Besides Roshell, she's my closest friend. Well, she was my closest friend. The incident put a strain on our relationship, and I fear it will never be the same.

I can't shake the suspicion she's hiding something from me, and a part of me wants to pursue it. Can I handle the truth, or will it wreck me?

A sudden gasp yanks me from my thoughts. My teammates have risen from their seats, staring out the window with excited squeals. There's a cop wrestling with a suspect across the street. It takes two other cops to subdue him. I shift my eyes as they chuck him in the backseat of the squad car.

I don't like cops. Most of them are decent people, hardworking and brave, but my terrible experience left a bitterness that made me paint them all with the same brush. It was the worst night of my life. What should have been a simple interview turned into humiliating interrogation when the officer asked, *"what were you wearing before he attacked you?"*

His expression did not hide his inner thoughts. *I asked for it*. Tempting a man with my skimpily-clad body was my sin. The only sin. My rapist was only reacting as a man. The officer didn't say those exact words, but I read between the lines. When Dineo suggested we drop the case, I didn't argue. I dreaded the thought of going back to the precinct. It was easier to take the money and move on.

Now, it's different. My feelings have changed. There's no doubt I made a mistake. I sold my soul to the Murphys for nothing, because he's back, and from the anxiety in my mother's voice, I'm worried he's up to no good. Can I trust what Dineo said? Will he stay away like he promised, or will I continue to live in fear?

"Hey." I turn my head toward the deep voice. It's the IT guy, staring at me with a soft smile. . I force a smile at him, and he takes it as an invitation to move to the seat next to me.

"You okay?" he asks.

I hunch my shoulders. "So-so."

"You look like you could use a drink. Or two."

For the first time, I give him my full attention, taking him in. He isn't quintessentially good-looking but there's something about his thick lips that makes him attractive. His dark hair is shaped into a mohawk with highlights at the tips. He's slim, but in a tall, athletic way.

Leaning back in my seat, I give him a genuine smile. "What's your name?"

"Ethan," he replies.

"Okay, Ethan. How do you feel about clubs?"

14

Gabriel

God, I need a life.

It's nine o'clock on a Saturday in Vegas and I'm in my hotel room, working myself to the bone. No. I can't do this anymore. I rub my stinging eyes with a weary sigh, then power down my computer. A bunch of the other executives are having dinner in the restaurant downstairs and if I hurry, I can still catch the main course. The thing is, I don't want to. The thought of hanging around the superficial business-people, hearing them talk of nothing but their charmed lives, doesn't appeal to me. It never did. I'd rather hang with a down-to-earth group, people who are genuinely enjoying themselves.

Someone like Zyon.

I've been taking Noah's advice and keeping my distance, but it's difficult. Not when there's a connection between us that draws me in, whether or not I want it. I want to be in her space all the time. Being around her feels *so good*. I'm often tempted to ignore my self-imposed rule to not get involved, but the warning in my head is always active, screaming at me to leave her alone.

But we're in Vegas. The perfect place to forget the rules and warnings. I want to have dinner with Zyon. Just dinner. No ulterior motives. There's no harm in dinner, right?

I reach for my phone before I change my mind. The line opens on the third ring and her giggling bathes my ear.

"Gabriel! Hiiiiieeeeee! Whatcha up to?"

From the noise in the background, she's already out. Bummer. I consider hanging up, but that would be rude. Plus, there's something in her voice that puts me on the alert. Zyon is usually upbeat, but not like this. She's either drunk or high, or both.

Damn it. None of them are good news for a tiny, vulnerable girl in a big city, where men prowl like wolves seeking their next victim. Just like the night we met, I can't relax knowing she's not safe.

"Where are you?" I ask, mentally weaving my way through the city. There are plenty of nightclubs along the strip. She can't be far.

"Why? Coming to join me?" I can hear a slight slur in her voice which confirms I'm right. Definitely wasted.

"I'm taking you back to the hotel. Come on, tell me where you are."

"No. The night's still young, party pooper, and I'm having fun."

"Zyon."

"I said no, goddamnit." A sudden curse leaves her mouth, then she says, "Ow."

"Are you okay?"

"What do you care?" she asks. "Don't you have something better to do? I'm sure there are more important things to worry about than a girl like me."

"I care about what happens to you, Zyon. I don't think you're safe."

"Oh, bullshit. You don't care about me. No one does. Because guess what? I'm nobody. Just a useless object. So just let me live my fucking useless life!"

She hangs up before I can get another word in. I try calling back a few times, but she doesn't pick up. Frustrated, I consider combing every club until I find her, but it would be a waste of time. I'm hoping she's just down the strip but there's no telling where she really is. There's only one solution. It's the last thing I want to do, but I have no choice. Scrolling through my phone, I dial Marcus' number.

"I need you to find a phone," I say when he picks up. "Like yesterday, please."

Marcus snorts. "You're walking around with a two-thousand-dollar phone *without* a tracking feature? Man, you're crazy."

"It's not mine."

"Whose is it?"

Even though I know Marcus has my back, it takes me a beat to say, "Zyon."

"Alright... why do you need to find her phone?"

"Because she's somewhere drunk and she's not picking up."

"What, you want to go get her?"

"Isn't that obvious?"

Marcus sighs. "Come on, Gabriel. Even I can't endorse a move like that. She's been drinking. That's dangerous for you."

“Stop treating me like a fragile flower, Marcus. I can control myself; been doing so for five years.”

“Four. Remember your relapse?”

“Are you going to help me or not?”

Marcus sighs again. “Give me a few.”

I hang up and change into a pair of dark jeans and a long-sleeved V-neck shirt. I grab a baseball cap at the last minute. In case there are employees hanging out in the lobby, I’m hoping this will be enough to conceal my face. I don’t know how I’ll find Zyon when I get to her, or what extraction method I'll need to bring her back to the hotel. Knowing her, it will probably involve kicking and screaming, especially if she’s as drunk as I suspect.

I move to the balcony while I wait for Marcus, taking in my view, from the bright city lights creating a temporary sky glow to the fast-paced movement of the pedestrians and cruising traffic. The music coming from the strip is loud enough to trigger a rhythmic beat in my pulse and send a familiar buzz through me, but I won’t allow it to influence me. Not tonight. Not here, in the city that made me lose myself so many times before. My mind returns to Zyon, and I think about our phone call. Something makes me suspect this isn’t the typical Vegas binge. She's going through something. Whatever it is, she can’t escape. I know, because I faced those demons, too, and I was lucky to emerge on top. They’re still lurking, seeking a chink in my armor to take me down. It's a risk walking into an alcohol-soaked club but I can handle myself. Zyon needs me, even if she hasn’t realized it yet.

Marcus calls me back a minute later. "She's at Fiction. I just texted you the address. I know you don't want to hear this, but please be careful."

"Thanks man. I will."

I hang up the phone and order an Uber. By the time I reach the front of the hotel, they're already parked and waiting. I keep trying Zyon's phone on the short ride over. She doesn't answer, and I try not to think of her hurt, or worse.

We arrive at the club and I'm out the door before the car even comes to a stop. Seeing the bouncer at the door gives me a small tinge of relief. If there are security guards around, chances are she's safe. I hope.

After flashing my ID and paying the cover charge, I take a short flight of stairs to the main area. It's hard to make out much inside, with multi-colored lights mainly focused on the dance floor. I move through the heavy crowd, looking for a five-foot, curly-haired figure but only finding different versions of her, none who quite match. I'm reaching for my phone when I hear an uproar up ahead. Patrons stand in a circle staring at something in the center. *Someone.* My instincts push me forward and, sure enough, it's Zyon, wasted as fuck, giving a guy a lap dance in the middle of the dance floor. She bends over, giving me a peek of her upper thighs. The asshole under her is getting a view of much more. He's clearly taking advantage of her vulnerability, caressing her thighs, moving his fingers up, up—

Oh, fuck, no.

I part the crowd, ignoring the angry exclamations as I storm onto the dance floor. The crowd boos when I pull Zyon off the man's lap. She frowns at me, but it's not an angry frown. It's like she's trying to figure out if I'm real. She gives me a dreamy smile and presses her body close to mine. The alcohol is practically oozing from her and it floods my senses, bringing back the memories and the longing. I can almost taste the smooth scotch filling my mouth, running down my throat and warming my insides.

Fuck.

I shake my head and ease her away from me, ignoring her drunken pout. She's not carrying a purse, nor is there any lying nearby. I hope this means she didn't leave the hotel with one. I take her upper arm, ready to steer her through the crowd when a hand on my shoulder stops me.

"Yo, dude. Where the fuck you going with my girl?"

I scoff, looking him up and down. He's a big guy, but I have height advantage. Unless he's a skilled fighter, I could knock his lights out easily. The old Gabriel would have already started a fight, but that guy is long gone. I don't want him resurrected again.

I ignore him and keep moving toward the exit, guiding Zyon in front of me. She's wobbling, overwhelmed by the alcohol in her system. We're almost to the bar when I decide to lift her in my arms, but when I dip to sweep my arm under her legs, I get a hard shove that sends me flying. My fingers brush the floor as I stop myself from falling completely. I straighten and turn as the same guy lunges at me, just as Zyon slumps to the floor. I turn my attention to her, and he slugs me in the face, sending me reeling backward. A violent fury surge through me. *Here we go.* I don't have time to recover before he's coming at me again. I shift to block his fist then respond with a solid blow to his nose. There's a sickening crunch and he howls, palming his face, blood seeping from between his fingers. If my experience serves me right, he's in a world of pain right now. Surprisingly, he's still standing, bouncing on his heels like a boxer preparing for a fight.

"Hey, man, if you know what's good for you, just walk away," I warn him. I'm really trying to keep it together, and I don't need this asshole fucking it all up for me.

"Why don't *you* walk away, you coward?" he huffs. "Or stay and fight me like a man."

Clicking my tongue, I turn toward Zyon once more. He moves around to face me, and I raise my arms in front of my face in time to block his strike. The crowd gasps when I grab his collar, giving him a head butt that sends him stumbling back. I follow that up with a hand to the neck. His eyes flutter closed as he drops to the ground with a hard thud. Breathing hard, I flex my fingers and stare down at him, waiting for him to rise so I can finish what I started. I won't hit a man when he's down, but fuck, I want to keep beating the crap out of him.

Asshole. Taking advantage of a vulnerable woman.

Shit. Zyon.

I whip around and she's already on her feet, leaning against a familiar-looking guy who's staring at me open-mouthed. It's not until I take Zyon from his arms that I recognize him. I'm still coming down from that post-fight high, but the adrenaline rush isn't enough to block my regret over losing my cool. The last thing I needed was for an employee to witness this. I lift Zyon in my arms, wishing I could take back the last two minutes of my life.

"Here's her purse," Zyon's companion says to me as we step out of the club. A blast of cool air hit us and Zyon curls into me. I ignore my body's response; this isn't the time to think about sex, or anything remotely related. My only goal is to get Zyon safely to her room.

"Hold on to it until the Uber gets here, will you?" I say to him. He nods, and I read the question in his eyes. He's wondering why I'm here, and I'm sure my fight will spread through the company grapevine if I don't nip this in the bud.

"What's your name?" I ask him.

"Ethan. I work in IT. I came to add the updates to your laptop last week—"

"Yes. I remember." I adjust Zyon in my arms. She stirs a little, only to press into me further. I'm starting to wonder if she's doing it on purpose. "I would appreciate it if you don't mention tonight to anyone, do you understand?"

He vigorously nods. "Sure thing, Mr. Cain."

"Gabriel."

He nods again.

"Did you come here together?" *Was this a date?* I want to add.

"Yeah... but she left her bag with me and disappeared after a while. I thought she went back to the hotel without me."

So this wasn't a date. I don't know why I feel such an immense relief. The car arrives, and I bundle Zyon in the backseat before getting in beside her. She instantly slumps against my shoulder and falls asleep. I shake my head at my reflection in the rearview mirror, at the bruise that's forming above my eye. The repercussions will be brutal. One look at my face and the boys will know I was in a fight. Over Zyon. This will only add weight to Noah's argument that she's trouble. I still disagree.

Zyon stirs when the Uber pulls up to the hotel, and this time, she wakes up fully. She lifts her head off my shoulder with a faraway look. "Where are we?"

"Away from trouble," I reply simply, opening the car door. I help her from the car, glad that she's awake and I don't have to carry her. I'd hate to draw attention to us while getting through the lobby. The executives are probably still hanging out in the restaurant, and I don't need them to see their CEO carrying a drunk woman upstairs.

Zyon wobbles a little when her feet hit the pavement. Her expression tells me she's about to pass out. *Shit.* I tap her cheek lightly with my palm. "Hey. You need to keep it together, okay? Just until we get upstairs. Can you do that?"

She gives me a slight nod then mumbles, "I think I'm about to throw up."

"Take a deep breath. Yes, that's it. Breathe." Her face settles, and I take her arm, gently guiding her through the lobby. I spot a few people from work staring in our direction, but I'm hoping they don't realize it's me. I pull the cap further down, just in case.

I imagine how we look. Me, with the pocket of my shirt half ripped off; Zyon, with her hair even messier than usual, although it's her dress that's pulling all the attention. The black fabric barely covers her thighs, and her breasts are almost spilling from the plunging neckline. I don't know how she survived in a club of thirsty animals.

It's almost eleven, so the elevators aren't in demand, giving us a private ride to her floor. She stumbles when we step inside, and I hold her against me on the ride up. It's the longest elevator ride of my life, total torture that leaves me struggling to keep my hormones in check. The doors finally open and she moans when I lift her in my arms.

"Which room?" I ask her, and she mumbles, "Three-eighty-four."

I set her down when we get there, handing her the purse. She reaches inside and starts feeling around, her movements becoming more frantic as the seconds pass.

"Where the fuck is my key?" she mutters, still rummaging, and I experience a sense of déjà vu. This entire night has happened before, but the ending can't be the same. I can't touch Zyon again. I won't.

"Come on." I put my arm around her and head back to the lift.

"Where are we going?"

"To my room. We'll call the front desk and have them replace your key." I don't want to risk going back downstairs.

She leans against the wall when we enter the lift again, her eyelashes fluttering on her cheeks. "I'm tired, Gabriel."

"Of course you are. You've been dancing all night."

She shakes her head. "You don't understand."

"Then make me understand."

She sighs and seems about to say something when the voice operator announces my floor. The doors open and I move toward the exit, but she remains in the elevator, staring at her feet.

"Coming?"

She hesitates for a moment then steps forward, following me out. We barely make it into the room when she rushes past me and disappears through the open bathroom door. I dial the front desk and order a new key while she empties her stomach in the bathroom.

Then there's silence.

I wait for her to emerge, but she doesn't. After waiting for a few minutes, I find her passed out on the floor. A quick check of her pulse tells me she's okay, so I place her on the bed and remove her shoes. After a debate with my conscience, I remove her dress too, averting my eyes as much as I can while I peel it from her body.

But only for a minute.

I feel like a perv, but I can't stop staring. It's not just her gorgeous figure gleaming under the dim light; it's the peaceful beauty on her face, her full lips that quiver as she sleeps. The tugging on my heartstrings isn't an unfamiliar reaction. In fact, it's a normal response whenever I look at her. I can't control it, and sometimes I don't want to. I like the way she makes me feel.

If only she wasn't my assistant.

She stirs. Just a little, curling onto her side. I cover her with the duvet before taking the couch for the night. A long, horny, twisted night.

A loud, agonized groan pulls me from sleep. I jump up with a start, ready to defend myself. There's no one in the room except me and Zyon, who's sitting up in bed, her fingers grinding into her temple.

"Ugh. My head..."

She seems disoriented, her hair a wild mess, her torso completely bare. I switch my gaze from her breasts to the bed while pushing the throw blanket off me.

"There's aspirin in the bathroom."

Her head jerks up and she yanks the sheet over her body, her eyes taking in my boxers and T-shirt. "What— wait— we... nothing happened, right?"

I chuckle. "Zyon, we both know you would have remembered if something happened."

She drops her head with a scoff, but I can see the hint of a smile on her lips. It fades as quickly as it came, her expression serious when she meets my gaze again.

"Your face."

I glance at my reflection in the mirror. The bruise is a purple welt now. "You should see the other guy."

She shakes her head. "It shouldn't have come to this. I hate that you got involved in a fight because of me. Again."

"Why?"

"Because I'm not worth the trouble." She shifts a little and the sheet slips down her chest, but she catches it. "Trust me."

"Zyon, that's the most ridiculous thing I've ever heard."

"It's true." Her eyes glisten and she quickly swipes at them. "I'm not worth fighting for."

I sigh, swinging my legs off the couch. "I don't know who hurt you, Zyon, but whatever they did will never change the truth." I lean forward, giving her a direct stare. "You are worthy. You are worth it. Don't ever let anyone tell you otherwise."

She sniffles and wipes at her face again. "Thanks for that. I needed to hear something positive after—" she takes a deep inhale and then slowly releases it. "After last night."

I wait for her to elaborate, but she doesn't, and I won't push her. I'm all too familiar with keeping secrets close to the chest. I recognize a familiar trait in Zyon, but if she doesn't get help, she will self-destruct like I did. It would be easy to tell her my story so she can learn from my mistakes, but I've never really shared the deepest parts of me with anyone, not even my friends. I don't want to go back down memory lane. It's too painful. I hope she'll figure it out like I did. Still, I don't want to shut her out. I get the feeling she could really use a friend.

"Zyon, if you ever need to talk, I'm here for you, okay?"

She cocks a brow at me, and I clarify at once. "No strings. Just friends."

"Okay. I might take you up on that offer, so I hope you mean it."

"Of course I do. But I charge for my time. And I don't come cheap."

She makes a weird sound before throwing a pillow at me. I duck with a laugh, and she joins in. Our eyes lock for a beat. Then another. I suppress the urge to pull the sheet from her body and taste every inch of her soft skin.

She breaks the gaze and fiddles with the corner of the sheet. "I could really use that aspirin."

I smile and rise from the couch, heading to the bathroom.

"And you need to put on some goddamn pants."

"My hotel room, my rules. Deal with it."

I can sense the pillow coming. This time I can't duck fast enough. It connects with the side of my face and Zyon giggles, pleased with herself.

God, that laugh, the genuine glee on her face. I'd love to do everything in my power to keep her in this state; happy, carefree.

But I can't.

15

Zyon

"I think I like someone," I say the second Anita takes her seat across from me. For the first time since I began therapy, I'm excited to share something about my life. If that isn't progress, I don't know what is.

Anita's eyebrows shoot up as she relaxes in the chair. "First of all, let's acknowledge that you actually spoke without me ripping the information from you—"

"That's a bit much, isn't it?"

"We both know it's not," she says, smiling. "But let's get back to what you just said. You like someone?"

"Yeah... well, I think so." Her lips are pursed and she's waiting for me to continue. "He's my boss."

Anita's expression is unreadable when she asks, "Did you sleep with him?"

"A long time ago." Well, three months ago, actually, but she doesn't need to know that.

"Can't be too long considering..." she sighs. "Are you sure it's lust and not love?"

"It's definitely not love, Anita, but I like him. He makes me feel safe. He cares about what happens to me. Unlike Dineo or my... sperm donor." I twist my fingers on my lap while thinking of something that never occurred to me before. "We attended a team conference last month and I—uh... went to the club. I had a few drinks, too." I ignore Anita's disapproving glare and go on. "I passed out in his hotel room, but he didn't take advantage of me."

"That surprises you."

I nod. "Most guys would take what they wanted, no question."

"So you think he's sent from heaven, right?" Anita asks, giving me a sarcastic smile.

"I don't think he's perfect. There's just something about him that sits well with my spirit."

I can't deny that something changed between us in Vegas. Gabriel seems a little more open to me. Friendly. He's still a back-breaking boss who's trying to get his money's worth out of me each month but, there's no more iciness. No more tension.

Well... that's not quite true.

There's a different kind of tension between us, a fiery sexual tension we both try to ignore, although it's getting stronger each day. Sharing a private space with a man I desperately want to sleep with is the worst kind of torture. I struggle to ignore the seductress inside me every single day. It's hard as hell, because all I want to do is climb him like a tree.

It's particularly difficult when he dresses in suits that hug his delicious body, leaving me parched all day. He constantly complains I'm too distracted by my phone when I'm running close to a deadline. If only he knew *he* is the reason I'm distracted. I'll keep that knowledge to myself for now. Who knows what the future holds?

"How does your interaction differ from the other guys you've been with?"

I blink, coming back to the present and Anita's inquisitive stare. "When I'm around him I feel… I don't know how to describe it… good. Right. It's nothing I conjure or control. It's just there. With other guys, the pain felt worse than ever."

She nods. "It's fine to like a guy, Zyon, but you are not ready for a relationship. Not until you heal."

"How will I know when I'm ready?"

"When you stop drinking and sleeping around to mask the pain. More importantly, when you start talking about what happened."

I rest my head on the back of the chair and close my eyes, processing her words. Yeah, I'm definitely not ready.

16

Gabriel

"For the last time, Noah, I'm not interested in a blind date. You want to make me happy? Give me the updated hotel mockup you promised."

Noah scoffs on the other end of the line. "I will, Mr. Workaholic, but you have to give Tiffany a chance, too. I promise, she's worth it. I'm not just talking about her looks. She's smart. Successful. No baggage."

"If she's so great, why don't you date her? Oh, wait, I forgot. You're still hung up on Ana. Pity she's getting married, huh?"

"Oh, screw you, Gabriel. Hitting below the belt when I'm trying to help you. Ungrateful son-of-a-bitch."

"I told you, I don't need your help."

"Right, because you're too busy banging your assistant."

"Are we doing this again? For the last time, I'm not sleeping with Zyon. We're just friends."

It's been an uphill battle trying to convince them that Zyon and I are just friends. There's no fucking around, not even a little, although the opportunities are there. Zyon and I have done hours of overtime in this office when the other employees have already left. There's an undeniable sexual tension, but my self-control won't let it happen. Our boss-employee relationship is still intact. There are no blurred lines. Things are just the way they're supposed to be.

"One of these days I'll have the pleasure of saying, I told you so," Noah says.

"Well, today is not that day. Talk to you later. Some of us have work to do."

I hang up in the middle of his snarky reply as a knock sounds at my door. I look up as Zyon pops her head inside. "I'm back, boss."

I give her a hard look and she returns a cheeky grin. I shouldn't have told her not to call me boss when she did it the first time. Now, she does it just to get under my skin.

"How's your grandma?" I ask. It's thoughtful of her to sacrifice her lunch hour once a month to spend time with her grandmother at the nursing home. Thoughtful and sweet. It doesn't help that I'm seeing her in a different light each day.

She gives me a genuine smile and her eyes sparkle a little. "She's doing great, as usual. Keeps asking how the great grandkids are. I think she's getting a little senile."

"Maybe she's trying to give you a nudge."

"Kids?" she shakes her head and makes a barfing sound.

"You don't like kids?"

"Oh, I like them very much, so long as they go home with their parents at the end of the day."

I chuckle and she shrugs, looking pleased at her joke. She's young, her feelings may eventually change. Zyon may not want to admit it, but she's a nurturer through and through. The way she goes out of her way to ensure I eat on time every day, how she rides me for working too late, the way she appears with those toe-curling back rubs when I'm extra stressed and need them so much... yes, a woman like Zyon may want kids someday. She just doesn't know it yet. For some reason, I can't help imagining her pregnant, sitting in a rocking chair rubbing her stomach. Our baby. The image gives me an unexpected thrill.

"Boss."

Zyon's voice brings me back to reality. "Are you going to stop calling me that?"

"Now that I know how much it irritates you? Nah. Not a chance." She giggles, and I can't help laughing with her. Then our eyes meet and awakens that longing again. Zyon's smile fades. So does mine.

"Anyway... so, I'm back a little early and I have some extra time on my hands, so feel free to use me however you want."

Zyon's words are clearly innocent, but they instantly summon the filthiest images in my mind. All I can think of is having her pinned beneath me, at my mercy, used by my cock, and with every deep, deliberate stroke I claim another piece of her until I own her completely.

"Gabriel."

"Mmm?"

"You're spacing out. You need to take a break."

I shake my head. "No, I'm fine."

"It's past your lunchtime."

"I don't have a lunchtime, Zyon. You insist on making it one o'clock, but that's not how I operate. I eat when I get a chance."

"I'm ordering takeout. Do you want a sandwich, or should I order from that Indian restaurant you like?"

Okay, so she's deliberately ignoring what I just said. I back down because it's easier to let her have her way. "I'll have a sandwich."

"Good."

"While you're at it, order one for yourself. You're giving me hell about not eating, yet you're guilty of doing the same."

"I don't habitually fast like you do, but thanks. I never say no to free food."

As I open my mouth to reply, my office phone rings. Zyon pivots and heads to exit as I take the call. The instant I hear the company attorney's voice, I know the conversation will be a long one.

"Hey, Zyon." I press the hold button on the phone as she turns around. "Are you free after work?"

She shrugs. "I guess. Why?"

"Have dinner with me."

"Oh...okay. You already know how I feel about free food."

I watch her walk out, her perfect ass swinging in that goddamn skirt. I don't know why I'm suddenly so nervous. It's just a casual dinner, not a date.

"So..." Zyon falls in step with me as we walk to the lift. "Where are we having dinner?"

"There's a Greek restaurant on fifty-fourth I've been to several times. The food is quite good."

"Sounds fancy."

"It is."

Her eyebrows bunch a little while I press the button for the lobby. "How about we not go there?" she says.

It's my turn to frown at her. "Why not?"

"I'm not big on fancy restaurants. Simplicity has always been my thing." She clicks her tongue. "But you don't know what that means, do you?"

"Of course. I can do simple."

The elevator comes and I guide her inside, ignoring the urge to keep my palm against the small of her back.

"Have you ever *done* simple? That's the question."

"I have."

"When was the last time you had a meal under thirty dollars?"

I give her a blank stare and she replies with, "Yeah. That changes tonight."

"Oh boy. I'm afraid to ask. What do you have in mind?"

A sly look brightens her face, then she shakes her head. "Nope. Not telling until we get there. You drive, I'll give directions."

"Something tells me I'll regret saying yes."

"That something might be right. The mystery is part of the fun, though!"

I've never liked surprises. They are too impulsive, and I hate not being in control. But there's something about Zyon that makes me willing to surrender to the unknown, something that makes me want to follow her anywhere. Everywhere. I don't want her out of my sight. I wipe my face with a sigh. I must be super exhausted to be thinking like this. What happened to just being her boss?

Zyon keeps the mystery going throughout our journey, only giving enough instructions to get to the next street. She soon directs me to park on the curb before a restaurant with a huge, tinted mirror and a wall painted green, red and yellow. There's a bright yellow sign marked *Dineo's* just above the entrance, and I can hear the blast of a DJ over a heavy, four-beat rhythm.

"That's reggae, FYI," Zyon says, watching my face.

"I know it is."

An amused smile tugs the corner of her lips, prompting me to ask, "What?"

"You don't seem the type to listen to that kind of music, that's all."

"I didn't say I listened."

"Ah. I got you." She turns and heads toward the entrance. I try not to look at her ass. Epic fail.

We enter the brightly lit space, where a tall, strapping woman stands by the hostess station. She lets out a loud squeal before pulling Zyon into a tight hug, then she eases back with a startling gasp. "What have you been eating, eh, child?"

"Food," Zyon says grumpily, but I can tell she's used to the head-to-toe scrutiny. She rolls her eyes as the woman spins her around while shaking her head.

"Nothing but skin and bones. No hips. No butt. How will you find a husband looking like this?"

She obviously needs glasses if she believes anything that just came out of her mouth. I scoff out loud. She glares at me while patting down Zyon's hair. Her expression softens as she gives me the same scrutinizing stare, her tongue swiping across her lower lip.

"So, Zyon, did you finally bring me a sugar daddy?"

Zyon laughs. "I think he's way too young, Aunt Zee." She makes a slight gesture to me. "This is Gabriel, my boss. Gabriel, this is my Aunt Zahra."

"Good to meet you, Zahra," I say, offering my hand, but instead, she wraps her plump arms around me, pulling me into a tight hug. She smells of cinnamon; subtle and pleasant.

"We don't shake hands around here, Sugar Daddy. We hug. Always hug," she says with a sneaky grin that reminds me of Zyon. "So... what brings you to our neck of the woods? Besides my gorgeousness, of course."

I smile as Zyon rolls her eyes again. "You're something else, Aunt Zee. I brought Gabriel to sample some real cooking. No offense to your mom or anything," she says to me. "This food will have you licking all ten fingers."

I don't ever see that happening, so I just say, "No offense taken." Especially since my mother has never cooked a day in her life.

Zahra and Zyon move to the dining area, so I dutifully follow while checking out the place. There's fresh yellow paint on the walls and the wooden tables and chairs look new. Even the chandeliers have a fresh sparkle, giving me the impression it was recently renovated. It's just a little after six and the room is almost packed.

"Your mother's in the back," Zahra says to Zyon, as we approach an empty table near a window. "Are you going to say hi?"

Zyon's shoulders stiffen, then she says, "I thought she was going up to Uncle Sipho's today."

"She canceled. What's the matter? Don't tell me you two got issues again."

Zyon glances over her shoulder at me. "I'll call you when I get home, okay?"

"Okay. Although I won't be holding my breath. I'm still waiting for that call after Aaron—"

"Later, Aunt Zee." Zyon's voice carries a firmness now, a slight edge to it. Zahra seems to catch the tone, too, because she glances at me before nodding.

"Let me get the server for you, okay?" she says, and Zyon gives her a tight nod. She sinks into the chair I pulled out for her with a loud sigh.

"Something tells me you already regret coming here," I say, taking my seat.

"Something would be right," she mumbles, looking a little gloomy.

"Want to talk about it?"

Zyon shakes her head. She mumbles something I can't hear then smiles, but it doesn't reach her eyes. She opens her menu and looks over the top at me.

"Have you ever tried suya?"

"I have no clue what that is."

"It's skewered beef with a dry rub. A little spicy, but really good. How about pepper soup?"

"Nope. I'm sensing a trend." I'm not averse to spice, but I don't enjoy food that leaves me battling with a burning mouth.

"Oh, my God. You clearly haven't lived," Zyon says, staring at me with wonder.

"I think I'm very much alive."

Tsk-ing at me, she waves to the server, who comes with her notepad and pen ready. She orders two servings of suya and pepper soup, and there's a sparkle in her eyes when she asks for extra spice.

"Something tells me I need to order a jug of milk too," I say to her when the server walks away.

"Nah. It's not as bad as you think."

"I don't know if I should trust your opinion, especially with that look on your face."

She grins, and this time it's real. "What look?"

"Like you're up to no good."

She raises her hand like she's swearing on the bible. "I promise, there's absolutely no mischief. I'm just dying to see your authentic response to a cuisine you've never tried before."

The server interrupts to take our drink order, then leaves again. Zyon watches me, her elbow resting on the table and her hand palming her jaw.

"What?"

"There's a story behind that cranberry juice you just ordered, right?"

"What makes you think there is?"

"It's after work. You've had a long, hectic day. Most men would order a glass of scotch, not juice. So, what's the story? A wild night in Vegas that made you do something stupid?"

My stomach tightens when I think of how close she is to the truth. I don't want to lie, but I don't want to talk about it, either. "How about you give me a little advice?"

She frowns, clearly realizing I want to sidestep her question. Surprisingly, she doesn't pursue it. "If this is a relationship question, count me out. I know jack-shit about them."

"I'm not in a relationship, so, you can relax. It's definitely not about that."

Her brows quickly lift as she smiles. "No special woman in Gabriel Cain's life? I'm surprised."

"Why? Have you forgotten how unusually long I work each day?" It seems she's about to ask a follow up, but I wave her off. "I need your advice," I remind her.

"Okay. Let's hear it."

"As you already know, my partners and I are expanding our business with an investment in a resort chain. I noticed you took several real estate courses at NYU. What advice would you give us to proceed?"

It's not that I need her advice. It's just the only thing to distract her from asking me another personal question.

She chuckles. "Will my answer affect my appraisal score at the end of the year?"

"No."

"Then I'll give you an honest answer. I have no clue."

I gape at her and she laughs out loud. "I only did those courses for the credits, sorry. I think I left every bit of information back at school. But," she quickly raises her index finger when I'm about to reply, "I know quite a lot about resorts, considering I've gone on vacation a couple times."

"Okay... so, where would you consider the best location?"

"The Caribbean, hands down."

"Why?"

"Don't you travel?"

"Yes, but I've never been to the Caribbean."

"I keep telling you how much you're missing out. The Caribbean's warm practically year round. The beaches are so beautiful it makes you want to cry, trust me. There's such a rich mix of culture and vibes... ugh, I'm tempted to request a two-week leave right now."

"Don't even think about it. Where have you visited?"

"I went to the Dominican Republic a few years ago. St. Lucia last summer. I had the Bahamas in my plans, but it didn't work out."

"Why?"

"It just didn't."

"You told me your father came from Jamaica. How come you've never visited?"

She shrugs, but a dark look sweeps across her face. "Just never got to it, I guess."

I recognize the hardness on her lips, the emptiness in her eyes. There's definitely a story behind that expression. It makes me curious, but I won't push her. She spared me earlier, so I will do the same.

"So..." Her expression suddenly brightens, while the server returns with our drinks. "I saw an interesting article online today..."

The spark in her eyes prompts me to ask, "What article?"

"Like you haven't seen it."

"I wouldn't have asked if I did."

She spreads her hands like she's reading a billboard, "Brooklyn's most eligible bachelors take it off for charity."

"Oh. That's a very old article."

She narrows her eyes at me. "It was four months ago, a little before we met. By the way, did you take it *all* off? The article didn't say."

I shake my head and take a sip of the cranberry juice.

"Is that a blush?"

"It most certainly isn't."

"You're blushing. I think it's quite adorable. Especially since you're always so... intense."

"I smile, don't I?"

"Not really. You need to do it more often. You are way more approachable when you smile."

I give her a quick, fake grin and she giggles, her thick lips spreading across her face. My gaze latches on to them, and I grapple with the sudden urge to kiss her. I lift my eyes to meet hers and the giggle quickly stops. She takes a breath, her chest slowly falling as she releases it.

"I wish you would stop looking at me like that," she says, twirling the straw in her glass.

"How?"

"I don't know how to explain it. It's like you're staring deep inside me."

"Do you want me to stop staring at you?"

"How about you lower the intensity a little?"

I can't suppress the smile that spreads across my lips, and Zyon gasps.

"Wait a goddamn minute. Is that a real smile? Oh, hell no, it can't be."

"Did anyone ever tell you how over-the-top you are?"

"Just take my advice. Smile more often. It looks really good on you."

I want to tell her the truth; that I've had nothing to smile about for such a long time. Before I can gather up the nerve, our food arrives, stopping me from pouring out my heart on the table, and after an irritable prompting from Zyon, I place a piece of the beef in my mouth.

"This is quite good, actually," I say after taking several bites. "It reminds me of you. A little spicy, but definitely worth the taste."

Her brows instantly lift, and she sets her fork down. "Do you even remember what I taste like?"

"As if I could forget," comes my immediate response before I can stop myself. I do a facepalm in my head. *Fuck*. I'm toeing a line I don't want to cross.

Zyon's eyes soften, and her little pink tongue peeks out to wet her lips. "Good. You shouldn't. You've got to do more than buy me dinner if you want another taste."

Oh, boy.

I want to believe it's just mild flirting, harmless, but Zyon's wearing an expression that tells me that's not the case. Even worse, it's conjuring images in my head that are definitely not safe. Like my lips grazing her upper thighs, making its way to her waiting flesh, tasting that sweet—

"Zyon, honey, you weren't going to leave without seeing your mommy, were you?"

I lift my gaze as the splitting image of Zyon comes toward us. She's taller, older and curvier. Her dreadlocked hair brushes her hips. From my peripheral view, I notice Zyon dropping her fork to the plate with a sharp clang, and I shift my eyes to her once more. Her face looks pinched, her mouth tight. I've never seen her so tense.

"Hello, Mommy." Her tone is so cold, it could make ice. Her eyes aren't much better. Her mother doesn't seem to notice; maybe she doesn't care. She leans down and wraps her arms around Zyon's shoulders, smacking a loud kiss on her cheek. Zyon's hand lifts to wipe her cheek when her mother pulls away, but she stops short and returns her hand to the table.

"Were you really going to leave without seeing me first?"

"Of course not," Zyon replies, but I'm positive she's lying.

Her mother twists and her cool eyes sweep over me. "So, you brought a friend." She says the word 'friend' like its more than that. Like I'm a lover.

"He's not my friend. He's my boss. Gabriel, meet my mother, Dineo."

Dineo assesses me even closer now. The indifference is gone. Now, there's full-blown interest. "Your boss, huh?" She sticks out her hand and I take it. "Nice to meet you, *boss*." She winks at me. "It seems my daughter is quite the asset if you're taking her out for dinner."

"Oh, fuck my life," Zyon mumbles, palming her face. Dineo gives her a sharp look but says nothing.

"She's quite the asset, of course. Invaluable. We're really grateful to have her on the team."

"I'm glad. You better treat her right, got it? Or you will have to answer to me. She's all I have in this world, you know."

It's obvious Dineo believes this is more than a boss-employee relationship. I don't care to convince her it's not. Especially when I'm not sure what's going on in my head. It's clear Zyon's not taking her response well. She is *pissed*. She shoots up from the chair, earning annoyed glances from diners nearby. Her chest violently bounces as she stares at her mom, her breath audible in her frustration.

"Don't even think about it," Dineo murmurs, and Zyon takes a deep breath.

"Gabriel, I'm ready to go. Can we get out of here, please?"

"Of course. Don't worry about the bill," I say to Dineo. "Just send an invoice to Zyon and I'll take care of it." I don't want to wait. I need to get Zyon out of here. She looks like a bomb about to explode. It's not good for Dineo's business, nor their relationship, as tattered as it seems to be.

Dineo gives her customers a reassuring smile as she follows us to the exit. She stops at the hostess' station to watch us walk out. I give her a wave goodbye and her return wave seems sad. I want to feel sorry for her, but I suspect she's the villain in this story. It brings me back to Vegas and how out-of-control Zyon was. Did Dineo hurt her?

"I'm sorry about that," Zyon says when we reach the car. "I shouldn't have lost my cool."

"That wasn't even close to losing it, believe me."

"Oh, yeah," she says with a dry snicker. "I remember Vegas."

"Not my finest moment, but yes, you get the idea. I think you controlled yourself quite well."

She sighs and leans against the car door. "What do you think about me, Gabriel? I'm not talking about me as your assistant. Me, as in Zyon Stewart."

My eyes peruse up her body as I mull over my answer. From her cute little feet in those pumps, to the skirt that hugs her body, finally taking in her simple buttoned shirt. I know she isn't asking about the physical Zyon, but what's deep inside.

"I think there's a soft, vulnerable woman under that tough exterior. That wall, I believe it's a front. You feel safer behind it because of the demons on the other side."

"Oh, God," she says with a choked sob, dropping her face into her palms.

"That wall, Zyon..." I remove her hands so I can see her face. "It's not healthy. It's a just temporary fix. You need to face those demons head-on or settle for a constant battle for the rest of your life." I wipe the tears from her cheeks with a sigh, my thumbs gently brushing her cheekbones. "I'm saying this to you, but I'm telling myself, too. I didn't realize until now that I still have work to do."

Zyon sniffles and wipes her face. "You are the most in-control person I know. Don't tell me you have demons, too."

"More than you can imagine," I say, opening her door. "A whole lot more."

We drive in silence, Zyon curled up on the seat and staring out the window. I decide to leave her alone. There's a lot on my mind, too. For the first time since Daniel died, I want to talk about what happened that night. There's also my attraction to Zyon to contend with. Denying it to my friends is one thing, but I can't fool my body. It's hungry for her, *desperate*. I desire no one else but her.

The question is, do I want to do something about it?

No. I can't. Zyon is fire, and I'm fuel. No good will come from us being together. We are both living in the dark. I need a woman who can bring me a ray of light. At least, that's the thought in my head, but the rest of me doesn't agree. The internal battle will continue until God knows when. Maybe it's time to take Noah's advice and get back out there, meet new women and start dating again. It doesn't hold much appeal, but it seems like the safest thing to do.

I pull up to the curb in front of Zyon's apartment and she lets out a weary sigh before reaching for the handle.

"Wait," I say to her.

She replies with a slight nod, but her expression tells me she's not really here. Leaving the car, I walk around the front and open her door. She blinks, takes my hand, and eases from the car. I should take a step back, but I don't. Her body grazes mine, just a little, but it's enough to send blood rushing to my cock. I feel delirious, just from that single, two-second touch.

She lifts her chin and meets my gaze. Arousal fills her face, and it's contagious, running from my head to the tip of my toes. My body feels like there's an electric charge surging through me, simmering under my skin. Her scent floods my senses, making me even giddier. I'm slowly losing control.

Fuck. I need to step away.

We're standing so close; I only need to lean in an inch and our lips would collide. The warning bell in my head goes off like an ambulance siren, but I'm too far gone to listen.

"You need to move, Gabriel," Zyon whispers. "Before I lose my mind, or I'll do something that we'll probably regret."

I could point out that she has the option of stepping to the other side and walking away, but I don't, because I want her here. I want to touch her, to taste her lips again, to—

A soft moan leaves Zyon's lips as her palms flatten against my chest. "Can't say I didn't warn you," she whispers against my lips before capturing my mouth.

There's no resistance, not when I've been wanting to taste her so badly. My hands find her ass and I grip her hard, crushing her against me. She loops her arms around my neck, deepening the strokes of her tongue, her fingers combing the hair at the back of my neck. I need more than our lips colliding, more than the taste of her sweet mouth. More than her clothed body pressed to mine. Her apartment is just several feet away; do I dare?

No. This is far enough.

I break the kiss as the front door opens, a dark-skinned girl with braided hair stepping out, looking down at us with a smile. "Now I know why I couldn't get you on the phone," she says.

Zyon shakes her head with a grimace, but there's still residue of lust on her face. "Rosh, this is Gabriel. Gabriel, meet my best friend, Roshell."

Roshell stops in front of me, giving me that same scrutinizing stare as the women I met today. She sticks out her hand, treating me to a firm handshake. “I’ve heard great things, Gabriel. Great things.”

“No, you have not,” Zyon bites out, pushing her away. “Don’t you have something more important to do?”

“Nope, I don’t, but I don’t want to ruin whatever’s going on here, so I’ll take my leave. Nice to meet you Gabriel. I’m looking forward to seeing you more often.”

“Oh, God.” Zyon palms her face.

“Wait a minute. Do you talk about me?” I ask her, amused, as Roshell walks away.

She shrugs. “Not really. I just mentioned how much of a tyrant boss you are.”

“I can’t be that much of a tyrant if you agree to have dinner with me.”

“Didn’t I tell you how much I love free food?” she replies, and I laugh. A short silence settles between us until she backs away. “Night, boss. See you on Monday.”

“Goodnight, Zyon.” I watch her climb the steps, and I try not to stare at her ass. My eyes latch on to her legs instead, but that’s even worse. I immediately imagine them wrapped tightly around my waist, and I can hear her soft moans as my cock drills into her. Her fingernails running along my back feel so real; I can almost taste her creamy skin as I lick her breasts.

Zyon’s front door closes with a loud click, bringing me back to reality. Shaking my head, I return to the car, away from the spot where my head just lost the battle against my body. I’m in trouble. The warning bells in my head are stronger than ever as I drive away. Do I keep ignoring them, or is it time to finally listen, to stay away from Zyon for good?

17

Zyon

"Let's get back to your parents, Zyon," Anita says, interrupting my daydream. I straighten myself on the couch and give her my undivided attention. At least, I'm trying to. I can't stop thinking about last night, Gabriel backing me against his car, devouring my mouth...

Does this mean what I think? Is Gabriel ready for me? His attraction is obvious. I've caught him several times taking me in, the hunger on his face leaving no room for confusion. I sense an inner conflict, though. There's a barrier preventing him from making a move. Is it too much to hope he'll overcome that barrier, that he'll finally surrender to what he feels for me?

"Zyon."

"Yeah, sorry Anita. You were saying?"

“Last time, we spoke about your father and how he's been trying to reach out to you. Did you consider meeting him halfway like you promised?”

Shaking my head, I give her a thumbs-down sign. “Negative.”

I’ve ignored his messages on Facebook since he started reaching out two months ago. I don’t need his apology for leaving us. Too little, too late. I will never believe he truly loves me. You don’t leave the people you love. Not if you can help it. It didn't matter if Dineo left Miami and returned to Brooklyn without leaving a forwarding address. She went back to her family, where she and my father met. If he wanted to find me, he would have. In the end, he only cared about his new family. Not me.

“Why don’t you want to reach out to him? Is it because of your mother?”

I open my eyes, giving Anita a frown. “What about her?”

She’s been calling my phone since last night, but I sent her an ‘*I’m okay, not ready to talk’* text then turned the ringer off my phone. I’m still pissed at her and I don’t know how to get over it.

“Do you think she'll feel betrayed if you contact your father?” Anita asks.

“I couldn't care less about what Dineo thinks. She doesn’t give a shit about me.”

“I thought you were on the mend. You both came here, did the work, made progress. What changed?”

“Besides her blaming me for what happened that night?”

Anita’s eyes narrow with a skeptic expression on her face. “No, she didn’t.”

“You’re her friend, Anita. Of course you would take her side.”

“I’m not taking sides, Zyon. It just doesn’t sound like something Dineo would do.”

“I guess you don’t know her as well as you thought, huh?”

“Maybe you’re right,” she says with a shrug. “But this isn’t about me. Have you spoken to her about it?”

“No. I’m still waiting for a half-decent apology, at the very least. I also think she’s keeping a secret from me. I don’t have a clue what it could be, but I suspect it involves...” I give my hand the impatient flick I always use whenever I mention my aggressor.

“Aaron,” Anita supplies.

I wince.

“You’re giving power to a man who doesn’t deserve it, Zyon. You will never be truly free until you say his name.”

“I know... but I just can’t.”

Anita nods and types on her tablet.

“Tell me more about what you suspect about Aaron and your mom.”

“I don’t know. Something just doesn’t add up. It’s not just now; it’s been since the moment he moved in. He's loaded and so are his parents, so why would a guy like him need a place to stay, especially in a matchbox apartment in Brooklyn?”

“What did your mother explain back then?”

“She only told me he had issues with his roommate and needed a place to crash while he searched for a new apartment. It wasn’t until... after when I found out how wealthy he is.”

“What did she say then?”

"Nothing that made sense to me. To top it all off, I find out she's been talking to him since he returned to the city. I feel betrayed, like I can't trust her."

Anita sighs. "Maybe it's time to arrange another joint session."

"I'm not interested."

"Zyon—"

"Can we change the subject? Do you mind?"

Anita scrunches her lips, the displeasure clear on her face. "Yes, I do mind, Zyon," she snaps. "I wish you would stop telling me how to do my job."

"I'm sorry. That's not what I'm trying to do, I swear. I'm just—it's hard to talk about. Resurrecting that pain makes me want to freak out."

She remains silent for a moment, staring me down, her stern gaze reducing me to the five-year-old I was when we first met. I pick at the arm of the cushion, waiting for her to toss me out, or at least reprimand me more. God knows I deserve it.

"I'm sorry," I apologize again, and she nods this time in acceptance.

"You still haven't told me how you feel about Aaron coming back to town."

"I don't know... terrified? I keep imagining him lurking in every dark corner. I'm scared of going home and finding him on my doorstep or hiding in my room. I can't sleep with the lights off or my door unlocked. I hear his voice everywhere I go."

"Have you seen him around?"

I shake my head with a deep sigh. "No, I haven't, but I can't rule out that he's watching me."

Anita puts her tablet down. "Have you considered taking self-defense lessons?"

"I thought about it, but I haven't gotten around to getting it done. I'm trying to save money so I can get my own apartment." Living with Roshell is great, but she and Terrence are getting closer. I'm sure she will eventually need her space.

"Okay. In the meantime, just be alert wherever you go. For your homework, I want you to talk to your mother. I want you to reach out to your father, too."

I raise my brows at her, and she scoffs. "Try, at least. Your unhealthy relationship with your parents is affecting your healing process. You may not believe me, but it's true."

"Okay," I reply, standing up. "I'll see what I can do."

Anita looks weary and I don't blame her. I've been resistant and defiant in every session. She's just trying to do the job she's paid to do.

"Look, I'm sorry for giving you a hard time. I'm just..." I throw my hands in the air as the words fail me. Anita nods like she understands.

"I never take it personally, Zyon. There are many people who don't survive what you endured. But you are here, trying to get over it, so that counts for something. I just want you to work at it, okay?"

"Okay."

This time, I really mean it. I'm sick of being angry all the time. Sick of living in fear. I want to sleep with the lights off and my door unlocked, to not look over my shoulder wherever I go. Hell, I want to fall in love with a man who accepts me, flaws and all. Anita's right; I won't get a breakthrough until I put in the effort to change.

On the ride home, I think about the homework Anita gave me. Am I ready to reach out to my father, or have a heart to heart with my mother? The rebel in me doesn't want to, but it's time to leave that girl behind. Seriously. I'm ready to find the light, ready to face these demons. First step: make peace with my parents. Then, I need to open up about what Aaron did to me.

Shit.

I just said his name, even if it's in my head. For the first time since that night, I'm not afraid to say it again, and again.

"Aaron."

"Aaron."

The driver twists his head to glance at me as I burst into a giggle. Saying Aaron's name doesn't trigger an instant transformation, but I feel lighter inside, like I'm ready to welcome the old Zyon back into my life.

18

Zyon

"You, me, lunch in five. How does that sound?" Olivia asks the minute I answer my office phone. We've gotten close since I started working here, but our schedules clash too often for us to really hang out. Today is a rare day where we're free at the same time.

"Sounds like Dietrich called in sick today," I reply. Dietrich is her office husband slash BFF. They're essentially joined at the hip.

"Girl, I'm not on the rebound, but yes. Dietrich's partner broke his ankle last night and he took a few days off to play doctor. So, what do you say about lunch?"

I shrug, although she can't see it. "Yeah, sure."

"Great! Meet you down in the lobby?"

"Okay, cool."

I hang up and stick my head through Gabriel's door to tell him I'll be out for lunch. He barely acknowledges me with a flick of his wrist.

His eyes are glued to the screen before him. I don't understand why he's been so distant all day. Correction: he's been distant since our kiss last Friday night.

I'm still annoyed at his behavior. It wasn't what I expected coming in to work after such a wonderful night. Gabriel kissed me. His hands roamed all over my body. I felt his hard cock pressing against my stomach. He wanted me. What changed?

I wear my best outfit, a body-hugging dress with a cute little side slit and a bateau neckline. I take extra time to perfect my makeup. I even detangle my hair and straighten it a little. Why? Because I thought our kiss meant something. I thought my boss was finally ready for me.

To my chagrin, I arrive to work to a freezer. Gabriel has returned to his old ways, icing me out, behaving like that kiss didn't happen. I have the overwhelming urge to slap some sense into his flip-flopping ass, but I need my job.

God, I'm so angry.

What is wrong with me? Am I not good enough for him? Is that why he didn't touch me in Vegas? The way he kissed me in front of my apartment, that wasn't a man with no interest. I refuse to believe it. *What's his problem*? I pull my bag from a drawer and slam it shut. A part of me hopes the sound will pull Gabriel from his office so we can hash this out, but it doesn't work. Damn it. I need to get my head together and move on. Gabriel doesn't want me.

If only my stupid heart would get the message.

I exit the main door and head to the elevator. I'm praying its empty because I can't seem to temper the anger inside me; I'm sure it's clear on my face. The universe seems to be out for me today because the elevator arrives with the last person I want to see. I resist rolling my eyes at Deacon beaming down at me.

"Hello, friend." His smile disappears as he stares into my face. "You okay?"

"Just peachy." I reach to press the button for the lobby and notice it's already lit.

"Going for lunch?" he asks.

"Yup." I consider placing my EarPods in, but that would be rude. He's a senior manager in the company—in HR—and I'm not interested in putting myself in his bad books. Although he's probably ready to write me off after I rejected his advances. How many times have I said no since I started working here? Eight? Ten? I've lost count.

"I'm heading to lunch too," he says. "Care to join me?"

"Sorry," I reply as the elevator doors open. "I already have plans."

"Lucky guy." He gives me a sweet smile that makes me feel bad. "Maybe next time."

"Maybe." I probably won't, but I've done enough to hurt his feelings today. I watch him walk away, wishing I could feel something for him. I need that distraction in my life right now.

"Be careful of that one," Olivia's voice sounds from behind me, making me jump.

I swivel to her with a glare. "Olivia, don't sneak up on me like that."

"Sorry. We're in a crowded lobby, so..." She shrugs, and I sigh out the tension.

"It's okay. I'm just on a little edge today. What were you saying about Deacon?"

"Shh. Keep your voice down. He's right over there."

I glance over to the security post where Deacon's dropping off a package. "He can't hear us. What?"

"Stay away from him. He's trouble," she mumbles.

"That's the vaguest warning I've ever gotten. They say I'm trouble, too. Maybe he needs to stay away from me," I retort, chuckling at my own joke.

Olivia doesn't smile back. "It's not a joke, Zyon."

"Okay, fine, but I need to know why." Now I'm really curious because Gabriel's given me the same warning, more than once. At first I thought he was jealous, or he couldn't stand Deacon. Watching their interactions over the months I've been working here, I've realized there's no love lost between them. I'm dying to know what happened, but Gabriel's lips are like a vault. Maybe Olivia can shed some light.

"I can't give you details, because I signed a non-disclosure agreement," she says.

"Oh, wow." It's definitely serious. What the hell did Deacon do?

"Just take my word for it, Zyon. You don't want to mess around with him."

"Okay, okay. I won't. He's not my type, anyway."

"Oh, please. I saw you checking him out on your first day."

"That's standard procedure. Nothing to it." I slip my arm through hers and we move toward the front door as Deacon leaves the security post. "So, where are we having lunch?"

"I'm in the mood for pasta. How about you?"

"Sounds good."

Ahead of us, Deacon's head swivels to watch a stunning blonde who just walked past him. He catches my gaze and grins; I shake my head. *Men*. Always after pussy, loyalty be damned.

Olivia nudges my side when the blonde walks past us. "That's Nicole Cambridge. Emily's best friend. I'd bet my last dollar she's here to see Gabriel."

My pulse immediately trips. "Gabriel? Why?"

"They are kind of a thing. Childhood friends turned lovers or something like that. I mean, Gabriel's been out with tons of women, but she's the only constant in his life."

My heart falls to the floor of my stomach and it suddenly feels hard to breathe. "Oh."

We walk through the turnstile out to the street, and it feels like someone's punched me in the gut. The ache grows worse as Olivia keeps talking.

"Rumor has it he's planning to propose. I don't know if it's true, but if even if it's not, Nicole's a lucky bitch. A man like Gabriel and I'd be set for life."

"I'm sure that's not true."

"About what, me being set for life? Girl, do you know how much he's worth? I'm talking even without his parents' money. He runs his own company. You're his assistant. How come you don't know that?"

"I'm talking about the proposal. Nicole."

It can't be true. There's no way Gabriel kissed me while seeing someone else. No way. We had a moment. *Several* moments. The way he looked at me, it meant something, didn't it?

"They are definitely screwing. I know that much."

I try to arrange a neutral expression, but it's an epic failure. Inside I'm hurt and angry, at myself *and* Gabriel. I can't decide who's more to blame: me, for allowing myself to feel something more than lust, or Gabriel for pulling me in like he actually cared?

"Either way, I think Nicole will get her wish."

"You think so?" God, I'm doing a terrible job keeping myself together. I can hear the quiver in my voice. Thank God Olivia doesn't seem to notice.

"Of course. You should see them together. The way he looks at her; God, I would give anything for my boyfriend to care about me half as much."

Tears sting my eyes and I blink them away. Gabriel doesn't want to be with me. He's already seeing someone else. It's time to finally get the message and move on.

"For someone on the verge of starvation half hour ago, you sure left a lot on that plate," Olivia says after the server takes my half-eaten pasta away.

"I lost my appetite."

At her raised brows I roll my eyes. "Oh, don't give me that look," I snap.

Again, Olivia's brows lift. "What's gotten your panties in a bunch?"

"Nothing," I reply. "Can we go?"

"I thought you were waiting on your doggie bag."

"Forget it." The chair scrapes as I stand and march from the restaurant.

"Did I say something to offend you?" Olivia asks, jogging to keep up with me.

I slow down with a heavy sigh. "No, you didn't. I just have a lot on my mind." Like confronting Gabriel. Did he think I wouldn't find out? *Ugh*. Men! Assholes, the bunch of them. Gabriel's the worst of the lot. It's all a farce. He's not a sweet, kind man like I thought. He's a snake.

Deacon falls in step with us as we approach our office building. "If I didn't know better, I'd think you ladies were stalking me," he says, grinning.

"Good thing you know better, right?" Olivia says with a smirk. She takes my hand, pulling me along with her.

Deacon moves from Olivia's side to mine. "Come on. Zyon, what's the rush? Being a few minutes late won't get you a slap on the wrist."

"Ignore him," Oliva whispers, her grip tightening on my wrist. I almost trip over my legs as she rushes us forward.

The elevator doors open as we cross the lobby. My heart pauses when Gabriel steps out with Nicole. He doesn't look my way as they head to the executive parking lot. His hand brushes her lower back, guiding her along. They seem close. *Intimate*. The ache in my stomach feels even worse, like I'm going to throw up. I can feel the tears welling in my eyes, making them sting, and I resist the urge to wipe them away. Screw this. I'm not going to cry over a guy. That's not my style.

I shift my eyes from the exit when Olivia nudges me in the side. The elevator, *right*. I'm thankful when Deacon doesn't enter—small victories. The way I'm feeling right now, I'll probably go off if he keeps coming on to me. I just want to get to my desk and simmer while I remind myself why I'm here, which is to earn a paycheck, not screw my boss.

I immediately spot a sticky note attached to my computer. It's Gabriel's handwriting, and for a split second, I harbor a little hope. It vanishes when I read the contents. It's just a stupid instruction to book the conference room upstairs for tomorrow's board meeting. I crumple the note in my palm then throw it against his office door, wishing I could tell him where to stick it.

I hate him. He's not the good guy he claims to be. Good guys don't lead a woman on with sweet kisses and soft touches, only to leave her heart on the floor in pieces. He's a bad man, just like every other. I need to remember this feeling if he ever tries to touch me again. These walls are staying up.

19

Gabriel

The thud of files dropping to my desk catches me by surprise. I look up to meet Zyon's dark glare.

"The bearer from Rosemead just dropped these off. Figured you were waiting for them."

"Thanks." I straighten in my seat as she spins around with a curse, storming toward the door. "Zyon, stop."

"What?" Her tone is like acid, stinging me where it lands.

It takes a moment to sink in that she'd been this way all morning; dark and sullen, barely saying a word, which isn't like her. I had been so caught up with work I didn't even notice until now.

"Are you okay?" Stupid question, considering that she looks like she has murder on the brain.

"Just *peachy*." She turns around to leave again and I rise from my seat.

"Zyon."

"I said I'm fine, okay? Don't worry about it."

I grab her around the waist before she steps through the door, pulling her against me. I knew it was a terrible idea even before I left my desk. Her ass grazes my front, short-circuiting my brain and sending an electric charge through my body. My cock is functioning with a mind of its own. Without thinking, I wrap my arms around her, pulling her closer, not caring about my decision to keep my distance.

"Stop struggling."

"Then let me go," she snaps.

"Not until you tell me what's wrong."

Zyon stops writhing in my arms and lets out a harsh breath. "There's nothing wrong, okay? Just let me get back to work."

I twist her around, searching her face. "You've been quiet all morning. Distracted. You filled my coffee order wrong. Twice."

"It won't happen again, I promise."

"I don't care about the goddamn coffee, Zyon. I care about you. What's wrong?"

Zyon laughs, but it sounds hollow and dry. "You care about me... wow."

"It's the truth."

"It's a load of sh—" She takes a deep breath and tries to pull from my arms. I don't want my grip to bruise her, so I let her go.

"Are you going to tell me what's wrong?"

"Why don't you try figuring it out?"

"Zyon, come on."

"I swear to God, I'm trying to be professional right now. You, Gabriel Cain, you are nothing but a fucking liar."

"Wait, what?" I grab her arm before she can move off. "When did I lie to you?"

"After dinner the other night. Remember that?"

How the hell could I forget? I didn't sleep that night. All I could think of was her softness pressed against me, the heat in her eyes that left no room for misunderstanding. I kicked myself for not surrendering to my desire for her, but in the morning, I was relieved when my common sense kicked in. I can't fuck Zyon again. We're both burning for each other right now, but when reality hits, when our baggage becomes too heavy for us to handle, we'll fizzle like a campfire in the rain. I don't want to lose another assistant, especially not one as efficient as Zyon. Business before pleasure. That's my motto.

"You said there's no special woman in your life. You lied to me."

I frown at her, even more puzzled than before. "I didn't lie to you."

"Really?" she says, cocking her head. "Then who is Nicole Cambridge?"

The hell? "Nicole and I have been friends since we were kids. What does she have to do with this?"

"Your childhood friend, huh? Is that what you call the woman you plan to propose to?"

"*What*?"

"Yeah, I heard it through the grapevine. I shouldn't even be mad. It's not like there's anything going on between us. You proved to me that all men do is lie and cheat, taking what doesn't belong to them. It's your way or no way at all. You're no different. You're just like the rest of them!"

"Zyon—" I grab her again when she tries to leave. This time, I pin her against the wall by her shoulders. She gives me a glare sharp enough to cut steel. "First of all, do not call me a liar. I'm not perfect, but I try my best to be honest."

"Let me go." She tries to push me away, but my hands lock her down.

"Nicole and I aren't getting married. We aren't a thing. Whoever told you that, they are *wrong*."

"I don't care. Seriously."

"Now who's the liar, Zyon?"

My brain screams at me to let her go. It warns me I could lose control if I don't walk away, but I don't listen. I don't want to listen or obey. I only want to feel. Fuck the reasons for keeping my distance. The only thing that matters is Zyon's lips, and how I'd been dying to taste them again, and how totally accessible they are right now. I'd be a fool to let her go.

Just one more taste.

"I told you, I don't care—"

Reaching behind her head, I grip a handful of her hair and capture her lips. They meld perfectly with mine, just like before. She moans against my mouth before letting me in, and I devour her with pent-up hunger. I've been desperate for this. *Starving*. My hands wander, lifting the hem of her skirt, bunching it at her waist. My lips make a trail down her throat while my fingers move up her thighs, stroking the soft skin. Her body quivers when I cup her through her silk panties. Our eyes meet as I gently press forward, feeling the dampness that lets me know she's wet. Really, *really* wet. I shift her panties aside to slide two fingers inside her, and sure enough, she's soaking. The musky scent of her arousal is tempting me to bury my cock inside her. My fingers go to work, giving her the slow, twisting thrusts I know will drive her as crazy as I'm feeling right now.

"Fuck, Gabriel…" Zyon's body jerks and her fingers sink into my shoulders. She rocks her hips, matching the steady rhythm of my fingers. I curve my fingertips, trying to find the spot that will make her see stars, and she curses again. "You're gonna make me come…"

I want nothing more than to move her to my couch and *really* make her come. I want to see the desire in her eyes as I fill her. Her tight pussy around my cock—I *need* it. Those sexy lips screaming my name; I'd give anything to hear her husky moans.

Damn it, I'm already breaking one rule by touching Zyon. I'm not too far gone to realize I'm making a mistake. I remove my fingers and Zyon makes a strangled sound. Her questioning expression simmers as the office phone rings. I let her go and back away with a regretful sigh. I can't deny how aroused I am. That kiss wasn't enough. I want more.

I need more.

But *fuck*, I can't.

Zyon's hair looks more frizzy than usual, her eyes wild, her chest heaving as she takes deep breaths to calm herself. She looks so desirable. Totally fuckable. I want nothing more than to answer her body's call for me. Again, I remind myself it's the worst decision I could make. Shaking my head, I take a few more steps back, ignoring the disappointment on her face. She dashes from the room while I reach for the phone. It's Nicole, and I roll my eyes at the co-incidence. My fight with Zyon began because she thought Nicole and I were a thing, and

Nicole's call interrupted us. It's funny how I'm sandwiched between two women I'll never be with.

"Hey Nicole, what's up?" I greet her.

"Hey, I tried reaching you on your cell phone. It went straight to voicemail."

"I didn't want the distraction, so I turned it off." That's a lie; my biggest distraction was only a few feet outside my office door. "Everything okay?"

"Couldn't be better. Just heard the wonderful news that Rosemead got nominated for the rising star award. Congrats! You and the boys must be thrilled."

"Yeah, we are. Thanks." I really don't care about winning at the corporate awards this weekend. It sounds cliché but being nominated is enough validation for the impact we've made in such a short time.

"As you know, Daddy is being honored for his contribution to the city, so I will be there. I was wondering if you and I could ride together."

"Uh... I'm taking Lauren, and you know how she takes forever getting ready. I'd hate to keep you waiting." I don't mention that Zyon's going too. It's not important. I'm arranging a separate car for her.

"Oh. I forgot Cain Industries got nominated for employer of the year."

"Yup." I was hoping Dad would end his hiatus and represent the company—his company—but he's still MIA. It reinforces the suspicion that he's trying to drive me nuts. There's no other reason, and it's pissing me off. I'm approaching a point where I'm unwilling to care about what my parents think because my company needs me more than I need their approval.

"Okay, so I'll see you on Saturday? You better save me a dance," Nicole says.

"Of course." I hang up the phone and my mind immediately returns to Zyon. It's time to tell her that what just happened was a mistake. I don't want her getting the wrong idea because this can never happen again. I open the door to an empty chair and her laptop already powered down. She's gone. I shake my head, not sure if what I'm feeling is relief or disappointment. Whatever it is, the truth remains the same. I need to leave Zyon alone.

20

Zyon

"Let's get one thing straight," Roshell says as I twirl in the mirror. "You, my friend, are getting laid tonight. There's no way Gabriel will be able to resist you in this dress."

I shake my head at her, but my eyes are still glued to my reflection. I spent hours shopping for an outfit for the corporate award ceremony I'm attending tonight, and I'm quite pleased with my blood-red, off-the-shoulder dress with a daring side split. Roshell offered to straighten my hair and I'm glad I let her, because I love how silky it feels draping over my shoulders. She did my makeup too, and although it's a little heavier than I usually wear, I can't deny how fantastic I look.

"What, no response?" Roshell asks.

"Gabriel isn't interested in sleeping with me again." I turn around to look at her perched on my bed. "But who knows? I'm sexy as hell and I'm wearing no panties. I just might get laid, anyway."

Roshell's not smiling at my joke like I expected her to be. "I thought we were done with the random sex."

"Sleeping with Gabriel would be random, too, wouldn't it?"

"No, it wouldn't. It would mean something."

I give her a hard stare. "What would it mean, Roshell? Do you think I'm desperate? I'm not an afterthought. I won't settle for Gabriel's scraps."

"*Whoa*. This conversation is taking a turn I didn't expect, honey," Roshell says, looking at me with concern. "Did something happen that you forgot to tell me about?"

I throw my hands in the air. "Plenty happened, girl. You were so busy with Terrence and everything seemed so perfect between you two. I didn't want to ruin your good energy."

"Okay." She leaves the bed to stand by the mirror. "Terrence will be away for an entire month handling business in South Carolina. I'm all yours. Tell me what happened."

"As you already know, Gabriel and I had a moment outside last week. I thought it meant something, but I was wrong. He's seeing someone else."

"Wait—what?"

I shrug. "He claims they're just friends, but I don't know, Rosh. I saw them together. You could cut the tension with a knife."

"You've always had an overactive imagination, Zyon," she says, staring at me like I have an incurable disease. "Maybe you read too much into what you saw."

"I'm not an idiot."

"I never said you were."

“If I’m wrong like you say, how do you explain the way he’s behaved toward me? Even after we kissed in his office, he—”

“Wait a minute. I thought you only kissed after dinner last week.”

Oh shit. I forgot she doesn’t know about *that*. “We...kind of hooked up in his office after I saw him with his friend.” I make air quotes and roll my eyes. I don't believe it for a minute. Men are liars through and through.

“So, you ‘kind of hooked up,’ whatever that means, and kissed multiple times, yet you still think it means nothing.”

“It doesn’t. He’s been cold to me ever since. We talk about work, nothing else. He doesn’t even call me into his office anymore. It's clear he doesn’t want to be alone with me.” I whip around, searching for my purse. “But I don’t care. There's plenty of fish in the sea.”

“Sounds like you care plenty,” Roshell says with a grin.

I lash her with a death glare. “Do you want me to slap you?”

“If it gets you to admit how you really feel, fine. I’ll take it.”

My cell phone buzzes on the table. It’s a text from Gabriel telling me the car is a few minutes away. Another sign he's keeping his distance. We are going to the event together; why wouldn’t he just pick me up? I send him a reply that I’m ready and waiting, and I push the negative feelings aside. Tonight is a celebration, not a funeral. I won’t let the bad vibes get me down.

“Admit it, Zyon. You’re falling for him.”

“I won’t admit shit.”

“Mmm-hmm,” Roshell says with a knowing look. I keep forgetting she knows me better than I even know myself. “I don’t know, Zyon. Why would he invite you to an exclusive function if he’s not into you?”

"It's an exclusive *work* function and I'm his assistant. It goes without saying. He's taking his sister too. It's nothing special, believe me."

"I wish you would stop selling yourself short."

"I'm being realistic, Rosh."

My cell phone beeps again. The car has arrived. I take a deep breath as Roshell gives me a once over and declares I'm one hundred percent red carpet ready. For the first time, I'm nervous, because the more time passes, the more I'm thinking about what Roshell said.

Am I falling for Gabriel? Is this why there are a million butterflies in my stomach when I think of him, or why I'm so hurt over seeing him and Nicole together? Is this why I'm so angry that he's giving me the cold shoulder? I don't know. I've never been in love before.

Fuck. Love? When did that become an option?

Even if it's true, it'll have to be my little secret. No one can ever know. Not even Roshell. Definitely not Gabriel.

It feels like hours have passed since the car picked me up, but it's only been half an hour when we pull up to the hotel. I was lost to my thoughts the entire journey, wrestling with the urge to go back home. I don't want to see Gabriel. I don't want him see *me*. I feel like I'm wearing my emotions on my face tonight, and if that's true, then I won't be able to hide my feelings for him. He can't ever know I'm halfway in love with him.

There. I fucking said it.

I'm falling in love with Gabriel Cain.

Shit.

I'm falling in love with a man who's probably taken. A liar. God, I don't need this right now.

The passenger door opens, and the driver sticks his hand inside to help me out. He releases me on the sidewalk, then tips his hat and returns to the car. Another round of nerves follow me into the beautifully decorated lobby with signs pointing to the top floor. The elevator takes me upstairs and I give the hostess my invite, joining the cocktail hour already in full swing.

My eyes instantly search the crowd for Gabriel, spotting a cute brunette waving in my direction. There's no one behind me, so I assume she's beckoning at me. I move forward and she copies me, but I'm surprised when she pulls me into a tight squeeze.

"Hi! I'm Lauren, Gabriel's sister. I've been dying to meet you," she says after finally letting me go. I can't help staring at her like she's crazy.

"Why?" I ask, and she chuckles. *Oops, that was blunt.*

"Because you are the only assistant who's lasted beyond a week since Matt left and I've been really, really curious why." She looks me over with a nod. "Now it makes perfect sense. You are *stunning*."

"Thanks. You look beautiful too." She's wearing a champagne-colored gown with thin, crystal-studded straps, and her thick hair hangs in loose waves over her shoulder. She has Gabriel's eyes, but hers are softer, friendlier. I already like her.

She takes my hand, pulling me forward. "Come on. The guys are over there."

I follow the jerk of her head to a table at the front. Noah, Marcus, and Gabriel are standing in a huddle with glasses clutched in their hands, Gabriel with his signature cranberry juice. I approach with Lauren, my eyes glued to Gabriel's broad back. The flutters are back, now accompanied by the inability to breathe.

Marcus sees us coming and whispers to the others. I'm aware of Noah's presence, but I'm not looking at him. My eyes are on Gabriel and only Gabriel. I'm looking for an imperfection, something to make him less desirable, *anything*. Who am I kidding? He could be wearing a potato sack and I would still find him attractive. My body would still burn for him. I swear, my temperature has risen several degrees within a minute. He's wearing a dark suit clearly made for him, and he's gotten a haircut since yesterday. It's freshly faded at the sides and neatly combed on top. There's not a strand out of place. I don't know where the urge comes from, but all I want to do is run my fingers through it, tousle it a bit, just to see his reaction.

Gabriel's checking me out too, his eyes doing a slow-motion scan of my body, lingering at my thigh-high side split for a beat before continuing upwards. He meets my gaze and gives me a casual nod. "You made it," he remarks.

No, 'you look amazing' or, 'that dress really suits you'. I'll even take a compliment on my hair, but he gives me nothing. It irritates me, because deep down, I did this all for him.

Fuck him.

"I almost changed my mind," I reply, and he frowns.

"So, Zyon. Didn't I tell you we'd meet again?" Marcus asks, cutting into the tension between me and Gabriel.

I shift my eyes to him and force a smile. "You did. Do you mind giving me the lottery numbers for the weekend draw?"

"Of course. I'll hook a sister up."

"Appreciate it."

"Guys, I'll be back," Lauren says. "Just saw an old friend from high school."

She moves off and I notice Marcus watching her leave. There's a tenderness in his eyes that wasn't there before, and he slips a guilty look at Gabriel, who is still staring at me, oblivious at his best friend pining after his sister. Instead, he's still frowning. What is his problem?

Determined to ignore him, I turn to Noah, who's been silent. My instinct tells me he's not a fan of mine, although it makes no sense. We've only met once. He's politely staring at me with a dry smile. Well, two can play that fake game. I summon my brightest smile.

"Lovely to see you again, dear Noah," I say, and his features lighten a little.

All he says is, "Hi, Zyon," before raising his tumbler.

"How come this dickhead gets such an elaborate greeting and mine was dry as a bone?" Marcus pouts, making him look even more attractive.

It's a pity he's Gabriel's friend, or else I wouldn't hesitate. It's also a pity he's head over heels in love with Lauren. For some reason, he seems vested in keeping it a secret. I'm curious. I would love to know why. I mentally smack myself. Enough with wishing he was a random stranger I could take home tonight. I'm trying to be done with that. It's not healthy. Anita's right and so is Roshell. My focus should be on healing, not getting laid. My eyes drift to Gabriel, staring at something behind me. My secondary focus is to get over him.

I hate this feeling. It's like I can't breathe; I have this insane ache for him to touch me. I suspect I'll just come apart if he does. I catch a fresh, flowery scent before feeling a presence behind me. I twist to see a woman walk past me and slip her arms around Gabriel. Nicole. Yeah, there's no doubt in my mind about their relationship status. Friends don't snuggle up to each other like that, and Gabriel doesn't seem interested in creating space between them. In fact, he looks very comfortable.

Time for a drink. Or two. Tonight is going to be a long one.

Nicole takes me in as she asks, "Who's our new friend?"

Gabriel detangles his arm and I cock my brows. *Our* new friend? No ma'am. I'd rather lose a finger.

"Nicole, meet Zyon Stewart, my assistant. Zyon, this is my good friend, Nicole Cambridge."

Nicole shoots him a puzzled glance before giving me a quick smile. "A pleasure."

I can't say the same. At least Gabriel introduced her as his friend. "Hello," I reply, my tone deliberately dry.

The organizer comes on the microphone to announce they're ready to get started.

"I'll see you later?" Nicole turns to Gabriel, and he replies with a sharp nod. She reaches up to give him a peck on his cheek and immediately looks at me. I understand her meaning. *He's mine.*

It's not funny, not even for a moment, but I giggle to myself. If the old Zyon was still around, she would give Nicole a run for her money. Old Zyon would bring Gabriel to his knees and leave him begging. Nicole has no clue who she's messing with. Since the old Zyon no longer exists, and because the new Zyon wants no drama, I'll leave it alone. The plan still hasn't changed; I intend to get over him and move on.

I'm just waiting for my heart to get the message.

I manage to get through dinner and halfway through the ceremony without looking at Gabriel. Our seats help a little, but it's still a struggle, especially when I feel him watching me. I catch an eyeful when he gets up to collect the employer of choice award. Looking around, I realize I'm not the only one. Almost every woman has her eyes glued to him. Could I handle being with a man who attracts attention like that? I'm jealous as hell and I hate sharing, so probably not. All the more reason to get over him.

The band starts playing and people begin moving to the dance floor. I'm surprised when Gabriel stands and offers me his hand.

"What?" I ask.

"Come on, let's dance."

I don't want to make a scene by refusing, so I take his hand. The classic music isn't my style, but it can work. Gabriel slips his hand behind my back and links my fingers with his free hand, and we sway with the music for a while. He seems lost in his thoughts while I'm working to turn off my emotions. Having him this close makes it so hard.

"Are you okay?" he asks.

I glance up at him. "Don't I look okay to you?"

"No. You're tense."

"So are you."

"I have my reasons. What's your excuse?"

"I thought we came to dance, not share our feelings."

"We can do both."

"Not interested. I'm not amused by this hot-and-cold attitude you've been giving me. You want to treat me like an employee? Fine. That's why I'm here. To work. But don't keep flip-flopping with me. It's annoying as—" I take a deep breath to calm myself.

"I thought we weren't here to share our feelings," he says with a sparkle in his eyes. He's amused; I'm not.

"Screw you, Gabriel," I say under my breath, and the sparkle disappears, replaced by undeniable lust. I know what he's thinking. I'm already thinking about fucking him, too. The fantasy is so vivid I can almost feel his cock inside me.

Oh God.

I need to get away from him. *Now.*

The set finally ends, and I'm able to walk away without making a scene. I don't return to the table. Instead, I head to the ladies' room to compose myself. I wish I'd brought my purse with me to freshen up my makeup and delay going back. Being in love sucks.

Extracting soap from the dispenser, I slowly wash my hands, scrubbing my palms, rubbing between my fingers. The bathroom door opens, and I glance up, doing a double take when I realize who it is. I drop my gaze back to the sink, turning on the tap and quickly rinsing the soap from my hands. I want to go home. There's nowhere safe in this goddamn building.

"Ziah, isn't it?" Nicole says, closing the bathroom door.

I scoff. "It's whatever you want it to be." I'm positive Nicole remembers my name. I hastily dry my hands because I know where this is going. She didn't come to use the restroom. She came to size me up, to warn me. I'm not in the mood for her games, nor do I want the police involved if I lose my temper and rip her hair out.

I head to the door, but she blocks my path with a smile. "Your hair is a little frizzy. Right there. Let me get that for you."

She reaches up to touch my hair and I swat her hand away. "I'll get it. Thanks." I move back to the mirror and smooth my hair down.

"You're not his type, you know," she says behind me, and I meet her gaze in the mirror.

I scoff. *Here we go.* "Whatever." I attempt to leave, but again she blocks my way. "Can you move?"

"You're trying to act casual, but I saw the way you looked at him on the dance floor. He's not into you," Nicole says, her eyes filled with malice.

"And you came all this way to tell me that because...?"

She looks me up and down with a smirk I'm itching to slap off her face. "Just helping a fellow girl out, you know. Rejection's a bitch. I'd hate to see you go through it."

"You don't know me. Why do you care?"

"I don't care. I'm just—"

"Marking your territory, right? Because you're insecure. You're trying to cancel the competition. Am I right?"

"Oh, please, you are not competition. Gabriel pitied you and gave you that crappy assistant job. You don't belong in our world, nowhere on my level—"

"Yet, you feel threatened enough to seek me out, to—what did you call it? Help a girl out. Oh, please. Get the fuck out of my face."

Her expression tightens. "You're so rude."

"And you're a bitch, so we're even. Don't you dare try to intimidate me again." I push past her and storm toward the ballroom, then I change my mind and turn the opposite direction. I don't know where this hallway leads but I just want to get out of here, away from Gabriel and my feelings for him. Away from his obvious friends-with-benefits relationship with Nicole. I walk down the cobblestone pathway that leads to the gardens and I plop down onto a bench with a heavy sigh. It's time to start looking for a new job.

21

Gabriel

"I'm surprised you brought a complete stranger to an event like this," Nicole's voice comes from behind me.

I turn to her with a puzzled frown. "A stranger? Who are you talking about?"

"Your assistant, of course."

"She's my employee, not a stranger." I impatiently tug at my tie while scanning the room. Where the hell is Zyon? She left ages ago without her cellphone or purse. Is she okay?

"She's not family, either, or even a long-term employee. Why would you invite her to an event like this?"

"I wanted to. Is that enough for you?"

"Don't be sarcastic, Gabriel. It's rude," Nicole replies, pushing my hand away and fiddling with my tie until its straightened again. "Congrats on the employer of choice award, by the way. I'm sure Sam and Charlotte will be over the moon about it."

"Thanks. Now I'm ready for Dad to take his company back. It's time to give my full attention to mine."

A flash of red catches my attention and I turn my head to look. It's not Zyon. Damn it. *Where the hell is she?*

"Are you sure about that? You've been doing a fantastic job." Nicole rubs my shoulder. "Did I tell you how amazing you are?"

"You did. Maybe about a dozen times."

"I really mean it. What are you doing after this? Me and a few guys from Dad's office are going to celebrate. You remember that club we visited before I left for Paris?"

"The one I left after five minutes? I'll pass. Besides, I need to take Zyon and Lauren home."

The smile disappears from her face immediately. "Marcus already offered Lauren a ride home, so she's in safe hands. Zyon can take an Uber. She's your employee, not your friend."

"I want to take her home." My voice sounds a bit firmer than I intend, and Nicole seems more than a little offended. I soften my voice. "I'm really not into clubbing, anyway. We'll hang out some other time, okay?"

"Sure." Her response sounds dry and she's wearing a tight smile. Her eyes carry a chill that tells me she's irritated. This isn't my first time rejecting her, so her behavior has me on edge.

"What's up?" I ask her, and she shakes her head.

"Nothing," she says, but her face is still tight.

"Come on, Nicole. It's me you're talking to. We go way back, remember? I know when something's bothering you."

"I don't know, Gabriel. It just feels like we've drifted apart, ever since I left for Paris. I thought it was the distance, but it's been worse since I got back. When was the last time we hung out? Don't say your father's wedding because that doesn't count."

"You know I've been busy."

"Yet you find time to hang out with those two." She jerks her head at Marcus and Noah sandwiching Lauren on the dance floor.

"We run a business together, remember?"

"Oh, don't give me that."

I reach over and take her hand. "Here's my promise. When Dad returns from his hiatus, we'll have a BFF Day Out, I promise. I'll even paint your nails if you want."

Nicole laughs, the familiar sparkle brightening her eyes. "No, you won't."

"Yes, you're right." I pull her into a quick hug, then let her go. "Are we good?"

"Yup. Solid." The smile disappears from her face as she looks behind me. I catch a whiff of Zyon's scent before she appears by my side.

"Hey, boss," she says as Nicole walks away. "I'm about to take off. See you on Monday."

"Wait a minute." I reach for her upper arm to stop her from leaving. She looks down at my hand then back up at me with a raised brow. I drop my hand, but she doesn't move when I let her go. "I'm taking you home," I say.

"No thanks. I called an Uber."

"I insist. Cancel it." She gives me that 'excuse me?' stare and I soften my tone a little. "Cancel it. Please." We need to talk. I don't want to wait until Monday, and I have an inkling she won't answer my calls over the weekend. She's here with me now; it's the perfect time to set things straight between us.

"Fine." She walks to the dance floor to tell Lauren and Marcus goodbye. I notice she ignores Noah. She probably senses he's not her biggest fan. She walks by me without a word, heading to the elevators. Shaking my head, I follow her out, and I'm glad when we're the only ones in the lift. It's time to say what's on my mind.

"Zyon. About what happened in my office on Tuesday..."

She's staring straight ahead at the aluminum doors. "What about it?"

It was a mistake. You are my employee. I shouldn't have crossed the line. The words won't leave my mouth, no matter how I try to coax them out. My tongue is like lead in my mouth.

"What about it?" Her voice slightly raised, she turns and stares directly into my face. She's pissed, and I haven't even said the words out loud, but they need to be said.

"Zyon, you are —"

The elevator jerks to a halt and the lights immediately flicker out. I wait for things to get going again, but there's nothing. We are in total darkness.

"The fuck is this?" Zyon mumbles, and she brushes past me. I turn my cellphone flashlight on as she presses the emergency button.

"It must be a blackout. I'm sure the hotel has a generator. Just wait a few minutes."

Sighing, Zyon backs up to the wall. "I hate this."

"What, particularly?"

"Being confined. It triggers me."

I wait for her to continue but she doesn't. It makes me curious, so I ask, "Why?"

"Just an incident I don't want to get into." She opens her eyes and looks at me. "What were you saying about that," she makes air quotes before continuing, "moment in your office?"

"It shouldn't have happened, Zyon. I shouldn't have kissed you."

"Oh, yeah, of course not," she says with an eye roll.

"Why the sarcasm?"

"Because it was more than a kiss. I remember your fingers inside—"

"Okay. I get it." I heave a deep sigh before saying, "Yes, it was more than a kiss. It was still a mistake, Zyon."

"Oh." A range of emotions flash across her face so fast I can't quite catch them, then her expression goes blank. She turns from me and looks straight ahead.

An awkward silence settles between us. The generator should have kicked in by now, which means something's gone wrong. I try Marcus's cell phone and it goes straight to voicemail. There's no getting through to Noah, either. He's not picking up. I dial Nicole's number and she answers on the first ring.

"Please tell me you already left the hotel," she says, sounding breathless.

"No. We're trapped in the elevator. What's going on?"

"There's been a city wide blackout, Gabriel. The hotel's backup system's down too. We're all taking the stairs to the lobby."

"Shit."

"The hotel team is doing everything they can to get everyone out. Hang tight, okay? I'll update you in a few minutes."

"Thanks, Nicole." I end the call and glance over at Zyon, now sitting on her coat. Her legs are tucked to the side under her dress. She looks stunning in the dim light. Desirable. "There's been a—"

"I heard."

"Okay."

Silence.

I lean against the wall, cross my ankles, and tuck my hands in my pockets, hoping the wait won't be long. There's too much tension in this tiny space. I can feel the anger rolling off from Zyon like waves in a violent storm. It's giving me anxiety, the kind that makes me want a drink to calm myself.

A soft sniffle pulls my attention to Zyon on the floor. I thought it was my imagination, but I hear it again, then again. I drop to a squat, lifting her chin. The light from my phone gives me a clear view of her tear-stained face and it tugs on my heart like it's being wrenched from my chest. I suppress the urge to hold her and make the hurt go away. Based on her expression, she'll probably slap me if I try.

"Look, Zyon, I'm sorry. I didn't mean to hurt you."

She pulls her chin from my hand with a loud sniff. "Oh, please, get over yourself. This isn't about you." She pulls her legs to her chest and rests her chin on top, wrapping her arms around her shins. I set my coat on the floor beside her and take a seat.

"There's plenty of space over there," she mumbles, still not looking at me.

"I'm quite fine where I am, thank you. Now, are you going to tell me what's making you cry?"

"No."

"Look, we're both stuck in here for God knows how long. For the sake of our mental health, let's talk it out."

She sniffles again, then leans against the wall, releasing a conceding sigh. "I just hate being in here. It feels like I can't breathe."

"Talk to me. Tell me why."

"It brings back terrible memories, that's all."

"That's not all, Zyon. Come on, it helps to talk." The words leave my mouth before I realize the irony. When was the last time I talked it out?

"Yeah, right. Says the man who won't tell me why he doesn't drink," Zyon says.

Her response takes me by surprise, and my chest tightens when I remember Daniel's fast approaching death-anniversary. Each year solidifies the confirmation that he's not around because of me, and the guilt feels that much worse. The grief rises, flooding my system. I close my eyes to absorb the pain.

"You and I are more alike than you think, Gabriel. We live at different ends of the spectrum but we've both been through shit and keep our secrets close to our hearts." I hear a rustle as she shifts, and her fragrance washes over me. "I think that's where they should stay," she whispers.

I open my eyes and the tears spill out. Zyon's on her knees beside me, her dark eyes searching my face. She cups my cheek tenderly, sending a rush of emotions through me. For a moment, we just stare at each other, then I close my eyes again as she wipes my tears away. My stomach flips from her gentle touch. She runs her thumb over my lips, and I can hardly breathe. There's no controlling bone left in my body. Every limb and organ have their own mind.

Still, I don't kiss her. Not until she licks her lips. That single act sends me into a frenzy, and I grab her cheeks as our mouths collide. Zyon moans, the sound fueling me forward. I devour her mouth like a starving man. Which I guess I am. I've been hungry all week. Thirsty. Desperate for her and only her. No other woman has ever triggered this burning desire inside me.

Zyon eases up, pushing me to the floor, seizing my lips even before my back hits the tiles. I'm so caught up in the kiss, I'm not even aware that she straddled me. Not until she grinds herself against my hard cock. I groan, the sensation almost too much to bear. My hips rise to meet her slow, deliberate grinding. Dry humping never felt so fucking good. Zyon pauses on top of me, her hair even wilder than before, her eyes blazing like fire.

"I need you to fuck me, Gabriel. Please."

I still under her, her words shocking me into silence. My common sense awakens when her fingers move to my belt, undoing it so fast, it's almost open when I grip her wrist.

"Stop."

Zyon frowns impatiently. "What? Why?" She tries to wring her hand out from mine, but I tighten my hold.

"Look, if you're worried about protection, I got you, okay? I always carry condoms in my purse."

Why the fuck is she carrying condoms in her purse? No. Screw that. I shouldn't care. I already crossed a line tonight, but there's still time to salvage it. Sitting up, I gently ease her off me.

"I'm not sleeping with you, Zyon. Not tonight, or ever again. I'm sorry."

Zyon sucks in a breath, and the pain on her face makes my heart sink. I didn't want to hurt her, especially after the heartfelt moment we just shared, but Zyon isn't the kind of woman easily deterred. Being straightforward and tough is the only way to get through to her.

"God, I'm such a fucking fool," she mumbles.

"You're not a fool, Zyon. It's just that you're—"

"Not in your league, right? I'm not a cute ivy league blonde. I'm the girl from the other side of town. Rough around the edges. I could never fit in your elite little circle."

"I didn't say that."

"Your actions speak louder than any words you could ever say. I get it. I'll never come on to you again."

"Zyon—"

"Don't talk to me, Gabriel. From this moment on, I'm your employee, nothing more. You do not speak to me unless it's connected to the job you're paying me to do."

The elevator jerks and the lights come on. I can clearly see the unshed tears in her eyes, and I feel like a complete asshole for being the one to put them there.

"I wasn't trying to hurt you, Zyon."

"You didn't. I promise you, there are many men who would love to take your place." She clicks her tongue while pushing to her feet, mumbling, "Fuck outta here."

Just thinking about those other men makes me want to shut this elevator down and fuck her until every thought of them disappears.

I don't want another man touching her. It's crazy. I'm going crazy. Confused as hell, that's what I am. I'm denying my longing for a woman I need more than air.

Fuck.

I don't want to want Zyon so much. God, it's so strong I can taste it on my tongue.

The doors open and she dashes out, pausing when she sees Nicole standing there. It doesn't help when Nicole rushes forward and wraps her arms around me. "Thank God you're okay! I almost lost my mind down here!"

I quickly return Nicole's hug as Zyon storms through the exit. "Thanks Nicole. Talk to you later, okay?"

Marcus, Noah, and Lauren are right behind her. I give them a quick thumbs up before I chase after Zyon, but she moves fast, even in those heels. By the time I clear the automatic doors and get onto the busy sidewalk, she's already gone.

Damn it. Damn it to hell.

22

Gabriel

"For a moment I thought you planned on backing out of brunch. Again," my father murmurs as he opens his apartment door.

"Of course not. Karyn told me she's making fried chicken. I wouldn't miss it for the world." I accept the hug he gives me, then thrust the employer of choice award at him. "Thought you'd want to see it before they put it in the display case."

He takes it and examines it with a smile that makes the corner of his gray eyes crinkle. "This is all you, Gabriel. You did this. In just one year, you turned the entire company around." He looks up at me with a genuine expression. "I'm really proud of you, son."

I blink at him, thinking I misheard what he just said. It's been years. I've worked for years to hear those words. I didn't know how much I needed them until now. "I appreciate it, Dad. Truly."

I barely step into the apartment when Karyn comes waddling into my arms. I can't get over how much she reminds me of Zyon; same wild hair, tiny body, just as feisty and headstrong.

I let her go, giving her baby bump a rub. "Almost there, huh?"

"Can't wait! Your baby brother is already giving me a hard time with his vicious kicks." She takes my arm and leads me to the dining area. "Before you boys start talking shop, let's have a decent meal. I made a spread you're really going to love."

"Oh, boy. Something tells me I'll need to book an extra session at the gym after this."

"You're a growing boy. You need to eat."

"I'm a grown *man*, Karyn," I grumble.

She turns and looks at me fondly. "That you are, Gabriel. I stand corrected."

"So, Gabriel," Dad begins while pulling out his chair at the head of the table. "What have you been up to?"

I shrug. "Not much. Thanks to you and your hiatus, I don't have a life outside of work."

"I'm sure that's not true."

"Have you already forgotten the hours you used to spend at the office? Nothing's changed since then, believe me."

There's a slight pause and Dad gives me a direct stare, and I sense a little discomfort. "Speaking of hiatus... I'm considering taking a permanent leave of absence from work."

I frown at him. "What do you mean?"

"I thought we weren't talking about work," Karyn says, placing a plate of fried chicken in the center of the table.

"Just giving Gabriel a little heads up, honey." He squeezes her hand with an affectionate smile as she takes her seat beside him. "We can talk about the details later, but I want you to take over Cain Industries for good."

A temporary silence settles as I stare at him, my mouth slightly ajar. "What?"

"Boys, please. Can we not do this right now?" Karyn says.

"In a minute, honey." Dad turns his gaze back to me. "Listen, I know it's a huge responsibility—"

"That I don't want to handle anymore," I interrupt. "I have my own company to run, Dad."

"You have a partnership with your friends, one that can easily be broken. I'm sure Marcus and Noah will do a fantastic job running Rosemead on their own."

Tension erupts in my stomach, threatening to spill over. "Dad, do you remember when I told you I wanted to start my own company?"

"Of course I do. You wanted to make your own way, and you did it. Quite an exemplary job, I might add. Now it's time to take your rightful place."

"Rosemead is my rightful place."

Dad sighs. "Do you know how many kids would jump at the opportunity to run a multi-million dollar company? Don't be ungrateful, Gabriel. Besides, you owe me."

I don't need him to elaborate. He's talking about what I did to Daniel, I'm sure. "I already paid my dues. I managed your company for an entire year without taking a paycheck—"

"That was your decision, not mine," Dad says.

"Yes, you're right." So stupid of me, too. Back then, I wanted to impress him, to find my way back into his good books. Turns out I sold myself short. "Dad, I'm grateful for your consideration, but I can't accept the offer. There are tons of qualified people around. I'll even assist with the search."

"No need." Dad reaches for his fork, a clear sign that he's ending the conversation. "I'll appoint Deacon instead."

"What? Deacon? Oh, hell no, Dad. He's not qualified to run the company. We both know that." He isn't even qualified for his current post. I still don't understand how someone without a college degree is holding a senior position in the company when it's a requirement for everyone else. Even more, it still puzzles me how he popped out from nowhere and slipped under Dad's wing. Why is my father mentoring a stranger? How did Deacon climb the company ranks so fast?

That's a discussion for another day. Right now, I'm focused on this horrific piece of news my dad just dropped. "Why would you want Deacon to run your company? He has no experience."

"Deacon's like family. He's smart. I'm sure he'll catch on fast."

"This is ridiculous. Deacon's no family of mine. He's nothing but a sexual predator you bent over backward to protect."

"Gabriel—"

I interrupt Karyn with a flash of my hand. "What does Deacon have on you, Dad? Huh? What secrets have you been keeping from me?"

"Gabriel!" Karyn shouts.

Dad's face pales but his eyes are steel. "You're out of line."

"Am I? Why is Deacon still working with us after what he did? He should be rotting in prison. Why did you protect him?"

"I don't owe you an explanation. You don't want to run my company, fine. Thanks to you, I don't have another son to pass it to, so I'll choose the next best thing."

I drop my fork on the table. "Oh, fuck this."

"Gabriel, come on," Karyn says as I stand.

"I'm sorry, Karyn. I need to go."

She stands too, coming around the table to block my way. "No. You're going nowhere. I spent hours preparing this meal, so you're going to sit your butt down and we're all going to have a decent brunch. Okay?"

I cock an eyebrow at her.

"Please?" she adds, and I concede with a sigh and return to my seat.

"It's obvious there are things that need to be said, so why don't we get them out. Gabriel, say what's on your mind. Whatever's bothering you. Sam, you're going to listen. No interruptions."

"Yes, ma'am," Dad replies, turning his attention to me.

"What happened with Daniel was a mistake," I begin. "My mistake. I have been paying for it since the night he died. I've done everything you asked me to do without question, but I still think you're trying to punish me."

Dad rolls his eyes. "Do really you think that's what I've been doing?"

"Yes! You know how much my company means to me, yet you want me to give it up for a dream that's not mine. I don't appreciate you trying to mess with my head. Using Deacon to bait me, mentioning Daniel to make me feel guilty. That's low, Dad, and I didn't expect it from you."

"Okay, Gabriel, give your father time to respond—"

"I'm not done!" I bang my fist on the table and Karyn's eyes widen. Fuck. The last thing I want to do is scare her.

"Just calm down, son," Dad says in a soothing voice that irritates me. I take a deep breath and look at Karyn.

"I'm sorry. You should have let me leave."

"I don't want you to go, Gabriel. You're hurting. Sam is here, listening, and I'm sure he wants to fix things. Right, Sam?"

"Of course, I do."

I don't believe him. He's just putting on a front for Karyn, trying to prove he deserves the father of the year award. I refuse to pretend anymore. Again, I stand, and this time, Karyn doesn't stop me.

"I hope we can talk about this one day, son," Dad says to my back. "I really want to fix things between us."

I pause at the door, giving him a casual shrug. "We'll see."

I don't feel optimistic. Not even a little. I close the door with a bang. I'm almost at the elevator before I realize another source of my anger. Zyon. She hasn't been taking my calls. I'm pissed at how tempted I am to drive to her apartment. Chasing after women is not my thing. For the first time, I want to step out of my comfort zone, just to see her, to talk about *us*.

I won't, though. Zyon's mad at me, which is exactly what I want. It means she won't try to seduce me again. That's what I need; that distance. I'm hoping it's enough to make me forget.

Sadly, it doubt forgetting is possible. Zyon has already left a permanent mark on my soul.

23

Zyon

"Zyon, I need the expense report on my desk in ten," Gabriel says, his head sticking out his office door. He doesn't wait for a response. I cut my eyes away as he closes the door.

Asshole.

Sighing, I open the expense report he requested and briefly scan the contents. No, he's even worse than an asshole. How can he reject me, then ice me out when I get pissed off about it? Don't I have every right to be upset?

It's been a week since he ripped my heart to shreds in the elevator and I'm still devastated. I've never cried over a man until that night. It still hurts. The pain is just as raw. A part of me doesn't want to work here anymore, but I need the money. A decent job like this will be impossible to find on short notice, and I don't want to go back to relying on the blood money Dineo has stashed in her bank account. That chapter of my life is finally closed.

Still, how can I survive being around Gabriel? Can I handle interacting with the man I'm in love with but can't have? God, I want to turn these feelings off so badly, but they are getting stronger each day. I feel like I'm about to lose my mind.

I send off the report to Gabriel, then start a document for the executive meeting tomorrow. I just need to focus on work. That's it. If I'm too busy then I won't think about him. Nights are a different story; plenty of sleepless ones ahead.

I'm halfway through my work when it hits me. I forgot to add the charge for a business luncheon he had last week. I dial his extension to give him a warning that it's incorrect and I'll be sending the adjusted report soon. When he doesn't answer the phone, I decide to go to him. I'm about to knock on his office door when I hear my name. I press my ear to the door and listen. He's definitely talking to someone. Why is he mentioning me?

"Noah, I need you to chill. This grumpy grandpa bit is getting a little old. I'm a grown man. I can handle my personal life."

There's a brief silence and he sighs. "Are you still on that? The story has already faded into oblivion. I made sure of it."

Another beat. I shift my weight to the other foot and lean against the door to listen better. What story is he talking about?

"No. The blog didn't mention me fighting over a woman. It said I was involved in an altercation, that's all. Don't try putting Zyon in the middle of this."

Oh, my God. Why didn't Gabriel tell me there was an article about what happened in Vegas? How bad was it? Maybe that explains his behavior. He doesn't want a woman whose actions reflect on him negatively.

"Okay, fine. She's the reason I went to the club that night. You're missing the point. The article didn't mention her at all. Noah—no, you listen. I'm done talking about this. I get the protective older brother thing you keep trying to do, but I don't need your protection. We already agreed Zyon is a trigger. I already decided to leave her alone. So quit riding my ass about what you think happened in the elevator last week. Give me a break."

Oh, wow.

Just... wow.

I back away from the door, the tears making it difficult to see. It's time for lunch, and although I'm not hungry, I need to get out of here. I grab my bag from the drawer and head out. Fuck Gabriel. Screw the expense report. To hell with everything.

I storm into the elevator, pressing the lobby button so hard it's a small wonder it doesn't break. I don't know why I'm so mad. Gabriel already made it clear he wanted nothing to do with me. It was hard hearing those words within the privacy of the elevator last week. Hearing him say them to someone else makes the hurt worse. I'm toxic, that's what he's saying.

The elevator pauses on the seventh floor and Deacon enters, beaming when he sees me. Not interested in a conversation, I give him a tight smile and pretend to be busy with my phone.

"I'm still waiting on that yes..." he says in a sing-song voice, staring at me over his shoulder.

"Good for you."

Deacon turns around to fully face me, just as the doors open again. He backs out, giving me a smile I'm sure make many women weak. I would have probably been among that batch a few months ago. Now, there's no appeal. Pity. Dating Deacon would definitely piss off Gabriel.

"Come on, Zyon. Have dinner with me."

The lightbulb in my passive-aggressive brain suddenly flips on. "You know, Deacon," I say, walking past him with a little sway of my hips, "I haven't yet heard you say please."

"You get off on men who beg, is that it?"

"Always."

I exit the lobby, and he falls in step beside me. "For me, it's usually the other way around," he says.

"First time for everything," I reply.

Deacon huffs; I wait for him to return inside but he keeps walking. "Fine. Zyon, will you have dinner with me, please?"

I stop and turn to him with a grin. "That wasn't too hard, was it?"

"Is that a yes?"

"It's an 'I'll think about it'."

Deacon throws his hands up with a frustrated sigh. "Zyon—"

"Okay, I'm messing with you. I'm saying yes to dinner. But only if I choose the restaurant."

"Deal." His radiant eyes wash over me as he backs away. "I'll make it worth your while. I promise."

"You better."

As I watch him leave, the smile slowly fading before I turn and walk away. I thought the decision would make me feel better, but it doesn't. Instead, there's an unsettling vibration in my stomach. Something's wrong. I can feel it. After wracking my brain, I can't put my finger on it, so I let it go. Maybe I'm just nervous about a date with Deacon. It's just a simple dinner. What harm could it do?

·♥·♥·♥·♥·♥·

"If someone told me six years ago I'd be decked out in makeup, having high tea on a tiny chair, I would probably put my paws on them," Deacon says. "But now, it's almost natural as breathing, trust me."

"You, wearing makeup?" I ask with a giggle. "I can't picture it."

"Thanks to technology, you don't need to," he says, dipping in his pocket for his phone.

He swipes against the screen then hands it to me. It's a photo of him wearing a tutu sitting around a tiny table with an adorable little girl. She looks about five, his spitting image. I chuckle at how ridiculous he looks with eyeshadow smeared over his eyebrows.

"You look really happy. Your daughter, she's really cute." I hand the phone back to him.

"Thanks. She's my world, and I would do anything for her. Her mom and I aren't together anymore, but I'm still in her life one hundred percent."

"That's truly amazing. Too often fathers disappear when the relationships end. It's like the kids don't exist anymore. I could never understand how they sleep at night. Like, don't they have a conscience?"

Deacon regards me for a moment. "Something tells me you're speaking from experience."

"Maybe," I reply with a shrug. "I don't want to talk about it."

"Talking helps, you know that, right?"

"You know what would help? Another drink." My head swivels as I search the restaurant for our server.

"Let me just grab drinks from the bar and add them to our tab," Deacon says.

I shake my head. "It's okay. I can wait for the server."

"I don't mind. You really look like you could use another drink, anyway."

I watch him go, realizing how much I'm enjoying our date. Surprise, surprise. Deacon has a great sense of humor, which is a huge plus. I appreciate a man who makes me laugh. He's a gentleman too, opening doors, helping me from the car, pulling out my chair. He seems alright, but he's not getting sex tonight. Not from me, anyway. There's still no spark, which puzzles me. Physically, Deacon is one hundred percent my type.

He's just not Gabriel.

When he palmed my back on our way inside the restaurant, it didn't trigger the urge to draw closer to him. His lingering gaze did nothing to heat my body. I didn't want his arms around me. I wanted Gabriel.

Fuck. I must be a masochist. Gabriel explicitly said he didn't want me and here I am, pining over him. Stupid.

Where the hell is Deacon with that drink?

I lean to the side, trying to spot him at the dimly lit bar. It looks empty. At least, the areas I can see. Relaxing with a sigh, I reach for my phone and notice several missed calls from Gabriel. A satisfying smile curves the corner of my lips when I read his text message.

You left without coming to me as I requested. Didn't I tell you I wanted to discuss the expense report?

I respond with a curt, professional answer. *You weren't in the office when the workday ended (5:00), and I had a date. See you on Monday, boss.*

I hardly press send when Gabriel begins typing his reply.

A date? With who?

I smirk as I type my reply. *Excuse me? That's personal information. Nothing to do with work.*

Again, he doesn't waste time responding. *Zyon, who are you out with?*

Maybe I should leave him wondering, but then again, I can't resist the temptation. For some reason, he's not a fan of Deacon.

Not that it's any of your business, but I'm on a date with Deacon.

My cellphone immediately starts to ring. I stare at his gorgeous, stern-faced photo before I cut the call. He tries again, and again I reject it. He gives up after the third try, and I drop the phone in my purse as Deacon returns with our drinks. I should be satisfied knowing Gabriel's at the office pissed as hell, but instead, there's an overwhelming ache in my stomach. Pissing him off doesn't give me closure. I doubt anything ever will.

"So... where were we?" Deacon asks after taking his seat.

"You were talking about your kid."

"No. You were about to tell me what happened with your old man."

I empty the entire cocktail in one go before saying, "He wasn't there. Full stop."

"Something tells me there's much more to this story."

"There isn't. Can we change the subject? How long have you been working at Cain Industries?"

"A little over five years. Came in without a college degree and worked my way to the top." He snaps his fingers. "Just like that."

"Wow, that's impressive."

"Thank you."

"I mean, you've done quite well for your age. Your parents must be proud."

Deacon sighs. "I'm sure they would be, if they were still here."

"Oh, no. I'm so sorry." I reach over and pat his hand. He captures it in his before I pull it back. I arrange a smile on my face; there's something about his touch that unsettles me. "Can I ask you something personal?"

A sneaky smile spreads across Deacon's face. "It's nine inches fully erect."

I gape at him then burst out laughing. "No. Don't be crude. I just wanted to know how you climbed the corporate ladder so quickly without a college degree."

"You can't get to the top without connections, Zyon, and Samuel Cain is the biggest one I know. He took me under his wing after my dad died and gave me a chance when no one else did. He's like a father figure to me."

"That's awesome." I'm tempted to ask about Gabriel's beef with him, but I don't bother. I don't want to talk about Gabriel.

A sudden yawn appears, giving me no time to cover my mouth. "Sorry. That took me by surprise."

"That's okay," he says, staring at me intently. "You look a little tired."

"Yeah... I think I am..." Is it me, or is the room spinning? "Does the room look like it's about to tilt?" I ask as Deacon chuckles.

"You're definitely out of it. Come on. It's time to take you home."

This feeling... wow, I've never experienced it before. It's not the familiar buzz of alcohol, the warm, soothing sensation that usually made me happy and light. It's definitely not the high that weed gives me. No. This is heavier, something that's stealing every ounce of my muscle control. I can hardly keep my eyes open as Deacon leads me to his car. What's happening to me? I was doing fine. Did Deacon put something in my drink? How, when we were together the entire time?

Panic flies up my throat as I grab the door handle. No, we weren't. Not when he left to get drinks from the bar. That's why he took so long, isn't it? He was drugging my drink! Oh, my God. He wants to—

No way in hell. I can't allow this to happen again. No, no, no!

Another wave of drowsiness hits me as I turn the handle to open the door, prepared to tuck and roll onto the street. Anything to escape whatever plans Deacon has for me. But the door remains closed. I shallow the sob that rises in my throat and try again. Shit. My limbs feel like jelly. There's this urge to close my eyes and sleep, but I can't. I need to survive this.

"What are you doing?" Deacon asks.

"Getting out. Please open the door," I mumble. I'm hoping he doesn't hear the panic in my voice, but I'm trying and failing to keep it together.

"Why? Did you leave something behind?"

"Yes, uh..." Shit, why can't I get my thoughts together? "Just let me out, please."

"I can't do that, Zyon."

"Why not?" I drop my head against the seat and succumb to the urge to close my eyes. "What did you do to me?"

He doesn't answer. The car jerks a little as he picks up speed. I'm too tired to fight, even though I need to. I've just gotten to a place where I don't feel like hurting myself and I can't go back to the darkness. Not again. I may not survive another attack. With my last ounce of strength, I launch myself at the wheel, which is probably the stupidest thing I've ever done, but I'd rather die than let Deacon have his way with me. Deacon curses as the car swerves and almost hits an oncoming truck, but he steers the car away just in time.

"Fucking stupid bitch," he mumbles, his elbow connecting with my face. I reel back from the blow, the pain blooming from my nose making my eyes water. My head hits the car door hard as I fall back with a gasp.

He glances over at me then swears again. "Chill the fuck out, Zyon. I don't want to hurt you."

"Then what are you doing, taking me against my will?"

"Stop acting like you don't want this. I've seen the way you check me out in the office."

"You're delusional," I whisper, trying to push myself upright and failing miserably.

I swallow the panic and push away the awful memories that threaten to increase my terror and leave me useless. This isn't the time for fear. I can't go down like this. Unfortunately, my willpower is no match for whatever Deacon gave me. I'm getting weaker, sleepy. The anxiety is fading away. I start pinching my arm to stay awake while thinking of a way to escape. What am I going to do when we get to wherever he's going?

I can feel the darkness on the edges of my vision, and I summon every ounce of energy to keep it at bay. It's not enough. I'm tired, so tired. I'll just close my eyes for a minute.

·♥·♥·♥·♥·♥·

My eyes flutter open as I land on something soft and bouncy. It's a bed. Deacon's bed. His blurry form is standing at the foot of it, staring down at me.

"Good. You're awake. It's never fun when they sleep through it all, you know? I like my women alert. That way, we can both enjoy the fun." He raps his knuckles against his temple with a tsk. "In hindsight, I probably shouldn't have drugged you."

"You're crazy," I whisper. "Don't you dare put your hands on me."

His face curls into a deranged sneer. "Do you know how many women would kill for me to take them home?"

"Willingly. They would willingly get in your bed, Deacon. I don't want to be here. Let me go!"

Deacon reaches down to caress my thigh, and I'm grateful that I'm wearing pants. "Relax. You will love what I have in store for you, trust me." He slowly removes his shirt, giving me a lustful stare. "I have a feeling you're about to make me work for it, Zyon," he says with a smirk. "I'm so looking forward to that."

"Just let me go, Deacon. Please. I'm begging you."

He leans over me, his disgusting smirk still firmly in place. "Who's begging now, Zyon?"

The sudden pealing of the doorbell makes me breathe a sigh of relief, but it doesn't last long. Deacon ignores the sound, trailing his fingers up my leg, licking his lips in a way that makes my stomach churn. Why did I ever think he was a decent guy?

The doorbell rings again, more urgently this time. Deacon rolls his eyes and eases off me. He disappears through the bedroom door and closes it behind him. I immediately try to get off the bed; whoever is at the door could be my savior. Try as I might, I can barely move. There's no energy left in me. The sounds are hushed coming through the closed door, but I can still hear the banging of the front door against the wall, then a stifled grunt from Deacon.

"Where the fuck is Zyon?"

Gabriel. Oh my God. It's Gabriel!

I roll off the bed and drop to the floor with a thud, hoping Gabriel hears the sound. I doubt he does when there are no running footsteps coming to rescue me. God, please, don't let him leave.

"Who?" Deacon asks.

"Don't fuck with me, Deacon. I know Zyon's here. I remember what happened to the last girl you had in your apartment."

"I don't know what you're talking about."

"Yes, keep pretending. If you hurt a hair on Zyon's head, I swear to God, no NDA will save you this time. My family won't back you again."

Lifting my head from the floor, I push up on my elbows while processing what I just heard. Was this why he warned me away from

Deacon? Did he hurt someone else? I leverage the side of the bed to push myself upright. It feels like a million years before I get to my feet.

"Take another step inside my apartment, Gabriel, and I'll call the cops."

"Do you think I give a fuck? Zyon!"

"Gabriel!" My voice comes out like a croak as I stagger to the door. I turn the knob, but it doesn't budge. I pound weakly on the wood, crying, "Gabriel! I'm in here!"

There's another thud and Deacon grunts again. I hear footsteps coming closer to the door. I beat on the door again, praying Gabriel can hear it. "In here!" I cry out once more.

"I hear you, Zyon," Gabriel says from the other side of the door. "Hang tight. I'll get you out."

It takes about a minute before the door opens, revealing a scowling Deacon and a red-faced Gabriel standing behind him. Gabriel shoves him aside and reaches for me, the relief on his face triggering my tears. I collapse against his chest, and the last thing I think before darkness consumes me is that I'm finally safe.

24

Gabriel

I raise my head as Doctor Singh closes the door to my guest bedroom. I've been pacing by the banister for the last half hour. I search her eyes for answers, but she nonchalantly stares at me.

"How is she?"

"Zyon's sleeping now, but she's fine. Except for a slight bruise on her face, there's nothing else that suggests she was assaulted. I took a urine sample to check what's in her system, but I have no doubt she's been drugged. I'd hate to think of the outcome if you hadn't gotten there in time."

I don't want to think about it either, so I gesture to the stairs. "Thanks again for coming at such short notice, Ana. I really appreciate it. Can I walk you out?"

I felt guilty calling Ana earlier, mainly because we haven't spoken since she and Noah broke up, but she's the only doctor I could call on a night like this. I haven't set foot in a hospital since the night Daniel died, and I'll do everything in my power not to go back. I can't handle the memories.

Ana replies with a curt nod, moving ahead of me as we descend the stairs. "Anytime, Gabriel. You need to report this to the cops. Deacon shouldn't get away with this."

"I fired him—"

"That's not enough. We both know that. You told me he's done this before, and if he's not stopped, God knows what else he will do."

"You're right, of course. I'll convince Zyon to report it tomorrow."

She pauses at the door, looking me over. "You should have let me dress that wound."

I twist my knuckle and sigh. "It's fine. I'll take care of it."

"While you're at it, take care of that temper, too."

"What temper?"

"The one that left those bruises on your knuckles. I can't imagine what Deacon's face looks like."

"I'm fine, Ana. Besides, Deacon got what was coming to him."

"From what I've seen, he deserves more than a beatdown. From what Noah's said, this isn't your first fight. Or your second. I thought you were done with that life."

"Wait a minute. You've been talking to Noah?" I ask in disbelief. Their relationship did not end well last year. I'm surprised she's even saying his name out loud.

"Of course we talk. We're exes, not enemies."

"Good for you. Noah is nothing but a goddamn gossip," I grumble.

"He's just concerned, Gabriel. We all are. I remember the crazy shit that happened when you lost control—"

"I was twenty-three years old. A kid. And I had my reasons."

"Well, you're not a kid now." She purses her lips, giving me a stare full of pity before adding, "I'm not a psychiatrist, Gabriel, but if you don't release whatever's eating you up inside, it will destroy you."

"I know."

"Then do it."

I pull her into my arms for a quick hug. "Thanks for the pep talk, Ana. Don't be a stranger."

"Says the man who's canceled every invitation to lunch. I was starting to wonder if you'd chosen Noah's side."

"I'm just busy."

"So am I. Do you think running a private practice while working at the hospital is a walk in the park?"

"Okay, superwoman. Point made. I'll show up for lunch next time."

"I'll believe it when I see it," Ana says with a smile.

"Oh, and before I forget, congrats on your engagement. I hope Colin knows what a lucky man he is."

The smile slowly fades from her face and her gaze shifts to the floor before resting on the wall behind me. "Thanks, Gabriel. I hope he knows it, too."

She slips into her jacket and slings the bag strap over her shoulder, then she pats my cheek. "Good seeing you, Gabriel. Being in love looks amazing on you, by the way." She's gone before I can reply, and I close the door with a shake of my head. She's absurd. I'm not in love.

I return upstairs to the guest room. Zyon's curled into a ball, her gentle snores telling me she's fast asleep. I recline in the armchair and watch her. The violence in my soul has simmered a little. Back in Deacon's apartment, it was a category five hurricane. Now it's a tropical storm, still able to do irreversible damage, but at least somewhat tempered.

I've done enough for one night. Deacon's face was a bloodied mess when I left his apartment. He's lucky that's all I did after seeing Zyon's state. Glassy eyes. Blouse half-opened. The fucking bruise on her face. After taking Zyon to the car, I went back. He didn't expect me to return. His door was still half-open, and he had his phone pressed to his ear. I didn't spare the phone, either. It disintegrated when I smashed it against the wall.

"You're gonna wish you hadn't fucked with me," Deacon mumbled when I dropped him to the floor. "You just made the biggest mistake of your life."

Fuck him. Fuck his threats. I'm ready for any legal battle he wants to send my way. He didn't get to hurt Zyon, and that's all I care about right now.

I almost lost my mind when I found out she was on a date with Deacon. It brought a breath-stealing panic I'd only experienced the night Daniel died. I tried to tell myself the emotion only came from knowing she was in possible danger, but a part of me knew there was another contributing reason; the fear I'd finally pushed her away for good.

Wasn't that what I wanted?

It required every ounce of my willpower to reject Zyon the night we were trapped in the hotel elevator. Having her lips on mine, her softness grinding against me... it was so hard to say no. It's probably not a great idea to have her in my apartment right now, but there's no way I could rest without her under this roof, where I'm sure she's safe. She's been through enough. I have no problem keeping my hands to myself.

"Whatever you're thinking about, stop."

Zyon's sudden, croaky voice startles me. She turns on her side, resting her hands under her cheek. The tiny smile that grazes her lips illuminates her face, pushing the weariness away.

"What are you thinking about?"

"You. How I should have kicked Deacon's ass a little more."

She gives me a long look that I can't decipher. "Thank you for saving me."

"Don't mention it. I'm just glad you're okay."

Zyon sighs, pulling herself up to a sitting position. "What time is it?"

I check the time on my phone. "A little after three in the morning."

"Shit," she says, swinging her legs over the side of the bed. She staggers a little before righting herself. "I need to call an Uber."

"Like hell you will."

Her brows lift and she folds her arms across her chest. "I'd like to see you stop me."

"Zyon, stop. Use your common sense. You're still under the influence, still vulnerable. Why would you want to leave in the middle of the night?"

Her lips twist as she seems to contemplate my words. "Fine," she eventually replies. "I'll leave first thing in the morning."

I push to my feet, and she immediately takes several steps back. "Good," I say. "Now get some rest."

"I need a shower. I'm feeling icky after—"

With a sudden, swift movement, she hauls the blouse over her head, taking the rest of the words with her. Not that I would have heard them, anyway. My eyes are already busy scanning her torso, taking in the swell of her breasts spilling from her bra, the flatness of her stomach, the glittering navel ring and the cute tattoo I kissed that first night. The arousal that's heating my insides feels so wrong, it makes me sick. What the fuck is wrong with me?

My gaze shoots up and meets Zyon's. She scoffs, tossing the blouse onto the bed. "Take a photo. It will last longer."

"Goodnight, Zyon."

The door softly closes behind me and I take a deep breath, but it does nothing to douse the tension. I'm simmering with need, but I ignore the insane urge to return to Zyon's room. Instead, I take a long, icy shower, still battling with thoughts of Zyon riding my cock, her wild hair bouncing in time with her luscious breasts. I'm going to hell for this fantasy. I'm sure of it.

Fuck. There's no escaping my need for her. Not with her so close. With my lower lip clutched between my teeth, I grip my cock, succumbing to the urge to satisfy myself. It doesn't work; it only heightens the fantasy of Zyon's eyes locked with mine as she takes my entire length into her mouth.

Oh, hell.

The first spasm of pleasure runs through me. My hips rock as I pick up the pace, bracing for my release. The fantasy is still going strong.

Zyon runs her tongue up the base before giving my head a gentle lick, then another, before deep-throating me again. Groaning, I grind into my palm as hot spurts of cum seep through my fingers. Zyon's name becomes a whisper on my lips. I still need her. My body still aches for her. It's a burning itch only she can scratch. Why the hell am I still resisting the inevitable?

25

Gabriel

"Good morning."

Turning on my stool at the breakfast bar, I watch Zyon pad down the stairs. "Good morning," I reply. "Did you sleep well?"

"So-so. You?"

"I've had better nights."

She joins me at the bar and immediately helps herself to a croissant from my plate. She does it with ease, like it's a normal thing we do every morning, and it leaves me wishing it was. I wonder what it would be like to wake up to her, to share my breakfast and sweet kisses with her, to spread her legs on this kitchen island—

"You're giving me that look again," Zyon says, stopping my thoughts from getting even filthier.

"What look?"

"Like you want to eat me alive."

I chuckle and shake my head, knowing just how accurate she is. I don't want to eat her alive. Not all of her, anyway. Just the flesh between her thighs. I want to lick her clean when she comes for me. I want her moaning, trembling, begging for more.

Yeah, I'm definitely going to hell. Zyon was almost assaulted last night. The last thing she needs is a man touching her. I shouldn't want to touch her.

But I do.

Fuck, I can't deny what my body needs.

"What, no reply?" she asks.

I push the plate away from me and stand. "Zyon, if you knew half the thoughts going through my head right now, you would beeline for the front door."

She stands too and approaches me. "What does that mean?"

"It means you should put some clothes on. That T-shirt is doing too much." I turn to walk away but she grabs the back of my shirt.

"Why do you keep doing that?"

I reach around and disengage her hand, then turn to face her. "Do what?"

"Hot one minute, cold the next. You do things to rile me up, and when I react, you push me away."

I don't want to have this conversation with her nipples pressing against the shirt. She's turned on. So am I. No good can come from this, so I'm walking away.

She scoffs as I move. "Surprise, surprise. He's running."

"What do you want from me, Zyon?" I ask, whipping around.

"Why can't you admit you want me, that you feel something for me? Is it that daunting to think about?"

I sigh. "Zyon, you're not okay right now. You were attacked last night. You're probably still in shock. Confused. What you feel isn't real."

"Don't tell me that. You know nothing about what's going on inside my—" Her voice falters and she drags her hand through her hair. "Why do I keep doing this to myself?"

She mutters that last bit like she's speaking to herself, but I respond anyway. "Zyon, I'm trying my best not to lead you on, but you're making it so hard to say no."

"Am I? Because the word leaves your mouth quite easily. Just admit it. You want me, but you hate that you do."

"We're no good for each other, Zyon."

She seems to process my words, then gives me a nod. "Translation: I'm not good enough for you."

"It goes both ways."

"Bullshit." She pushes past me. "I get the message. I'll be out of your apartment in a few minutes."

"No. I need you to stay. I can't protect you out there."

"Protect me from what?"

I consider how much to reveal without alarming her, but I decide to go for it. The more she knows, the more vigilant she will be. "Deacon has something up his sleeve, but I don't know what it is, which is why I need you to stay."

Zyon's brows furrow and she crosses her arms against her chest. "What is he up to?"

"I just told you, I don't know. I'm not sure he won't try to hurt you again. Which reminds me; you need to report this to the cops."

"Nope. I'm not going. The cops won't help me."

"I'm sure that's not true."

She palms her hips and glares at me. "You're a privileged white man who has never had a run in with the cops, Gabriel. You have no clue—" she sucks in a breath and shakes her head. "You don't understand the shit people like me go through. I'm poor, I'm black, and I'm a woman. That's three strikes against me. Don't call me a liar when you have no clue!"

The sudden tears in her eyes tug at my heart. I reach for her, but she swats my hand away.

"Whatever Deacon has planned can't be worse than what I've gone through. Let him do his worst."

"I can't leave you at his mercy. You're going to the police."

She pivots and moves to the stairs. "Don't give me orders, Gabriel. I don't do well with that. Discussion's over. I'm not going!"

"Fucking hell, Zyon. I wish you weren't so goddamn stubborn. Can't you see I'm just trying to ensure your safety? You need to get him off the streets so he can't hurt you or someone else."

She pauses on the stairs and looks down at me. "I get it. You're trying to do the noble thing you think defines who you are. I've been taking care of myself for a while now. I don't need your help. I don't need you at all."

"Oh, fuck it. If you don't want to press charges, then don't. Whatever happens is on you."

I turn around and descend the stairs. I hear her heavy panting as she follows me. “Stop acting like you care, Gabriel, when all that matters is your image.”

“What are you talking about?”

“The same reason you don’t want to sleep with me again. Why you were quick to distance yourself while talking to Noah. You are ashamed of me. Aren’t you worried what people will think about me being here?”

I take a step toward her, then stop with a huff. “If you think that’s true then you don’t know me at all.”

“I don’t know you, Gabriel. How can I, when you keep pushing me away?”

“Right... because you're an open book.”

“I don’t need to listen to this. I’m going.”

She takes several steps before I grab her arm again. This time, I spin her to face me and the fire in her eyes sends heat straight to my cock.

“Who are you, Zyon Stewart? What are you trying to hide?”

“Not a damn—”

My lips capture hers, cutting her words short. My thoughts turn to mush when she moans and presses her body against mine. I deepen the kiss, tasting the sweetness from strawberry jam mixed with the lingering minty taste of toothpaste.

With our lips still joined, I lift her into my arms, and she wraps her legs around my waist. Her butt barely hits the counter before I break the kiss and haul the T-shirt over her head. My tongue trails down her neck, licking its way to her perfect breasts. She moans my name when I tweak her nipples with my teeth, and I can’t recall ever hearing my name sound so sexy. I continue downwards, licking the butterfly tattoo above her hips. She flinches when I trace my finger over a scar right below it. It's completely healed, which means it was there the first night we had sex. I must have missed it somehow.

"What's the story behind this scar?" I ask.

She moves my hand, placing it between her thighs. Her lips carry a smile, but her eyes appear troubled. "There's no story. Nothing worth telling anyway."

I grunt in response, planting gentle kisses on her inner thighs, moving closer to her drenched pussy. With her hand braced on the counter, Zyon widens her legs, giving me better access to her hot flesh. The first lash of my tongue makes her shudder. A soft, long hiss leaves her mouth as my tongue parts her, moving upwards. She grips a handful of my hair when I sink two fingers inside her and take her swollen clit into my mouth.

"Ohhh..." Her grip tightens on my hair. "Harder. Faster. That's it, Gabriel... yeah, right there. Please, don't stop." Her hips roll as I increase the pressure. "Fuck. Your fingers feel like heaven inside me."

I grip the tip of her clit with my teeth and give it a gentle pull while my fingers work inside her, moving slowly, teasing, intentionally driving her insane. Her pussy tightens around my digits while her fingers tweak her nipples, unbridled lust on her face. She makes a soft, sensual sound when I suck her clit, her juices dripping down my fingers.

"Gabriel... oh my god...oh!" she breathes, her thrusting out of control.

I pick up the pace, twisting my fingers inside her, lapping her clit with fervor, pushing her toward the edge. From the agony on her face and the way she’s moaning my name, she's coming hard. I lick her clean, my tongue slowing down when she does. She drops her head to my shoulder, breathing hard.

“Such a wicked tongue,” she says between pants. “So are those fingers.”

She gasps when I jerk her off the counter, but her legs immediately wrap around me again. My cock is like a steel pipe in my pants. I’m so turned on, I’m positive I won’t last long inside her. I almost certain I won’t make it to the bedroom either, so I lay her on the living room carpet, removing my shirt and pajama pants at breakneck speed. Zyon opens up for me, and I’m settling between her thighs when a heart-stopping thought occurs to me.

“Shit...” I drop my head to her chest. Zyon groans, and I can hear the disappointment in her voice.

“Gabriel please...”

“I’m still out of condoms, Zyon.”

“Fuck,” she whispers. “So am I.”

Her response leaves me relieved. If Zyon's not walking around with condoms, it means she has no intention of getting laid. I don’t know why it matters to me, but I’m glad to hear it.

“I’m on the pill, okay? I’m clean, too,” Zyon says, lifting her hips and grinding her pussy against me, re-igniting my arousal. “Fuck me, Gabriel. No holding back.” She rolls her body again and I softly curse from the agony. “Fuck me hard. Please.”

I grunt, grazing my cock against her entrance. Our eyes connect just before I press inside her, and I experience an emotional rush that sends my heart rate flying. It gets more intense as I bury myself further inside her.

"Oh, shit." Zyon's eyelids flutter and she throws her head back against the carpet. Whatever this is, I suspect she's feeling it too. Ecstasy. Pure, unfiltered ecstasy. It's coursing through every single vein in my body, and I haven't even started fucking her yet. She rocks her hips, prompting me to move, but I fear it would only take a single thrust for me to finish inside her. She feels perfect around me. She feels *right*.

Hell, I'm definitely whipped. That's the only explanation for this insanity.

Zyon rocks her hips again and gives me a worried stare. "Don't tell me you're having second thoughts. Please."

"Not even in the slightest." I grit my teeth and press inside her again, and by the third thrust, I know I won't last much longer. I've never left a woman unsatisfied, and this is the worst time to start. I press back on my legs so I can access her clit without stopping, and I slow down my strokes, summoning every ounce of self-control so I can last. Zyon moans when I gently flick the most sensitive part of her clit at the same time as my cock glides through her wet heat. Each thrust and each flick brings us both closer to our peak. Zyon's thrashing beneath me, her mouth releasing the filthiest words I've ever heard her say. Her pussy grips my cock like a glove, draining my control. Our moans fill the room as we both come apart, losing ourselves in each other.

Pulling her body against mine, I silently confess the truth. I'm not just whipped. I have feelings for Zyon.

26

ZYON

I awake with my head resting on a hard, warm surface, the sunlight from the window bathing my face. That last thing I remember is falling asleep curled up next to Gabriel on the carpet downstairs. Lifting my head from his chest, I stare at his sleeping face. Even in sleep he looks stern, his eyebrows close together, his mouth in a permanent pout. Oh, that mouth... I can't stop thinking about the filthy things it did to me. My body comes alive, triggered by the memories of his tongue, his fingers, and his thick cock hitting all the right spots, giving me head to toe pleasure like I'd never experienced before.

I check the time as I wrap my leg over his. It's almost eleven. I have an afternoon session with Anita, but it can wait. Right now, I need another taste of Gabriel, and it just might be the last. With his track record, I'm sure he'll regret touching me.

I run my palm over his chest, and he stirs with a sigh, his eyelashes fluttering. He doesn't wake up, so I straddle his hips, rocking back and forth, rubbing my bare pussy against the front of his pajama pants. It takes no time for his cock to stiffen, pressing into me. His eyes slowly open, lashing me with a burning lust that sets me off. I ease up and tug at his pants. He lifts his hips and allows me to pull them off. They are at his ankles in seconds, and on the floor in another, then I'm back to straddling him, claiming his mouth for a quick kiss. He grips me tighter when I attempt to move away, deepening the kiss with a passion that arouses me even more.

He eventually slackens his grip and I break the kiss to nibble his chin before moving down his chest, planting gentle kisses to his skin along the way. He pushes up on his elbows when my lips move past his belly button, his eyes watching me intently. I stare into them as I teasingly lick his tip and he throws his head back with a groan.

"Zyon... shit."

I concentrate on the head, making slow, deliberate circles with my tongue, grazing the slit before taking his cock in my mouth.

"Fuck, yes," Gabriel murmurs as I swallow him to the base. "That feels so good. My cock looks so *fucking* good in your mouth."

Moaning in response, I move back to the tip and repeat the motion, my hair bouncing on my shoulders as I pick up speed, determined for him to finish in my mouth. From the sounds coming from his lips, I don't think he's too far off. I've never seen him lose control like this; his hips jerking upwards, his face screwed in concentration as he violently fucks my mouth. I release his cock for a moment and direct my attention to his balls, cupping them gently, then lightly licking the scrotum before taking both in my mouth.

“God in heaven,” Gabriel hisses. “You’re so good. You’re so fucking— Christ!”

He goes wild when I continue to suck his balls while pumping his cock. A strangled cry leaves him as his legs quiver. I return my full attention to his cock, and he clutches my hair with both hands, his cock gliding through my hot, willing mouth as I swallow every drop of his thick, salty cum.

“Fuck,” he whispers, his chest bouncing as he watches me lick my lips. “I can't believe you swallowed. That was so fucking hot.”

“Stick around,” I reply, leaning toward him. “There’s plenty more where that came from.”

It's just a teasing remark, but I realize he doesn’t get it. There's no responding smile. He just pulls me in a for a slow kiss that leaves me weak in the knees.

“I want you riding me right now,” he whispers against my mouth. Glancing down, I realize he’s still fully erect and it amazes me, considering how hard he came just now.

I straddle him, using the opportunity to run my hands over his chest once more. I can't help giving his sleek, toned abs a little attention, too. Gabriel watches me, his hands linked behind his head, his eyes saying everything and yet nothing at all. He releases a soft groan when I pinch his nipples, his lower body lifting, prompting me to slide down. I capture his gaze as I rub my pussy across the tip of his cock, lubricating it with my juices. His jawline hardens and he grips my waist, jerking upwards to impale me.

"Oh, fuck," Gabriel whispers at the same time as I moan. The passion in his eyes steal my breath away, and I close my eyes to focus on the moment. I can't look at him. He makes me feel too much. These emotions are getting me nowhere.

Gripping his shoulders, I ease up and sink back down, building a rhythm, increasing the tempo with each thrust. The sensation from my clit grinding against his front sends ripples of pleasure through my body. Gabriel thrusts upwards each time I sink down, his cock gliding through me like a hot knife through butter. Together we move, moan, sweat, surrender to the ecstasy that's so good it should be illegal.

The pre-climax wave isn't the only sensation taking over. Each solid stroke of Gabriel's cock sends my emotions to another level, and they're getting so intense it's hard to breathe. I can feel the stinging in my eyes from unshed tears. No. I won't cry. This is just sex, nothing else.

Gabriel tightens his grip on my waist. "Zyon, look at me."

I shake my head, my eyes still squeezed shut. "No." Tears spill down my cheeks, blowing my cover. The sheet rustles as Gabriel sits upright.

"Look at me."

Slowly, reluctantly I open my eyes. "What?"

"Why are you crying?" he asks, his face filled with concern.

"Nothing. I'm fine." I rock my hips to get us going again, but he pins me with an iron-clad grip. Frustrated, I try to break free.

"I'm not letting you go until you tell me what's wrong."

"God." I exhale harshly, staring at the ceiling to avoid looking at him. "You want to know what's wrong? I'm in love with a man who's emotionally unavailable."

I glance down at him, and his shuttered expression makes my heart sink. Fuck. I shouldn't have said that. Why the hell did I open my big mouth?

It's the truth. I'm falling for him. So hard. There's absolutely no doubt in my mind. It's not because he's the best lover I've been with, although that's quite a plus. It's amazing how my life has changed for better since I met him. He gave me a job. He saved my ass—more than once, and he was always there with a listening ear when I needed one.

Still, it's clear he's not ready for me. It will be okay. All I want is an orgasm before I move on.

"Okay, no more talking." I smile brightly to lighten the mood. He's still not looking at me. I brush the hair from his face, and his expression is as calm as the midnight sea. I hate that I can't tell what he's feeling.

"Yeah, no more talking," he mutters, flipping me onto my stomach. He roughly pulls up my knees, taking me from behind so swiftly I lose my breath. There's no restraint. No mercy. It's like he's punishing me. He's making me pay for being honest with my feelings. Feelings he can't reciprocate.

It hurts, yet it feels so fucking good. I am definitely a glutton for punishment. With my ass in the air and my pussy exposed, I take every inch of his rough strokes like the champion I am. My orgasm rips through me like a hurricane, just as wild and devastating. I can't help screaming his name, telling him how much I want him. God, I'm such an idiot, but I can't stop the words. Maybe this is what I need; to get it all out so I can finally move on.

Gabriel tightens his arms around me, and I close my eyes. My body is still quivering from the emotional climax. I'm still shattered. I doubt

I'll ever be whole again. He kisses the back of my neck, my shoulder, the line of my jaw, and I hear the heavy sigh that leaves his mouth.

"Zyon," he whispers.

I turn to face him, taking in his expression. I recognize the agony, the internal battle he's trying to overcome. I know Gabriel wants me. We just had the best sex I've ever had, and probably ever will again, but I'm not sure if he wants the emotions that come with it. I don't think he wants to fall for me.

"Hey... it's okay. I'm not looking for reciprocation, trust me. I just needed to get it off my chest."

"I know, but—"

The sudden rapping on the door sends me grabbing for the covers and throwing them around me.

"Shit," Gabriel mutters, confirming what I suspected. The door isn't locked. He flies off the bed, rushing to the door while shouting, "Don't open!"

But it's too late.

He's almost at the door when it opens, revealing a tall, slender woman with her platinum hair in an updo and the coldest eyes I've ever seen. She's wearing high-waist pants and a simple tucked-in buttoned blouse I'm sure costs my entire month's salary. She looks fit for the cover of any magazine.

Gabriel immediately spins around to me, covering his crotch. "What are you doing here, Mom?"

"Do I need a reason to see my son?" she replies, but she's not looking at Gabriel. She's staring at me. Yeah, her eyes are definitely cold, but there's something else within them that I can't put my finger on, and it's setting me on edge.

"Do you really need me to answer that?" Gabriel snaps, and I sense the tension between them. I'm not the only one with mommy issues, it seems.

"I'll be downstairs when you're done with... whatever this is," she replies.

The door slams behind her and Gabriel's hands drop to his side. "Sorry about that," he says wearily.

"I'm fine. It's not like I'm the one who flashed your mom."

He reaches for his sweatpants with a smile that doesn't reach his eyes. "I'll be back in a few minutes, okay? Then we'll talk. Really talk."

"Okay."

A bit of hope balloons in my chest but I allow it to deflate. I don't want to read too much into that, but I'm keeping my fingers crossed, anyway.

27

GABRIEL

"What do you think you're doing?" Mom asks as I descend the stairs to the living room. She's perched on the couch like a queen on her throne, dressed like she's about to attend an event, as usual.

"I'm not going to assume what you're asking me, so please elaborate."

"Since when do your one-night stands spend the night?"

"Never." I walk past her and head to the kitchen. "She's not a one-night stand."

I can hear the rustle of her pants as she follows me. "That's a joke, right?"

"Am I laughing?"

"Who is she?"

"There you are, getting all personal again. Doesn't it feel weird?"

She rolls her eyes and attempts to take a seat on the bar stool, but she changes her mind. "It's not funny, Gabriel. Do you think about how Nicole would feel if she knew about this?"

"I can't imagine why she'd feel anything other than happy for me."

"We both know she's in love with you, Gabriel. Don't play dumb."

"Can I get you something to drink?" I ask, turning to the fridge. Something tells me we'll be here for a while. I'm not looking forward to the reason she came unannounced to my house. My interest solely lies in talking to Zyon about what happened between us. She's in love with me. *Fuck*. Those were the last words I expected to hear from her mouth. Maybe it was the sex, but if I'm being honest, what happened was more emotional than that. I need to figure out what it means.

"Bottled water will be fine," Mom says, and I hand one to her. "You didn't answer my question."

"Of course I did. Nicole knows we can never be a thing."

"Does she?"

"I've never led her on, Mom."

"You promised me you'd think about dating her, didn't you?"

My brows tighten as I turn my attention from the fridge to her. "You know, I've been trying to figure out why Nicole has been so clingy lately... did you tell her what I said?"

"Of course I did, Gabriel. When are you going to get it? She's been in love since you were both teenagers."

"What? That can't be true."

"It is. You keep missing what's right in front of you. Wake up, Gabriel. She's the one."

"God..."

"I'm just confused. Is that girl the reason you can't be with Nicole?"

I take a deep breath, feeling my patience slipping and trying to keep it under control. "It's not a can't. It's a won't. I have no desire to be with Nicole. She's like a sister to me. She's also still hung up on Lukas."

"The girl upstairs. Who is she?"

I sigh, then take a swig from the water bottle. There's no use in hiding the truth. She'll hear about Zyon soon enough. "She's my assistant."

"For God's sake, Gabriel," she says, throwing up her hands. Very unorthodox of her. She's never lost control.

"What is it?"

She's staring like she has never seen me before. "Why do you keep letting me down?"

My hand tightens around the bottle. "Have I?"

"I don't get it. There's a beautiful, successful sweetheart who would love to be your wife someday, yet here you are sleeping with Deacon's leftovers."

Whoa. It's like I'm being bitch-slapped by her response. "What did you say?"

"You heard me."

"So, it's obvious you already know who she is. Are you aware that Deacon tried to rape her last night?"

"That's why I came to talk to you, not knowing you were wrapped up in bed with the girl who's trying to smear his name."

My mouth falls open. I'm not aware that I've crushed the water bottle until it crunches beneath my palm. I look down at it, then back at her. "*What did you just say?*"

"Do you need to get your ears checked? She's lying. Deacon doesn't need to rape anyone. He's a handsome young man, perfectly capable of getting any woman he wants."

"So, all those accusations, the ones you and Dad went to great lengths to cover up, they are just coincidences, right? What the hell does Deacon have on you and Dad?"

She stares at me, lips pursed.

"You better think long and hard about your response."

"No, you think about it, Gabriel. They went on a date, one that lasted for hours. Then he takes her to his apartment—"

"Under the influence. She was already under the influence. *He drugged her.*" The fury swells within me, and I feel like I'm about to combust. I take another deep breath.

"Is that what you she told you? Come on. You've known Deacon for years. Are you going to take the word of someone you just met over him?"

"I'm not taking her word for it. I saw her, Mom. The fucking asshole—" Again, another deep breath. "Her face was bruised. She could barely stand. In fact, she passed out before we got to the car."

"That's not what Deacon told me."

"It seems he gave you quite an earful."

"He told me she consented, and I believe him."

My eyes narrow at her. "You need to think really carefully before you say another word."

"I'm not taking it back. That girl is a tramp trying to tarnish a good man's name. She enticed him then cried foul because you showed up. She's not a victim, Gabriel. Don't let her—"

The sudden pounding on the stairs pulls both our attention. Zyon's coming down, dressed in her outfit from the night before. She's furious; I recognize the slant of her mouth, the way her eyebrows bunch together. Her hand is a tight fist around the strap of her bag. I move from around the kitchen island as she storms toward the front door.

"Zyon." I hold on to her arm, but she shrugs me off. "Don't go. Please."

She makes an abrupt stop and whips around to me. "Look, I've got family drama of my own. I don't need to be here for this. I don't need to be here at all." She glances at Mom then back at me. "Have a nice day, Gabriel."

I quit trying to persuade her to stay. It would be useless. Zyon marches to the beat of her own drum. Once she's decided, there's no convincing her to change it. I'm not done with her. Not even by a long shot. We're having this conversation at some point. Whatever the outcome, we'll definitely hash it out.

I turn to my mom with a harsh glare. "Satisfied?"

She's shaking her head. "You disappoint me, Gabriel. I don't know why I'm surprised. You've been doing that all your life."

I turn away from her, unwilling to hear any more. "I can't do this with you. Just let yourself out. I'm done."

I'm halfway up the stairs when she says, "Daniel's death-anniversary is tomorrow, or have you forgotten?"

As if I could forget. The memories have been getting stronger all week, like they always do when the dreadful date comes near. Depression has been knocking at my door, too. It's certainly not the first time since Daniel died and it won't be the last, either.

"I remember," I say to her.

"That's it. *I remember*. No goddamn remorse."

"What do you want from me, Mom?" I ask, facing her once more.

"I want you to make me happy," she replies.

"That's all I've been doing since Daniel died, bending over backward to please you. What more do you want from me? How much longer will you punish me for what happened eight years ago?"

"I want you to reinstate Deacon and give Nicole a chance. That's all I ask."

She moves closer to the stairs, giving me an earnest stare that usually makes it difficult to refuse her requests. No; I can't allow her to manipulate me anymore. I'm standing my ground.

"No. Deacon is a rapist who deserves to go to prison. I can't have him working for us. For the last time, Mom, Nicole and I can only be friends. I'm sorry about that old-school fantasy you and Kelly have going on, but I can't help you. I'm not interested."

Mom sniffles and I roll my eyes. Here comes the tears. Oh, hell. Not the tears. Not my kryptonite.

She sniffles again, her eyes blinking furiously. "You took my son away from me, Gabriel. Yet, I forgave you. I welcomed you back in my life with open arms."

"Mom—"

"I ask for two simple things, and you're refusing me. Ungrateful, that's what you are."

"Mom, I'm done playing your games. How many times have I apologized for that night? I'm sorry." I descend the stairs and stop right in front of her. "If I could take Daniel's place, I would."

She swallows, and trickles of tears run down her cheeks. “I wish you could too,” she whispers. “I wish you had died that night instead of my sweet, precious boy.”

My head jerks back from the well-placed emotional blow and the tightening in my chest gets worse. I give her a slow nod. “Took you long enough to say it.”

She bursts into tears, but I don’t comfort her like I normally would. I head back up the stairs, lock my bedroom door, and collapse on the bed. Then I smell Zyon. Her scent is all over my sheets, reminding me of the toe-curling sex that feels like it happened a hundred years ago.

I don’t want to think about Zyon right now. Or Daniel. Or my manipulative parents. I don’t want to think about anything at all. What I need is a good, strong drink that will make me forget what a disappointment I am. I don’t want to face tomorrow sober. A drink will keep the guilt away for once.

28

Zyon

"Slow down, Zyon, and tell me what's going on. Why are you crying?" Roshell asks, jogging behind me as I rush to my room.

I push the door open and wipe my face. "I'm fine, Rosh. I just need to be alone for a while."

"Nuh-uh. Not after you went MIA last night, then show up with a bruised face. Was it Aaron? Did he hurt you again?"

"No. But it seems like I'm a magnet for these assholes." I tell her about what Deacon tried to do and how Gabriel saved me, and she stares at me, mouth agape.

"Oh my God, Zyon! I can't imagine what must have been going through your mind when—" she pauses and palms her face. "I'm so sorry that happened to you."

"Thanks, girl." I pull out a pair of panties and a T-shirt from my drawer. I just want to curl under the covers and hide from the world.

The only other option is to get wasted and do something crazy and I am done with that life.

"What happened at Gabriel's, Zyon?"

I pause at the doorway leading to the bathroom. "His mother happened. She barged into his bedroom while we were in bed."

"Oh, shit. That must have been so embarrassing."

"That's an understatement."

"I can't imagine you crying over Gabriel's mom seeing you naked though." Leave it to Roshell to keep prying when I'm obviously trying to avoid this conversation.

I didn't intend to eavesdrop on their conversation. I had just left Gabriel's room and was heading to the guest room when I heard my name, and the venom in his mother's tone sent a dagger through my heart. "She accused me of lying about the assault, Rosh. She said I wanted it."

"Oh my God. No, Zyon..."

Her concerned expression gets me all teary again. "It fucking hurts. It leaves me questioning myself because Dineo said the same thing. Am I to blame for what Aaron did to me?"

"No, no, no." Roshell moves forward and cups my cheeks with both hands, and I lose it. Loud sobs rip from my chest. "We are not doing this, you hear me? None of this is your fault. Aaron is the only one to blame. So is Deacon. Don't you ever think otherwise."

I respond with a nod, and she uses her thumbs to wipe the tears from my cheeks. "What did Gabriel say to her?"

"Oh, he was livid."

"Good."

"No, not good. Not for me." Sighing, I gently move her hands away. "I told Gabriel I loved him, Rosh."

Roshell gasps, covering her mouth with both hands. "You did not."

"Yup. Put my foot in my mouth and everything. Even then, I think we were on the verge of starting something, but that will never happen now."

"Why not?"

"Remember when you dated Troy and his mama didn't like you?"

"Oh." Roshell's face falls, and I suspect she remembers the hell Mrs. Davis put her through. "Yeah, I get your point."

"I think it's time to find a new job."

"Are you crazy? Where in hell will you find a job that pays half as much?"

I'm done choosing money over happiness. "Money isn't everything, Rosh. I'm not saying I don't need it, because we both know how much I do—but I can't work with Gabriel anymore. I can't handle being around him."

"Yes, you can. You're stronger than you think."

"I know that. But I don't *want* to be strong!"

She follows me into the bathroom and leans against the sink, watching me unravel.

"I don't want to be strong," I say it softer this time and I can hear the defeat in my voice. I haul the shirt over my head with a deep sigh. "I just want to be free."

Roshell sighs too. "Terrence's brother owns an employment agency. I could ask if there's something in your field. Promise me you won't leave until you get another job."

"Fine. I won't." But the promise is as empty as my insides. I'm already drafting my resignation letter in my head. "Do me a favor, Roshell. Call Anita. Let her know I won't make it today."

"Do you think that's the best idea?"

"No. But I'm so out of it today. I just need to rest."

"Okay. I'll do it." She turns to go, then pivots back to me. "Zyon, you really need to talk about what Aaron did to you. Maybe not to me, or Dineo, but you need to get it off your chest before it eats you alive."

I give her a quick nod and step into the shower. She's right, as usual. Suppressing the memories of that awful night has been tearing me apart. It's time to bring them to the surface, to heal once and for all.

First, I need to rest. I didn't lie about my reason for skipping therapy today. I really am beat. I shower and get my clothes on, then curl up under the covers, welcoming the sleep that, hopefully, will keep the tears at bay.

My ringing cell phone wakes me with a jolt. It feels like I've been sleeping for days, but checking the time, it's only been a few hours. I almost ignore the call when I see Gabriel's name on the screen. *Almost*. I need to hear his voice as much as I need air. I hate this stupid weakness for him, but I can't help it. I press the answer button and place it on speaker while propping myself up on my elbows.

"If this isn't about work, Gabriel, I'm hanging up," I say.

"This isn't Gabriel. It's Noah."

I sit up in bed, completely alarmed. Something's wrong. Noah wouldn't call me from Gabriel's phone if it wasn't. No, scratch that.

Noah wouldn't call me at all. He hates me. I've been too caught up with my own shit to figure out why.

"Is Gabriel okay?" I feel like it's a rhetorical question.

Noah sighs. "There's been an accident, Zyon. You need to come. Gabriel needs to see you."

·♥·♥·♥·♥·♥·

"He's in the bedroom," Noah says as I step into Gabriel's apartment. "Just some minor bruises, but he'll be okay."

"What happened?"

"He..." Noah hesitates and glances upstairs, his expression uncertain. "He crashed into a perimeter wall. I suspect he had been drinking. He won't admit it, though."

"Why wouldn't he admit it? He's not the first person to drive under the influence."

"No, he's not. But Gabriel has been sober for five years."

I pause with my arm still caught in the sleeve of my coat, gaping at Noah. "Oh my God, I didn't know," I finally say.

"Well, you do now," he replies gruffly, and I don't miss the accusation plain on his face. I hang the jacket on the rack and fold my arms across my chest, giving him an unflinching stare.

"Did I do something to offend you?"

He scoffs. "No. Why are you asking me that?"

"Because you've always been cold toward me whenever we meet. You told Gabriel I'm not good for him."

His face goes red, and he looks down at his toes then back up at me. "Did he tell you that?"

"No, I overheard your conversation on the phone."

"I have nothing against you, Zyon. Gabriel's my best friend and I need to protect him as much as I can."

"Protect him from what? Who? Me?"

"Yes!" He lets loose a harsh breath and runs both hands through his hair, staring at me with a mixture of anger and sadness. "He was doing fine until he met you. Five years sober. No anger, no fighting, until you brought the darkness back into his life. You opened the door and let all the demons back in."

"Oh, wow." The familiar ache returns to my chest as I reach for my coat. "Then why the fuck did you call me?"

"Hey, no—Zyon—" He grabs my arm as I head to the front door. "Don't go, please. Gabriel's going to kill me if I make you leave."

"There's no purpose for me here, Noah. I'm leaving, and I'm taking the darkness with me."

"Zyon, please. Just disregard my opinion for a moment, okay? This isn't about how I feel. I assure you, Gabriel doesn't feel the way I do."

I give him the longest, dirtiest stare I can muster. "Fine." I shove my coat against his chest and head upstairs.

29

Gabriel

Fuck. My head. It feels like someone took a sledgehammer to it. I roll onto my side, rubbing my temple to ease the tension, wincing as my fingers touch a bruise. I immediately recall the events of the night and it makes me groan.

Damn it. I can't believe I drank. Feeling the familiar burn of alcohol running down my throat, warming my insides; the satisfaction only lasted for the two hours I spent in that bar. I knew I was wasted when I left, but I was too far gone to care. After getting in my car, my only thought was Zyon. I had to see her. She's the only one I want to talk to about the shit that's been messing with my head. Zyon gets me. She's not scared if I lose my temper. She doesn't stare at me like it's time for an intervention. She's the only one who understands the darkness that's been plaguing me because it plagues her, too.

After leaving the bar, it slowly dawned on me that I was more fucked up than I thought. Within a minute, I lost control of the car and ran into the perimeter wall. Luckily, I only emerged with a small bruise from my head banging against the steering wheel, the front of the car only slightly dented. Noah wasn't my first choice to call for help because I knew he would judge me, but Marcus wasn't picking up. Noah was my next best option.

I push myself up to a seated position and swing my legs over the side of bed as the door opens. The sight of Zyon in the doorway puts an instant smile on my face. She's here. I can't believe it. After how she stormed out this morning, I didn't expect she would consider my wish. I didn't expect to feel so overjoyed to see her, either.

The anxiety fades from her face as she stops before me. "You look like hell," she says.

"Such a lovely compliment. Thank you very much." I groan while getting to my feet. My entire body is just so *sore*.

"It wasn't a compliment. I lost my license for the same shit. Take it from me. Drinking and driving is the stupidest decision you could ever make."

"It's not a habit, trust me."

"So I've heard." She gently turns my head and examines the bruise, then gives me a stinging slap on my arm.

"Ow!"

"Why didn't you tell me you were a recovering alcoholic?"

"Because it's not something I go around telling people, Zyon." I grab the aspirin Noah left for me on the side table, along with a glass of water. Zyon watches me as I gulp the aspirin down, sternness stamped across her face. Maybe its disappointment. I can't tell.

"Are you going to tell me what happened?" she asks.

"Besides you storming out without giving me a chance to explain?"

She scoffs. "I doubt you broke your sobriety over me."

"You're selling yourself short."

"I'm being realistic. Why did you ask to see me?"

I sigh, gesturing to the armchair near the window, but she shakes her head. "I wanted to talk about what happened this morning," I say.

"We really don't need to, Gabriel. What's more important is the reason you had a drink after *five years*. I'm curious. Concerned. If there's something eating you up inside, it won't stop until it destroys you." She suddenly stops and palms her cheeks, letting loose a loud sigh. "Shit."

"What?"

"Roshell told me the same thing a few hours ago," she says.

"I'm not the only one with something weighing on my soul, Zyon."

"Nope." She makes a popping sound with her mouth and gets this faraway look in her eyes. I stand before her, watching a myriad of emotions cross her face, before she closes her eyes with a long, shuddering breath.

"I was sexually assaulted last year."

Her words send an instant chill up my spine. I drop to a squat, running my hands through my hair, staring at her with shock. "Holy fuck, Zyon..."

She shakes her head, keeping her eyes shut tight. They are filled with tears when she opens them again. The sorrow on her face makes me want to comfort her, to hold her in my arms and chase the pain away. But that's not what she needs right now. She needs to let it out.

"I've never talked about that awful night, not in detail. I just wanted to forget it ever happened. But... the things I did while trying to escape... they fucked up my life."

Pushing up to stand, I back up until my knees hit the bed. I take a seat and watch her, patiently waiting for her to continue.

"It happened one night after I got home from work and did the usual; took a shower, grabbed a snack, and curled up on the couch to watch TV. He came downstairs, flirting with me like he always did but that night, I'd had enough."

"Wait a minute. Who is 'he?'" I hate interjecting, but this isn't how I expected the story to proceed. I thought someone broke into her house or she was attacked in a dark alley. This was someone she knew.

"His name is Aaron Murphy, and he was my mom's investor. Her restaurant wasn't doing well, and he offered to invest for a percentage of the profit. I don't know all the details. I'm not even sure how they met. Regardless, they were close, because he was always at the restaurant and sometimes she invited him to dinner. At first, I thought they had an affair going on, but they never seemed intimate. Just friendly. Plus, he's only a few years older than me. I doubt Dineo would fall for a younger man. He started flirting with me, which made me uncomfortable, so I asked Dineo to stop inviting him to dinner. He showed up on our doorstep with his bags a week later, asking for a temporary place to stay. He had an issue with his roommate or something. Dineo didn't hesitate to take him in."

"If he invested in your mother's business, then he has money," I say. "Why wouldn't he just get another apartment?" It's really a horse-already-left-the-gate kind of question, but my brain's trying to fit the pieces together, and they're not cohesive. There's something missing.

"That's exactly what I asked Dineo. We lived in a cramped apartment. The spare room is in the attic, filled with junk, but he was happy to take it. Dineo gave me a lecture about entertaining people who are angels in disguise. Bullshit. He was the devil."

She takes another deep breath, her fingers fiddling with the hem of her shirt. "I got up from the couch and he followed me, still flirting. I told him to fuck off, and he got nasty. He said I was nothing but a whore playing hard to get. I was a virgin."

Again, she pauses and a sob escapes, then another until her cries fill the room. She slides down the wall until her knees are under her chin, her arms wrapped around her shins. I get on my knees before her, taking her hands in mine.

"Hey. We can stop here okay?"

Zyon shakes her head through her tears. "No, I want to talk about it. I should have done this a long time ago." She flips her hands so she's squeezing mine now.

"He told me I wasn't worth the trouble. I didn't know what he meant. I still don't, but for some reason I think it's important to remember. I ignored him and opened my bedroom door, thinking he would go away. Instead, he forced his way inside and forced himself on me."

My hands tighten around hers. The emotion I'm feeling is more destructive than anger. I want to rip that asshole apart with my bare hands, give him a taste of the torture he put Zyon through.

"He destroyed me that night. Inside and out. The more I fought him, the angrier he got. He left me with bruises everywhere, especially my face. I had a broken arm and a concussion from when he slammed my head against the floor. The scar on my hip is from his knife when he cut my panties off."

"Please tell me he's serving a life sentence in prison," I mutter, seething inside.

"No. He's not." A fresh wave of tears smears her face. "He's not some regular guy, Gabriel. His family has money. Crazy money, which makes the entire situation strange."

I have a theory, but for Zyon's peace of mind I won't say what it is.

"One mention of his name and the cops got nasty. They asked if we were dating, what outfit was I wearing, questions that made me the villain, not the victim. The way they treated me was so unfair."

"Now I understand why you didn't want to press charges against Deacon—" Fuck. It didn't occur to me until just now that Deacon tried to do the same thing to her. I can't imagine the terror she experienced. "I'm so sorry that happened to you, Zyon."

She nods, sniffling. "There's more, but I'm too ashamed to tell you." She reaches up and wipes her face dry. "Now it's your turn."

A harsh sound leaves my mouth as I sit back on the bed, staring at my palms. "My brother lost his life because of me."

Zyon shakes her head, her eyes wide with shock. "Whoa. That's not the opening line I expected to hear."

"It happened eight years ago. I had just turned twenty; Daniel was eighteen. The boys and I were going to a party, and he wanted to come. Mom said no, but we snuck him out, anyway. I had a little too much to drink at the party and T-boned another car on the way home." I look out the window as my chest tightens, making it hard to breathe. "I got out with a broken leg and a concussion. Daniel didn't make it."

"Oh, my God, Gabriel."

The memories assault me, completely taking over. I'm transported back to that night, waking up to the terrible news, hearing Mom's wailing in the hospital hall. Her loud, primal cry pierced my soul, making me sick. I wanted to die that night, for years afterwards.

"Everyone blamed me, of course, especially my mother, but I blamed myself the most. If I hadn't disobeyed her, Daniel would still be alive. He just finished high school, and I wanted him to have a good time."

I hear the sobbing, but I didn't realize it came from me, not until Zyon rushes to me and wipes my face. The simple gesture opens the floodgates and I settle in her arms as my body shakes with tears. I haven't cried in ages. *Years*. Not since Daniel died. Even then, it wasn't like this; like a never-ending dam has been opened. Zyon's words are like a balm to my soul, slowly calming me down, her hands making soothing circles on my back. Her scent washes over me, flooding my senses. She pulls back, staring into my face.

"Pathetic," I grumble as she wipes my cheeks. "I don't know why the fuck I'm crying."

"Because you're a human with emotions, that's why. Doesn't it feel a little better?"

"Yeah, it does." I watch her as she returns to her spot on the wall.

"Seems we both have mommy issues, huh?" she says.

"Tell me about it."

"I think mine is keeping a secret from me. I'm too scared to find out what it is."

"My mother hates my guts. She blames me for taking her favorite son away." It's the first time I've said it out loud. Acknowledging my mother's negative feelings brings me to an unexpected crossroads. Do I try to fix our broken relationship or let it crumble?

"Have you tried reaching out to talk about it?"

I shake my head. "I've never really discussed Daniel until today. She was never up to it, anyway. One mention of his name and she would lose it. She's better now, but I don't want to take her back there."

"So you sweep it under the rug."

"Whatever it takes to coexist."

"That includes doing everything to please her, right?"

She catches my questioning frown and adds, "I overheard the conversation with your mom."

"I figured you did. Zyon, what she said about you asking for it, I don't think she meant it. Mom's been through a lot; losing Daniel, her divorce, Dad remarrying with another baby on the way. She's just angry at life. Bitter. If she knew your story—"

"You're defending her. Why am I not surprised?" Zyon says with a scoff, pushing to stand again.

I rush to block her exit, my arms spread to stop her. "That's not what I'm doing. I'm trying to explain her state of mind."

"I get it, she's been through hell. She still has no right to talk about me that way."

"I agree, one hundred percent. Just... don't write her off, please."

Zyon sighs, and a wave of sadness runs across her face. "Okay."

I take her hand. "Does that mean you'll stay?"

"I can't. I have an appointment with my therapist. Remember those visits to Grandma at the nursing home?"

"Yeah."

"They didn't exist. I was actually going to therapy to, you know..."

I nod, understanding what she leaves unsaid. I spent a year seeing a psychologist after Daniel died.

"Grandma really exists; she just lives in Nigeria. She really said that bit about the grandkids."

"She sounds like fun."

"She has her moments," she says with a small smile. She jams her thumb at the door. "I should go."

"Okay, but we really need to talk about this morning."

"I know." She bounces our joined hand in the air before pulling hers from mine. "We will. What you need right now is rest."

"I'm okay, one hundred percent."

"Says the man who just popped an aspirin to have a conversation." She pats my chest. "Get some rest. We'll talk when the time is right."

I back down. Pushing Zyon will get me nowhere. "Fine. Talk to you later, okay?"

She doesn't reply, just offers me her cheek. I plant a gentle kiss, wanting to do more. Instead of giving into my urges, I follow her out, and she gives me a squeezing hug before disappearing into the Uber. I return upstairs to take her advice and rest. I think about Mom, and the dozen unanswered calls from her on my cell phone. I believe she's sorry, and I've already forgiven her, but I would give anything for her to forgive me, too.

30

Zyon

It was a vow made in anger, but I meant every word. Never again would I set foot in my childhood home. That was then, when the pain was so raw, when I felt so betrayed, when I hated the entire world.

And now...

It's a new day. This is a new me. I'm not the girl who masked her pain with sex, alcohol, and an impulsive lifestyle. I'm not the self-destructive girl I was a few months ago. Now, I'm the woman who's ready to start over, to love myself, to do what's best for me. What's best for me is making peace with my mother. I can't move on if I'm still holding onto my anger against her.

Still, my heart feels like it's trying to burst out of my chest as the car pulls up in front of Dineo's apartment. I get out and close the door, shivering as the early morning chill envelopes my body. I should have worn a coat. I probably should have waited for daylight to leave my house, but the longer I waited, the more nervous I became. I'm not anxious about facing my mother. It's the demons waiting inside that leave me terrified. Why did I think I could do this?

Fuck it. I shouldn't have come.

Anita's words come back to me as I pull out my phone to order another Uber. I tuck it back in my pocket with a conceding sigh. I need to do this. It's the only way I can truly heal.

I remain on the street for a moment, staring at the front door, remembering how hard I slammed it that night. Dineo followed right behind me, her cries shattering the stillness of the night. I didn't care for her tears. All I thought about was my pain. Looking back, I realize I wasn't the only one hurting. I was her only child, and my life had just been ripped apart because she made a mistake. I'm mature enough to consider how devastated she must have been.

It's time to forgive. God, I hope it's enough to forget.

Reaching the top of the steps, I glance at the set of keys in my hand; it feels like I'm clutching a ten-pound weight. I almost tossed them in the garbage when I moved out, but I'm glad I didn't. They've been lounging at the bottom of my sock drawer all this time.

Taking a deep breath, I turn the key in the lock and the door to my past creaks open. When I cross the foyer, it feels like I've been transported to a stranger's living room. Dineo has done a massive makeover. Gone is the couch where Aaron started flirting with me, the dining table we used on the occasions she invited him to dinner, the carpet he tripped me onto when I tried to escape. Looking around, there's nothing that reminds me of my time here. Nothing that reminds me of him.

Except this house. It still holds the memories of that awful night. I don't want to run or be afraid. I'm here to face these demons head on.

The heavy thud of footsteps proceeds Dineo's presence at the top of the stairs. Her fingers are busy tying the belt of her robe as she stares down at me like she's seen a ghost. I'm not surprised. This is the last place I expected to be ever again.

"Zyon?" She's coming down the stairs now, in obvious shock from the way her wide, unblinking eyes take me in. She's still wearing her headscarf, and I remember how she was a stickler for removing it before she left her bedroom each morning. I imagine how alarmed she must have been when she heard the front door open.

I spread my arms with a tiny smile when she stops in front of me. "Yes, it's me, Mommy."

"You came," she whispers, her hand reaching to my face. Her fingers gently stroke my cheek, just once, before she drops her hand to her side. "I can't believe it. You're here."

"It was hard. Took everything inside me."

"I know, baby." Her eyes are shiny with unshed tears, tugging at my heartstrings.

"I'm here. I want to fix us. I'm ready to meet you halfway, okay?"

Dineo nods, bursting into a sob as she pulls me into a hug. I wrap my arms around her, too, inhaling the familiar lavender scent that made me feel so safe as a child. The floodgates open and I start bawling with my head resting against her chest. Our loud cries fill the room as we sway together for so long, I lose track of time.

"I'm sorry," Dineo whispers when we break apart. Still sniffling, she wipes the tears from my face. "I'm really, really sorry, baby. I shouldn't have let Aaron in our lives. I should have fought harder to get him imprisoned for what he did to you. I'm so sorry I blamed you for what happened. Baby, it's not your fault."

"I know that now. I've already forgiven you, Mommy. I've been angry for a long time, but I don't want to be that person anymore."

She hugs me again, giving my back a gentle rub before releasing me and moving toward the kitchen. "Did you have breakfast? I could whip up your favorite egg muffins."

"No I haven't, and yes, that sounds like heaven," I reply, following her.

"Great. I missed cooking for you."

"Not as much as I missed eating it. It's been hell having to cook every day; Roshell has been no help."

Dineo smiles. "How is Roshell? Is she still trying to find Mr. Right?"

"From the look of things, she may have found him. Fingers crossed he does nothing to fu— mess it up."

"I'm sure they will be fine." She pulls the eggs from the fridge, then pauses to look at me. "How about you? Are there any lucky suitors I should know about?"

I chuckle. "Suitors? That's so old fashioned. To answer your question, I'd rather not say." I don't know where Gabriel and I stand, not well enough to tell my mother. He says he wants to talk, but I've got some thinking to do before then.

"Okay, okay," Dineo says, raising her palms. "I won't push. I'm open to meeting him when you're ready."

"We'll see."

I take a seat at the kitchen counter as she gathers the ingredients for breakfast. The sun is finally rising, bathing the kitchen in a warm glow. It brings back happy memories of the years I spent in this very spot, watching her cook. I didn't know how much I missed it until now.

"I'm sorry I've been a pain in the ass."

Dineo shifts her attention from the stove to me. "Water under the bridge, baby. Time to move on, right?"

"Right." I fiddle with an orange from the bowl while asking, "What happened to the old furniture?"

Dineo glances at me again, her eyes sad when she murmurs, "I sold them. I didn't want—" she huffs, blinking rapidly, her eyes glistening with tears again. "I always hoped you would come home, and I wanted nothing in this house that reminded you of that night. If I could have replaced the entire house, I would."

"I appreciate that, Mommy. I know how much that stuff meant to you."

"Not as much as you, remember that. Nothing I've achieved means more to me than you."

We hang out in silence for a while; Dineo humming while she cooks, me psyching myself up to visit my old bedroom. The scene of the crime. Can I handle taking that step, or will it trigger the darkness again?

There's only one way to find out.

"Mommy, I'm heading upstairs," I announce as she pours the egg mixture into the pan. She looks up and gives me a slow nod, and I feel her eyes on me as I leave the room. Tiny flutters fill my stomach as I ascend the stairs, but I take a deep breath and force myself to move.

Like the living room, my old bedroom is completely transformed. There's a new bed, dresser, even the closet doors have been changed. I'm sure this must have cost a pretty penny, even if she made some money selling the old furniture. Did she use Aaron's money to buy the new stuff? God, I hope not.

Making a mental note to ask her, I scan the room again. My gaze latches on to the spot where Aaron ruined me. The instant flashback leaves a lump in my throat, but I'm not as flustered as I thought I would be. I'll never be the quiet, naïve girl who assumed she was safe within the walls of her own home. That innocent angel will never emerge again, but I'm at peace. *Finally*.

I return to find Dineo pulling the muffins from the oven. She looks up at me with a smile. "You've always had that supernormal ability to appear the second I'm done cooking. I can see you haven't gotten rusty."

I grin. "My timer is fully functional, I guess."

I gather the plates and forks for our meal and join her at the dining table. Of course, she makes me say grace, and although I haven't done it in a while, I still remember every word.

"I love this," she says when I'm done, and we start digging in. "Feels like old times."

I nod in response while shoving a forkful of food into my mouth.

"So, your aunt Zahra told me Anthony tried to reach out you," she continues. "Did you speak to him?"

I shake my head while I swallow. "Not yet. I promised Anita I would, and I will, but I'm not quite ready. How would you feel if I did?"

"You're an adult, free to do whatever you want. He's your father. There's no reason for me to stand in your way.."

I nod. "Can I ask you another question?"

"Of course, baby."

"Did you use Aaron's money to buy new furniture?"

She vigorously shakes her head. "Oh, not at all. The money came from my tax refund. I would never—" She drops her fork and gives me an earnest stare. "It was a terrible decision to take that money. Zyon, believe me, I did what I thought was best at the time."

"I know that. You weren't the only one who made that choice. I said yes to the money, too. If I had to do it all over again, I would have fought harder. I would have preferred losing a case than my integrity."

She reaches over and squeezes my hand. "Me too, honey."

"I have another question." My stomach churns as I say the words. I hate having to ask this, but I need to know.

Dineo wipes her mouth with the napkin, her expression guarded. "Go ahead."

"What did you and Aaron talk about when you saw him?"

"When?"

"After he got back in town."

"Nothing, really. I begged him to stay away from you. I wish I had more than his word that he wouldn't come back to Brooklyn, but there's nothing we can do to make him leave. We can't go to the cops because you already retracted your statement. I tried to appeal to his human side."

"Did it work?" I ask hopefully.

She nods. "I think so. You haven't seen him around, have you?"

"No."

"Good. It seems my appeal was effective after all."

I return her smile with a tiny one of my own. I hope she's right. The alternative is too hard to think about.

31

Gabriel

"Hey," Marcus taps on my office door. "Check your email."

I press the email icon on my phone and scan through the subject line of the unopened ones until I see one that makes my heart race. I open it and quickly read the contents, punching the air when I'm done. "Hell yeah!"

"We did it, bro."

Finally, we got the license to start construction on the island. Operation: Dominate is definitely on the way. I move to hug my best friend, giving him a hearty pat on the back. After spending the entire Sunday handling an emergency on one of our development sites and waking early this morning to juggle both my companies, I'm already feeling like hell warmed over, needing that rest Zyon told me to get. This great news is like caffeine in my blood. I'm suddenly more awake than before.

Marcus and I pull apart as Noah enters the room balancing a tray with three large coffee cups. "Celebration time, brothers!"

He hands each of us a cup then raises his. "To the biggest hotel chain in the Caribbean," he says.

"Amen to that," Marcus adds.

"Cheers," I chip in.

We knock our cups together then take a swig. "Now the real work begins," Noah says, sitting on the couch.

"Oh, quit it, killjoy," Marcus mumbles. "Let's enjoy this moment for a minute."

"Agreed." I sit at my desk and prop my feet up on the glass. "I have twenty minutes before I have to get to Cain Industries. For once, I don't want to talk about work."

"Fine by me," Marcus says at once. "I want to hear what you and Zyon talked about on Saturday."

"Oh, so you want to gossip," I reply, amused.

"Call it whatever you like. I want to hear details."

"Even I'm curious, Gabriel, so let's hear it," Noah says.

I give him a pointed stare. "I thought you would have stayed around to eavesdrop."

"Right, because I had nothing better to do." Noah rolls his eyes at me. "I wasn't interested in hearing you and Zyon fucking like rabbits, anyway."

"Nothing happened. We just talked. Listen guys, Zyon is a complicated woman, but there's a reason she's like this. If you heard her story, you would understand."

"Then tell us," Marcus says.

"I can't do that. It's private. Take it from me, she's been through some heavy shit. I think she's still suffering trauma from what happened to her."

"All the more reason for you to stay away," Noah says. "You don't need a damaged woman in your life. You've been sober for five years, man. It took one fallout with Zyon to make you start drinking again."

Scoffing, I cross my arms on my chest and give him a hard stare. "I already told you why I went to that bar, you dickhead. It wasn't because of Zyon. It was my mother's words that sent me there. You're hellbent on making Zyon the bad guy to strengthen your argument that I should leave her alone. Tell me, Noah, are you truly concerned about my welfare, or do you want me as lonely and miserable as you are?"

Noah's expression darkens too, and he gets up from the couch. "What are you saying, man?"

"Admit it. You've been acting like a jerk since Ana and Colin got engaged. It's not my fault you let her slip through your fingers, *bro.*"

"Okay, boys, let's not do this," Marcus chimes in.

"Do you think that's what this is?" Noah asks, coming closer to the desk. "I'm looking out for you, just like I've been doing since that night."

"Hey, Noah. Chill. There's no reason to bring up the past," Marcus says seriously.

"Why not?" Noah asks, whipping around to him. "I'm not jealous or bitter. I just have his best interests at heart, and I need to remind him why." He turns to me again as I stare up at him with a frown. "Remember when you got so wasted you trashed that club in Vegas?

Remember that week you spent in jail because you beat the club owner to a pulp when he tried to stop you? Your money saved you from prison and a criminal charge back then, but there's no guarantee it would save you now."

I close my eyes as the memories assault me. That was five years ago, the last time I drank—not counting Saturday night and the stupid mistake that could have cost my life. I understand where Noah's coming from because those were some dark times, but I would never go back there. *Ever*.

"Noah, I'm—"

"Fuck you, man. That was a low blow, and you know it."

I run my fingers through my hair, suddenly feeling like shit. Noah is a real one. I know he means well. I remember how devastated he was when Ana posted her engagement photos on Instagram. I shouldn't have gone there, especially knowing he's still in love with her.

"Sorry, dude. You're right. That was a low blow, but I need you to stop putting down Zyon for decisions I make. *Me*. I'm the one in control of my life."

He nods, but his forehead is still wrinkled, so I suspect he's not in total agreement with me. Still, he comes forward and hugs me. "It's all good. It's your life. Do whatever you want with it, man."

"Hell yeah. Group hug," Marcus says, wrapping his arms around us. "We're brothers. No arguing over women, got that?"

"Got it," Noah murmurs when we break apart. He seems more relaxed now. "I'm serious, Gabriel. If you want to date Zyon, fine. Just be careful. That's all I'm saying."

"Is that that a backhanded approval?" I ask with a smile.

"It's all you'll get, so take it. Not that it matters, anyway. You're already falling for her. My approval won't change a thing."

My hand gets busy moving the stapler on my desk, then I readjust my laptop. Honestly, I don't know what I feel for Zyon. I'm attracted to her, that's for sure. She's the last person on my mind as I drift off to sleep each night, and she's my first thought when I wake each morning. I look forward to getting to work because I know she's there, waiting to drive me insane with her sassy attitude and those body hugging outfits.

Listening her story broke my heart. I hate how powerless it made me feel. Yet, I'm grateful she trusted me enough to share it because I saw the real Zyon for the first time. She's still tough and feisty, but beneath that hard exterior is a soft, vulnerable woman just trying to find her way. Life has done her dirty, but she's survived the worst. She's a warrior, if you ask me. Definitely the kind of woman I'd like to date.

Noah scoffs and leans on the desk. Marcus chuckles from where he's standing by the window. "What?" I ask, twisting my head to take them both in.

"I was just pushing your buttons, Gabriel, but it seems I hit the nail on the head. Are you in love with Zyon?"

"No comment."

"Translation: yes," Marcus says.

I don't reply. I turn my attention to the document I'd been reading before Marcus came in.

"Have you told her how you feel?" Marcus asks.

"Don't you have something better to do than poke around in my personal life?" I close my laptop and reach for my bag. "I'm going over to Cain Industries. At least I'll have some peace over there."

"Not with Zyon around," Marcus jokes as I zip the bag shut. "I can't imagine how you lasted six months without banging her on your desk. You have the self-control of a fucking saint."

I shake my head at him. "I pity any woman who falls in love with you. She's in for a hell of a ride."

The smile disappears from his face, but there's still a hint of amusement in his tone when he says, "She would be so lucky." There's something he's not telling me, but I decide to table that conversation for a different day.

"See you boys in the pm. We need to officially celebrate."

We part ways at the door, and I take the lift to the underground garage, my thoughts solely on Zyon. We haven't spoken since she left my apartment on Saturday, but I'll see her in the office in a few minutes and we'll take the next step forward. I'm sure there will be complications along the way, but I want this. I want her.

I'm surprised when I get to the office and see Zyon's empty desk, but I don't think much of it. The workday has just begun, and she's been late before. After half an hour passes, then an hour, I start to get worried, particularly when calling her cell goes to voicemail. The worry surfaces. I think about Deacon going after her, getting revenge. There are a dozen things on my desk that need my attention, but I can't focus. I need to know she's okay.

I grab my phone and car keys and head to the door, but the office phone rings before I get to the handle. I consider ignoring it, but the workaholic in me makes an automatic turn toward my desk. It's Emily. Damn it. Why didn't I check the screen?

"You haven't replied to my email," she says once I answer.

"Whatever it is, can it wait? I have an emergency."

"This *is* an emergency, Gabriel. Your assistant resigned this morning, effective immediately."

There's a sudden ice-like feeling in my veins, and I tighten my grip around the cradle. "What?"

32

Gabriel

"What the hell are you doing up there, cousin?" Emily says. "This is the sixth assistant in a year. At this rate, you're going to go through the entire city."

I drop to my seat, opening my laptop to find the black and white evidence. Why would Zyon resign? She was fine on Saturday; what happened between then and now?

Sure enough, there's a letter with Zyon's signature attached at the end. She's gone. Just like that. No warning, no reason. Nothing.

"Gabriel."

"What?"

"I need you to go over the list of applicants I just sent you. The busy season is approaching, and we can't afford to be short-staffed right now. The sooner you help us shortlist, the quicker we'll find someone to take her place, okay?"

I don't want someone to take Zyon's place. I only want her. Not just in my personal life, but here in the office, where she gets my work ethic. I've never gelled like this with anyone, not even Matt. Fuck this. Zyon owes me an explanation. I won't accept her resignation until she tells me why—to my face. "Put a rain check on that list, Emily. I'll get back to you."

"But—"

The receiver hits the cradle before she finishes her sentence, but I don't care. I'm going see Zyon. I don't give a shit about anything else right now. I hurry down to the garage, my only intention to cut the half-hour drive to Zyon's apartment in half. As I close the door to my car, a man steps in front of it, and his malicious expression forces me to put the car in park before I can even back out of my parking spot. I get out, and the urge to give him another beatdown overwhelms me.

"The fuck do you want, Deacon?"

He grins, his left eye still swollen and his face badly bruised. He looks like the monster he truly is. I wish it was enough to keep women away from him, but Deacon is a charmer. Something needs to be done to stop him. *Permanently.*

"You have some nerve showing up here," I say when he stays silent, just grinning. "How the hell did you get past security, anyway?"

"They know your boy is innocent," he replies, and I wish I could scrape that pretentious smirk off his face with a knife. "They've got my back, what can I say?"

"You didn't answer my other question. What do you want?"

"My job back. No—I need a promotion. Consider it reparation for being wrongfully accused." Again, he flashes that disgusting grin that grates on my nerves. "How does two million dollars sound?"

I shake my head, making my way back to my car. "You're wasting my time. Have a good day, Deacon. Or a shitty one. I don't really care."

"Are you sure about that?"

"I don't give a shit about you. Never have, nor ever will. You're a disgusting excuse for a human being, and I don't care to know you."

"Well, I'm sure you care about your dad's reputation, right? And the company. How would you feel if he lost it all?"

I pause. "What are you getting at, Deacon?"

He comes closer, the glee on his face making me nervous. He knows something I don't. Something big.

"Have you ever wondered how your father made it big? How his company became a multi-million organization in just two years?"

"Why would I wonder about that?"

Deacon scoffs. "Come on, dude. You're way smarter than that. Think about it. No way did he build a manufacturing company from scratch and make it so big in such a short time. It's impossible."

There's a heaviness settling on my shoulders. I ease out from the car to stand before him. "Seems you know something I don't," I say.

"Finally, we're getting somewhere. Let me set the scene. It was a week before my pops died, and he called me to the hospital because he wanted to give me something—"

"Just get to the fucking point," I mutter through my teeth.

"Fine. He told me your father was a drug dealer back in the day. He started Cain Industries to launder his dirty money. After the second year when things started going really well, he went legit."

My hands curl into tight fists and I close the distance between me and Deacon. "That's bullshit. My father would never do anything illegal."

Deacon backs off with a scoff, but I don't miss the flash of fear in his good eye. "Are you swearing for your old man? Believe me, Gabriel, you don't know him at all. Why did you think he took me under his wing? It wasn't out of the goodness of his heart, I can tell you that."

"Then why did he take you in?"

"Because Pops sent me with the truth. Pops was one of his lieutenants back in the day. He knew where all the bodies are buried, and thanks to him, so do I."

My butt hits the hood of the car and I feel sick. Now it all makes sense; Deacon's smug behavior all these years, why Mom and Dad brushed the allegations of his assaults under the rug, why they have been riding my ass to reinstate him... fuck, he's telling the truth.

"I need to talk to my Dad."

"Trust me, he will have no objections. Just give me back my job, and we can forget we ever had this conversation. Don't forget my two million dollars."

I want to wipe the smugness from his face so badly, but instead I counter. "Two million dollars and I write a glowing recommendation." No way in hell is he coming back to work. Not while I'm still here. Not while Zyon is here—damn it, she no longer works here, either. I need to fix that.

Deacon shakes his head. “No fucking way. I'm not leaving Cain Industries.”

“I need to think about it.” In truth, I’m buying time until I figure out what to do.

“What is there to think about? You welcome me back with a huge promotion, or I go to the authorities with the evidence. It’s that simple. You don’t want to be the reason your dad’s in prison, do you?”

“How do I know you’re even telling the truth?” The sinking feeling in my gut and my parents’ behavior tells me he is, but he doesn’t need to know that.

“Ask your folks. They won’t deny it. I’m giving you twenty-four hours to get back to me. Don’t keep me waiting, Gabriel, or you’ll regret it.”

Just like that, he’s gone, leaving me wishing I’d done more than beat his ass that night.

I push the dark thoughts away and get into my car. This is not the time to think about what just happened. I need to get Zyon back. Right now, my only focus is to convince her to give us a chance.

33

Zyon

"Hey, sweetie," Roshell says, her head sticking around my bedroom door. "I got your text. You okay?"

"Yup, I'm fine," I reply, laying a pair of jeans on the bed. "Why wouldn't I be?"

Roshell comes in and closes the door, her forehead creased with a frown. "Isn't it obvious? Zyon, you just quit your job, the one you called 'the job of a lifetime'. It's quite reasonable of me to ask about your state of mind."

"I told you, I'm fine." I reach into the closet and pull out a long-sleeved shirt.

"Are you? Because of all the impulsive things you've ever done, this is the most extreme. Why didn't you think it through?"

"Who says I didn't?"

It's all I've thought about since I left Gabriel's home, and even then, it was still a hard decision to make. I'm in love with Gabriel. It makes no sense denying it anymore, but it doesn't change the fact we'll never be together. He will never reciprocate my feelings, and I can't handle working with a man who'll never love me back. Call me crazy or stupid, but my emotional health is more important than the perks. I loved that job, but I love myself more. It's for the best, even though it feels like my heart is being ripped from my chest. I'm fine. At least, I will be. Each day will diminish the memory of Gabriel. Soon, I'll forget we ever met.

I hope.

"I don't agree with your decision, but I've got your back," Roshell says, coming around to hug me. "I'm sure you'll be okay."

I wrap my arms around her, accepting her kiss on my cheek. "Thanks girl."

"What are you doing, anyway?" she asks when we break apart.

I gesture to the outfits on the bed. "I'm picking out clothes for my new gig."

"You already got a job?" she says with a gasp, gently shoving my shoulder. "Way to go! Why didn't you lead with that?"

"Because it's temporary. I'll be working with Dineo at the restaurant until something else pops up."

Dineo didn't bat an eye when I told her of my plans to leave Cain Industries, which I appreciated, because it's her nature to judge every decision I make. Her supportive response was the boost I needed to email the resignation letter this morning.

"Well, that's great, isn't it? This is the fresh start you both need. I'm sure you two will be as thick as thieves again."

"I guess." I don't feel half as cheerful as the girl staring back at me in the floor-length mirror. Maybe I never will again. It's only been a few hours and I already miss Gabriel. I hate that I still want him so much.

Roshell sits on the side of the bed, watching as I pull out a T-shirt from my drawer. I need a shower to clear my head.

"What about Gabriel? How did he take the news?"

I close the drawer with my knee. "I don't know. I didn't tell him."

Roshell's mouth flies open. "You can't be serious."

"I couldn't, Rosh. I... I just didn't know how."

"Damn... you're cold."

"Please don't make me feel worse than I already do," I say, pulling out a pair of panties.

"That's not what I'm trying to do, but after everything Gabriel's done for you, you owed him a heads-up. Blindsiding him like this... that's so wrong, Zyon."

"God..." I cover my face with the T-shirt. Roshell's right as she's always been. I owe Gabriel an apology, at least.

"It's not too late to right that wrong," my best friend, my constant voice of reason, says. How many times has she pushed me in the right direction, or saved me from going over the ledge? Did I ever properly thank her for taking me in without question when I had nowhere else to go?

"I'm going to fix it, I promise. Thank you so much, Rosh."

She flashes me off with a scoff. "Don't mention it, girl."

"For everything, I mean. You were there for me at the lowest point in my life and I wouldn't have made it through without you. I love you. Thanks for being a real friend."

I wrap my arms around her, and she hugs me back right away. "Well, you've done your fair share of hand holding and back rubbing too, don't forget," she says, her soft chuckle making me smile. "I love you too, girl."

We separate and I head to the bathroom to take a quick shower, but I lose track of time when I start thinking of Gabriel. I lean against the tiled wall, allowing the warm water to beat down on me, hoping it will erase the crazy thoughts in my head. Like the one that's making me regret my decision to leave my job, or the other wanting me to fight for him. It was easy to tell Roshell there's plenty more fish in the sea, but my soul wants him. *Only* him.

So, yeah, I'm definitely in a pickle.

The water trickles down my cleavage, over my stomach, caressing the flesh between my thighs. I would give anything to have his touch right now, his kiss, his cock inside me. Fuck, I don't need to be turned on right now. The arousal gets stronger, leaving me with a flood of sadness that points to struggling in the days ahead. How will I handle getting over him? How can I ever face him without falling apart?

The shower should have cleared my head, but I'm more confused than ever. Stepping out and into a fluffy towel, I head to the bedroom. I'm just about to haul the T-shirt over my head when Roshell barges in with an excited look. "Get some panties on, girl. And some pants. You have a visitor."

I stare at her blankly until she says, "It's Gabriel."

My heart does an instant somersault in my chest as my hands fly to my disheveled hair. "Oh, no, no, no. He can't see me like this."

"Come on, girl. You spent the night at his place. I'm sure he's seen worse."

She chuckles when I shoot her a withering glare. "He seems really concerned, and he came all this way. At least go see what he wants."

"I need to change, do something about my hair— damn it, Rosh, I need more time!"

"Hey! Breathe. If Gabriel can't accept you as you are, then he doesn't deserve you. Go on. You look fine."

I glance at my reflection in the mirror. For the first time, it's obvious my best friend's wrong. Not only does my hair resemble a deserted bird's nest, my T-shirt is a size too big, and there are dark circles around my puffy eyes, too. Who cares, anyway? Gabriel isn't here to pledge his undying love for me. I owe him an apology, but I don't need to be dolled up for that.

"Don't even think about keeping him waiting, or I'll pick you up and toss you downstairs."

"I'm going, okay? Gosh! You're worse than Dineo. I feel so sorry for any kid who calls you mom someday." I reach for a pair of biker shorts and drag them on, and I realize she hasn't said a word in reply. I turn around and there's a stupid grin on her face.

"No."

She nods, then squeals. I give her a hefty slap on the arm, and she glares at me. "What was that for?"

"For not telling me I have a niece or nephew on the way. How long have you known?"

"About a week."

"Seriously?"

"You were going through a rough patch, so I didn't— look, we'll talk about it when you're done with Gabriel, okay? Don't keep him waiting any longer."

"Okay." I give her a hug. "I'm really, really happy for you. You deserve it."

"Thanks. Now go!"

My heart feels like it's lodged in my throat as I descend the stairs, but I arrange a neutral expression on my face. I don't care how gorgeous or charming he is, I'm keeping my emotions in check. I'm done with wearing my heart on my sleeve.

But when he rises from the couch to meet me, the emotional floodgates fly open, giving me a heart-stopping ache for him. There's something about his presence that steals my control. It's not just his appearance, either, although he's wearing that dark suit quite well and his hair looks like he ran his fingers through it a dozen times, giving it that tousled look I love. It's more than that. There's this magnetism about him I can't resist, no matter how hard I try.

"Hi." I fold my arms across my chest as I stop just before I reach him, which in hindsight is a terrible idea. Being this close to him sends my walls crashing down in a heartbeat.

"Hi." His gaze takes me in before meeting my eyes. Yup. Definitely magnetic. I should have stayed in my room. I move away from him when he says, "Care to tell me why you blindsided me?"

Of course, he's here on business. Why am I not surprised? The hurt on his face suppresses my disappointment and pushes the guilt to another degree. "I'm sorry. The way I handled leaving was totally unprofessional. But it's not personal, Gabriel," I reply, hoping he doesn't read the blatant lie on my face. "I just needed to leave."

"Why?" He makes an impatient sound and steps toward me. "I don't understand. You told me you're in love with me, then you take several backward steps. I'm trying to get you, Zyon, but you're making it hard as hell."

"Why does it matter? It's not like you feel the same."

"I wouldn't be here if I didn't want to be with you."

I scoff. "You're here because you lost a good assistant, nothing else."

"Zyon—"

"You're going to have a hell of a time finding someone like me. So yeah, you're just trying to protect your interests."

"Just shut up and listen." He clasps my cheeks between his palms and captures my gaze with an intense stare. "I'm saying it loud and clear so there is no misinterpretation. I want to be with you, Zyon Stewart."

I blink at him, aware of my racing pulse and the gazillion butterflies in my stomach. *What the hell did he just say?*

"Did you hear me, Zyon?"

"You're not messing with me, are you? Trying to butter me up to come back to Cain Industries?"

He snickers. "I wouldn't dream of it. Although I'm not opposed to you retracting that stupid letter." The sparkle slowly fades from his eyes, replaced by a tenderness that tugs on my heartstrings. He runs his thumbs over my cheeks, and I hear the sharp intake of my breath. "I mean every word, Zyon."

It's easy to read the honesty on his face and I believe him, no doubt. But there's something niggling at my insides, something I can't put my finger on right now because he's licking his lips, stealing my focus.

"I'm going to kiss you now, okay?"

"Okay," I whisper, pushing up on my toes to meet him halfway.

The first taste of his lips immediately silences the niggling thought. Pressing against his rock-hard frame, I lose myself to the slow, teasing strokes of his tongue, inhaling the scent of his cologne; it's all turning me on even more. I needed this. Him. This feels like coming home.

Gabriel moans and tightens his arms around me, deepening the kiss, devouring my mouth with such skill, it makes my throbbing pussy jealous. If an explosion went off, I don't think I would hear it because I'm wrapped in head-to-toe ecstasy. God, I am so addicted to this man.

Groaning, I reach for his belt, undoing it so fast I even surprise myself. It falls on the floor with a clang, my T-shirt following immediately after. Gabriel undoes the button on his pants and as he dips to pull them down, his cell phone rings in the pocket of his jacket.

No, no, no. "Just ignore it," I say, tugging on his arm.

"I can't." He looks just as frustrated as I am but he's already dipping inside his pocket. "It's my mom."

Just like that, the niggling feelings resurrect, but this time I don't need to look far for the source. She's on the other side of the phone.

Buttoning his pants, Gabriel goes out back to take the call and I reach for my shirt on the floor. It's only been a few minutes since whatever this is we've got going on, and I'm already foreseeing a problem. A huge problem. Gabriel returns just before I wear a hole in the carpet from my incessant pacing. The bliss that overwhelmed me a few minutes ago is now annihilated by a deep-rooted sorrow. We will never work. Our attraction to each other isn't enough.

"Sorry about that," Gabriel says. "I needed to take that call."

"Its fine. I don't feel so good, anyway. Think I'm going to lie down for a bit."

A thick brow shoots up as he reaches for my hand when I start backing away. "Wait a minute. You were fine a few minutes ago. What changed?"

I consider pulling my hand from his and darting upstairs, but that's the old Zyon. There's no running away from my problems anymore. I'm going to face them head on.

"I don't think we're going to work, Gabriel," I reply.

Gabriel's face settles, and he tightens his hand around mine. "Why not?"

"I can't compete with your mom."

He stares at me for a beat then chuckles. "Why the hell would you want to compete with her, anyway?"

"Maybe I need to be clearer." I tug at my hand, and he lets me go without much effort. "After listening to the conversation with your mom on Saturday, I realize one thing; you're willing to go the extra mile for her."

He's staring at me, confused, his arms now crossed against his chest. "And?"

"And a mommy-pleaser is a problem for any relationship."

"That's ridiculous. I'm not a mommy pleaser."

"Says the guy who interrupted a make-out session to take his mom's call."

"When you put like that, it sounds a little extreme. I needed to take that call."

"Why?"

"I'd rather not say."

"In other words, it was a call that could have waited."

Gabriel sighs, frustration bathing his features. "Zyon, it feels like we're going around in circles. I don't understand your sudden change of heart."

"Nothing's changed inside me, Gabriel. I still want to be with you, but your mom hates me. You want to be on her good side. Are you seeing the conflict now, or should I spell it out again?"

I brush past him and walk to the kitchen, the soft clicking of his shoes letting me know he's right behind me. "Zyon, my mother does not dictate how I live my life. Sure, I've been trying to compensate for what happened to Daniel, but I wouldn't sacrifice my happiness to please her."

"You say that now. What if she starts pressuring you to break up with me?" I ask, turning to face him.

"She wouldn't." He doesn't look convinced, and that's not comforting.

"I don't want to take that risk, okay? I've been through enough. This is asking for heartbreak on a platter."

"Zyon, for God's sake. I just told you I want to be with you. Do you think I would do anything to hurt you? All I've done since we met is look out for you. That will never change."

I pause with my hand on the refrigerator door and take a deep breath.

“I need you, Zyon, so fucking much. That's not something I've said to any other woman.” He spins me around to face him, and the tenderness on his face makes my stomach flip. “Give us a chance. I'll make it worth your while, I promise.”

“If I say yes, I want you to promise me your mom will never come between us. Or Nicole.”

Gabriel lets loose a frustrated breath. “I told you; Nicole is just a good friend.”

“A good friend who’s in love with you.”

“She's just been programmed by my mom, that’s all—” His shuttered expression tells me he didn’t intend to reveal that tidbit of information, and it sends my heart crashing through the floor of my stomach.

“Your mom is trying to hook you guys up? Really?” I shove past him. “How the fuck can I compete with that?”

“Just stop for a goddamn moment. Don't allow your emotions to cloud your judgement. Does it matter what their intentions are? Think about mine, nothing else. I want you, only you. Let that sink in.”

I cover my face with both hands, angry and frustrated and wishing I hadn’t gotten my hopes up. His mother wants him and Nicole together. I’ve watched enough telenovelas to know how this could end. Do I walk away from the man I love, or do I trust him with my heart?

“I need to think about this, Gabriel.”

He releases a rough sigh, looking as disappointed as I feel. “How much time do you need?”

“I don’t know,” I reply with a shrug. “I’ll call you when I decide.”

There's a slight hesitation before he nods, his fingers gently stroking my cheek. I close my eyes as he murmurs, “I'll be waiting.”

I nod in response, then wait until I hear the front door close to open my eyes. Roshell descends the stairs as I take a seat on the couch and tuck my legs beneath me, and she joins me.

"Just want you to know, I overheard everything," she says.

"Meaning you were eavesdropping."

"Call it whatever you like, but I think you'd be making a mistake."

"I can't compete with his mom, Rosh."

"He's not asking you to. I'm not trying to discount your fears, but you can't let them stop you from experiencing real love." She takes my hand with a smile. "This is real, Zyon. Take it from me. Watching you two together... it is real."

I drop my head against the back of the couch and stare at the ceiling. She's right. I can't let fear block my happiness. I've been happy since meeting Gabriel. *So happy*. It took some time for it to sink in, but when he's around, the darkness stays away. He's into me. He wants to be with me. How can I say no that?

34

Zyon

"I could get used to this," I mumble, throwing my leg over Gabriel's thigh. "Evening sex is my new favorite thing."

Gabriel snorts. "Wearing me out, that's your new favorite thing."

Grinning, I run my hand down the hard plane of his lower abs, making my way to his cock and wrapping my hand around it. Gabriel groans as I stroke him, and within seconds, he's swelling in my hand. I look up at him with feigned shock. "Worn out? Not even close. You're insatiable."

We've hardly left the bed since I knocked on Gabriel's apartment door last night. There was no time for talking. Our clothes were on the floor almost instantaneously. We made up for that interrupted moment at my apartment and then some. A thrill runs up my spine as I remember Gabriel inside me on his balcony last night.

"Look who's talking." With his lower lip caught between his teeth, he flips me on my back and spreads my thighs. I moan when he slips his fingers inside me. "Already soaking wet."

"Wet for you," I whisper, riding his fingers. "Always for you."

Gabriel grunts and settles between my thighs, his eyes gleaming with lust as he roughly thrusts into me. With my legs locked around his waist, I lose myself to the hard, delicious strokes. He soon slows down, making love to me with an unhurried passion that makes me so emotional it sends tears to my eyes.

Gabriel pauses, staring down at me with amusement. "Not you and those tears again."

"Oh, just shut up and make love to me," I reply, rocking my hips. His smile recedes as he resumes his pace, this time with an unexpected urgency. He dips his head to take my nipple between his teeth, tugging hard as he thrusts into me. The sweet pain sends me over the edge within seconds. I feel myself clenching around him as waves of pleasure run through me. His quickened pace tells me he's not too far behind. A growl tears from his throat before he captures my lips for a deep, long kiss, making the descent from cloud nine that much sweeter.

"Dude, you're heavy," I mumble when he drops on top of me. He sighs and rolls off to the side, jumping out of bed for the bathroom. He soon returns with a wet towel and proceed to clean me off. I can't contain the feeling inside me. I brush the stray hair from his eyes so I can see him properly. "I know you don't feel the same, but I love you, Gabriel."

He smiles and gives me a quick peck on my cheek. "What I feel for you is more intoxicating than love. I'm sure I'll get there someday. We have all the time in the world."

"Okay."

I drop against the pillows with a happy sigh as Gabriel returns to the bathroom. This has been the most amazing twenty-four hours of my life, from the second Gabriel opened his front door. He's right. We have all the time in the world to grow, to learn, to fall in love. Right now, I just want to enjoy this moment. Gabriel rejoins me in bed, pulling me into his warmth. Another happy sigh escapes when he nibbles on my shoulder.

"Just so you know, I'm rejecting your resignation," he murmurs.

"Dineo is going to kill us both. I promised we'd work together for a while. Besides that, I have no objections."

"Good. Don't worry about your mom. I'll handle it," Gabriel replies.

"There's something else I need you to do," I say, turning to him. "I need you to go to AA meetings with me."

He softly sighs, then gently nods. A series of emotions flashes across his face, each only lasting a few seconds, except disappointment. It's still lingering even now. "I can imagine how crushed you must feel after staying sober for so long. We're human. Mistakes happen."

"I know," he replies as his cell phone chirps. Turning on his side, he reaches for the phone on the side table and slides his thumb across the screen. The angle gives me an opportunity to see the incoming message and although I shouldn't, I can't help but read it.

Time's up, Gabriel. Considering I haven't heard from you, you didn't plan on keeping your word. I won't go to the cops. Not yet. I'm giving you one more chance. In the meantime, I'm taking the one person who means the most to you in this world. Just as a bargaining tool. All I need is your compliance and I'll return her right back into your arms. It's that simple.

"Fuck." Gabriel flies out of bed while dialing a number. Perplexed, I push up on my knees, watching as he puts the phone to his ear and grabs a pair of boxers from his drawer.

"Mom? Oh, thank God. Where are you? Good, stay there. Don't come back to Brooklyn tonight. Please tell me Lauren's with you."

He listens for a beat then breathes, "Oh, thank God. No— Mom, listen, I'm fine. Just stay in Queens until I tell you it's safe to come back. Deacon's trying to get back at me for not reinstating him. He sent me a threatening message."

He pauses and listens, his expression growing impatient. "No, Mom, I won't take the blame for this. You and Dad are at fault for letting that sick, twisted bastard blackmail you, for covering up his crimes. Not me. All I'm doing is trying to make things right."

As I listen, entranced, it feels like I'm watching a scene from a soap opera. Blackmail? What the hell's going on in Gabriel's family?

"For the last time, Mom, I'm not giving Deacon his job back. I'm not feeding that monster. As soon as Dad gets home from the hospital with Karyn and the baby, we're going to talk about the secrets you've been keeping from me—yes Mom, I know all about Dad's drug dealing."

Drugs?

"Listen, just stay at Aunt Bella's for now. Inside, Mom, and don't open the door for anyone. Yes, I know you're not a child—"

Gabriel pauses, and his face goes pale. "Damn it. Let me call her now." He hangs up and turns his back to me as he gets on the phone again. There's a long beat. He's tapping his fingers on his thigh, shifting his weight from one side to the other, still not looking at me. Finally, he rests the phone on the dresser top and starts grabbing clothes from the drawers.

"What's happening, Gabriel?" I ask as he steps into a pair of jeans.

"Deacon's taken Nicole. I need to find her."

"Are you sure?"

Gabriel nods. "She's not answering her phone. Nicole always answers when I call." He hauls on his shirt and reaches for his phone. "I'm heading over to Deacon's apartment. Hopefully, he's stupid enough to take her there. I'll keep you posted."

"Got it," I mumble, reaching for my clothes on the armchair.

"In the meantime, I want you to lock up behind me—what are you doing?"

"Going home," I simply reply, pulling the dress over my head.

"Why? You're safer here than at your apartment. Please, Zyon, stay."

I shake my head. "I'd rather be with Roshell. Besides, if Deacon has Nicole, it's obvious he won't come after me." He's already gotten the person who means the most to Gabriel. Deacon knows something I don't, and whatever it is, it's making me anticipate problems ahead.

Gabriel looks like he wants to argue, but he shakes his head instead. "At least let me drop you home."

"No, I'm fine. You already have an urgent problem on your hands. I'll just order an Uber."

"Fine." He walks up to me and gently cups my cheeks. "I'll come get you when I'm done. Be safe, Zyon."

"Yeah, you too." I accept the brief kiss he gives me then reach for my purse. My hair is a mess, but I don't care. I just want to get out of here.

Gabriel keeps me company until the car arrives, then kisses me again and sends me on my way. The tears immediately spill when I ease into the backseat. I can't stop them. I'm wondering if it's safer to love him from a distance. The Uber pulls up to my apartment, and I immediately notice the darkened windows. Roshell's not home. Now I'm second guessing my impulsive decision to leave Gabriel's place. There's a deep sense of foreboding that's washing over me, that I'm walking into a trap.

It's all in my head. I'm perfectly safe. Deacon won't come after me.

Taking a deep breath, I climb the steps while reaching into my purse for my keys. A rustling sound makes me whip around to see a tall, muscular man behind me. His dark hair is caught in his signature messy man bun, but he's no longer clean-shaven. The scruff he's wearing makes him more dangerous-looking than before. I gasp, and my trembling hand drops the keys. I quickly bend to grab them, but he catches up to me by the time I get to the door. I bite my lips to stifle the terror climbing up my throat as he grabs the keys from my hand.

"Hey, stranger. I was wondering when you'd show up."

I back against the wall, my sharp breaths making me feel light-headed. "You promised to stay away."

Aaron chuckles, clearly enjoying how terrified I am. "Did I? What document did I sign?"

"What do you want?"

The slow scan he's giving my body makes me sick. I glance to the deserted street behind him, toying with the urge to scream. Would anyone hear me?

"Don't even think about it," he murmurs, catching the intention on my face. "I would hate to snap that pretty little neck."

My entire body weakens. I wet my chapped lips as tears roll down my face. "Please, don't hurt me."

He smiles, the action doing nothing to improve how threatening he looks. "It's your lucky night, Zyon. That's not why I'm here. There's something I need to tell you, something about your mother you really should know." He drops the keys in my palm, a move that surprises me. "Why don't you invite me in?"

Dear reader

Thanks for reading Intoxication! Hope you enjoyed it as much as I loved writing it.

Rest assured, Gabriel and Zyon's story isn't over. The continuation of their emotional romance is almost complete!

Look out for part 2 of the Damaged Hearts series ***Deception***, coming early summer 2022.

If you don't want to miss the updates, consider joining my spicy book club HERE or follow me on Instagram or TikTok.

Erika Bradley

Acknowledgments

This has been such an amazing journey; I still can't believe we're here! Intoxication is now a published novel! This milestone wouldn't have been achieved without the amazing people in my life.

To my superhero husband, I love you. Thanks for babysitting when I needed time to write. You have been my sounding board since Intoxication was a few scribbles on my notepad. This is your baby as much as it's mine.

To my straightforward beta team who helped shaped this story and found the plot holes I missed; thank you from the bottom of my heart! I appreciate the hours you spent discussing the draft with me.

Alexa, my amazing copy editor, who polished the rough edges and made this story so much better; I appreciate you!

To my wonderful arc readers; thanks for taking a chance on my book! Thank you for all the great feedback that validated my decision to write this story! Your kind words mean more than you'll ever know.

Intoxication is just the beginning. The best is yet to come!

About the Author

Erika Bradley has been an avid romance reader most of her life, long before she was even allowed to read steamy novels. Recently, she decided to step to the other side of the world she loved and wrote her first romance novel, Intoxication.

Erika writes steamy, suspenseful plots with flawed, emotional characters that will keep readers turning each page. Her aim is to give each reader a satisfying escape.

She lives in St. Andrew, Jamaica with her husband and son. When she's not writing, you may find her curled up with a book or gardening. She also enjoys island trotting during her extended breaks.

Want updates on Erika's upcoming novels? Follow her on:

Instagram- https://www.instagram.com/authorerikabradley

TikTok- tiktok.com/@author_erikabradley

Or click HERE to sign up to her spicy book club for deals on her new releases. (There will be no spamming or sharing of your email. promise!)

Made in the USA
Monee, IL
20 November 2023